Jane Rogers has written nine novels, including *Mr Wroe's Virgins* (which she dramatized as an award-winning BBC drama serial), *Her Living Image* (which won the Somerset Maugham Award), *Island* and *Promised Lands* (which won the Writers' Guild Best Fiction Award). Her most recent novel, *The Testament of Jessie Lamb*, was longlisted for the 2011 Man Booker Prize, and won the 2012 Arthur C. Clarke Award. Her short story collection, *Hitting Trees with Sticks*, was shortlisted for the 2013 Edge Hill Short Story Prize.

Jane also writes radio drama and adaptations, and has taught writing to a wide range of students. She is a mentor for Gold Dust (a unique mentoring scheme for writers) and a Fellow of the Royal Society of Literature.

www.janerogers.info

Conrad
&
Eleanor

JANE ROGERS

Atlantic Books
LONDON

First published in hardback in Great Britain in 2016 by Atlantic Books,
an imprint of Atlantic Books Ltd.
This edition published in paperback in 2017.

10 9 8 7 6 5 4 3 2 1

A CIP catalogue record for this book is available
from the British Library.

Paperback ISBN 9781782397939
E-book ISBN 9781782397946

Printed and bound by CPI Group (UK) Ltd, Croydon, CR0 4YY

Atlantic Books
An imprint of Atlantic Books Ltd
Ormond House
26–27 Boswell Street
London
WC1N 3JZ

For Mick

Prologue

CONRAD AND ELEANOR have been seeing each other for eleven months when Eleanor becomes pregnant. It is 1975. They are at Cambridge.

'Annie says the people at the university clinic are good,' Eleanor tells him. It is sunny and they are sitting on the wall outside the pub looking down into the river. Conrad watches a mother duck shepherding her brood in and out of the weeds at the water's edge.

'Good at what?'

'Advice. Fixing it.'

'Fixing what?' he asks stubbornly, knowing perfectly well that his slowness will only make her more impatient.

'Abortion, what do you think?' Eleanor looks across at the gangs of other students sprawled around the tables. 'Why are you being so dense?'

'I don't agree with abortion. I mean—' quickly, as she turns to face him, squaring up for the argument, 'yes, a woman's right to choose and all that, but unless it's a rape or something – I mean, within a relationship, shouldn't it be discussed?' His voice sounds craven in his own ears.

'What will we discuss?' she says in a reasonable tone. 'How

I'm going to look after it while I do my house job? Or you are, working eight hours a day in the lab? Or what we're going to use for money?'

'We can discuss it,' he says doggedly.

'Keep your voice down. There's no need to tell the world.'

'OK. Let's walk along the river.' If this is the only time it will be discussed, then they will discuss it now, for good or ill. But Eleanor is objecting.

'I've got to be back for a histology lecture at 2.'

'Fine. There's an hour.'

'You've got to inject your mice.'

'The mice can wait.' He stands aside to let her go down the steps to the path. It is too narrow to walk side by side.

'So what d'you think I should do? Give birth and have it adopted?'

'Of course not.'

'What then?'

He feels a sudden spacey unbalancedness, as if he were starting across a tightrope. Head up, one foot in front of the other; don't think of the drop. 'We could get married.'

'*Married?*'

'Yes.'

She keeps on walking in front of him, he can't see her face. The silence extends.

'Why not? People do. They – they get married and have children.'

'What for?'

He pretends to laugh. 'Because they want to.'

'Do you want to?'

'Yes.'

2

She turns. 'You really want to get married?'

The spark of anger he feels is a relief. 'Yes. Is that so strange? We're going out together, you're expecting my child, I want us to get married.'

'But it never entered my head.' She begins to walk on. After a while she says, 'I don't think it's a very good idea.'

'Why?'

'We're too young. I mean we'll both probably meet other people we like.'

He knows she will.

'And in terms of our careers the timing's terrible. If we *were* going to get married and have kids, in five years' time might be about right.'

'Yes, but this has happened now.'

'OK. But I could have an abortion now and we could still choose to get married and have a family in five years' time, if we really wanted.' Her tone shows him how unlikely she thinks that is.

'In five years' time one of us could be dead. The abortion might lead to sterility, you might never conceive again—'

'You're being ridiculous. The whole point is, women can have control of their fertility.'

'So what went wrong here then?'

'I don't know.' El is on the pill.

'I rest my case.' He can see what is going to happen as clearly as he can see the rubbish clogging the river up ahead. If she has an abortion it will lie between them. A mucky connection. She will use it to move herself on. But the more he cares, the easier it is for her not to. He has a vision of two kids on a see-saw, one clinging on fearfully, and the other, at the extreme end, gleefully

3

bumping and jolting up and down. He forces himself to speak lightly. 'You just had a proposal of marriage.'

'My third.' She turns and smiles at him, then leans in and touches her lips to his. 'I'm honoured. I'm going to histology, but I'll think about it.'

He wonders who the other two are. Philip Marlin would be one. But he doesn't know the other.

'Four actually,' she says, 'if you count Timothy Evans at primary school.'

'Fine. I'll see you tonight.'

When they meet after dinner Eleanor has already called at the counselling centre. 'I was cycling past at 5 and they were still open.'

'And?'

'If I said I didn't know who the father was, it would be simple.'

He can't think of a reply.

'You would never have considered marrying if this hadn't happened.'

She's right. Why is he thinking of it now? He hates her. Let her do what she wants. With every word he says to her he is exposing himself further. 'Yes, I would.'

She sighs theatrically and folds her arms. 'Oh yeah.'

'Look—' His mind is blank.

'I'm looking.'

'Look, it's simple. You're pregnant, let's get married.' He feels his hot blush rising.

'Is it some antiquated notion of honour? You've ruined my reputation so now you must do the decent thing? Is it that?'

'No. The reverse.' At last, lucidity. 'Exactly the reverse. I want us to make a commitment. I want to live with you. I want it to be permanent. It's not cool, it's not what any of our friends are doing. But you being pregnant – gives us the excuse.'

The tiny silence before her reply is encouraging. 'You were waiting for this to happen.'

'No. I didn't know it would. Of course not, you're on the pill. But now it *has* happened, I can see it's what I want.'

'What about me?'

'I don't know.' There is a relief in having said it. Whatever happens. In having stated his position.

'Neither do I.'

Gathering out of his relief, swelling with the force of it, comes a magnanimity which astonishes him: he can pity her. She doesn't know what she wants. He does. He loves her and that makes him vulnerable, she could damage him with her not caring. But now in a swoop the positions are reversed: he is fortunate, knowing what he wants. She is the lost one. In the safety of his secure footing he can wait, and whatever happens will not be all loss. 'OK. When you know, you can tell me.'

After a moment she bursts out laughing. 'Thanks. What if I never know?'

Her laughter has broken their immobility – it is possible to reach for her and pull her into a hug. Their bodies are warm together. 'You haven't got that luxury. You've got – what's the cut-off point? Fourteen weeks?'

She shakes her head. 'If I go in the next week they can do suction. I'd be in and out within the hour.'

'Like cleaning a car.'

'What?' She is laughing.

'Suction. One of those vacuums they have at garages.'

'That's disgusting.'

'Yes. Don't do it.' He kisses her. He can feel the power. It has transferred from her to him. He can kiss her, he can pin her arms to her sides, he can walk her slowly backwards and lower her to the bed; raising his face from hers he can tell her, 'Don't move', and undress her garment by garment while she lets him raise first arms then legs in his hands, watching him, her eyes almost blank with surprise and lust. For the first time, Con has the power.

Knowing it makes it happen. She says yes, as he knows she will. You can't make happen what you want to happen. But when you shift from wanting it to knowing it, it happens. It comes to you, whatever you desire, it comes and offers itself up.

Chapter 1

ELEANOR IS LATE setting off for home on Monday, 10 February 2003. She has had to hang on at work for the phone call from the symposium organisers, who seem to have forgotten the time difference between Chicago and the UK. When she finally gets to her car it is encrusted in two days' worth of melted and refrozen snow, with the de-icing spray locked inside and the lock iced up. She cannot remember what time Con's flight got in but it was almost certainly afternoon – he will be home by now. Sod it, she will leave the car and take a taxi.

But on this bitter winter night everyone has the same idea; the streets of Manchester are crawling with cabs all cosily packed with passengers. She picks her way to the corner shop, buys a new can of de-icer and some milk, and walks gingerly back down the slippery street to liberate the car.

It is 9 by the time she gets home, but there are no lights on in the house. For a moment she's bewildered. Then: good. Maybe his flight is delayed. Of course. Weather. There're no messages on the answerphone. For an hour she works rapidly, drawing curtains, turning up the heating, defrosting soup and bread, clearing the weekend's unopened post and newspapers, unpacking her bag and putting on a wash, making the house feel lived-in again. No one would guess she has spent a whole luxurious weekend with Louis. She checks Ringway arrivals; flights from Germany all seem to be on time, there was one from Munich at 17.05. By 10.15 it's too late to wait any longer and she eats half the soup and has a whisky, before going to check her email. Maybe he met up with someone at the conference and is stopping over. Maybe she actually got the day wrong. There are quite a few emails but mostly junk and none from Conrad. She has another whisky and listens to Radio 4 news at 11 (no plane crashes) then goes to bed: It's fine. It is as if she has been here all weekend.

In the morning she has a quick scout about to see if he left his flight times anywhere – on his desk? On the corkboard in the kitchen? She always leaves hers, it wouldn't have hurt him to. Before she heads for work she scrawls him a note.

Thought you'd be back last night. Give me a ring when you get in. Dinner with health service bigwigs, home late.
El xx

When she gets home that night the note is where she left it. She taps in his mobile number and, predictably, it goes straight to answerphone. He never switches it on, it's pointless him having a mobile. She sends a brief text: 'Where are u? E x', but he won't pick that up either. He must have gone on somewhere. Their daughter Cara is the most likely person to know. El rings her in the morning.

'Mum. D'you know what time it is?'

'It's 7.30 and I have to leave for work in two minutes.'

'Well, I don't.'

'Sorry. Listen, d'you know when your father's coming back?'

'I didn't know he was away.'

'That conference. He went to that conference in Munich.'

'Mum, I don't know, I haven't spoken to him – I'm going to have to pee now you've woken—'

'OK, I've got to go. Call me if he rings, will you? Bye.'

That night she returns early, half expecting the house still to be empty. It is. But there's a message on the answerphone. Tina, Con's research student. 'Hi Con, are you OK? Sorry to bother you at home but you said we'd go through my results today. D'you think you'll be in tomorrow?' So, he was expected back at work. El wants to talk to Louis, who she has not seen since the weekend, and she texts him but there's no reply.

After Eleanor's eaten she goes through Con's desk more thoroughly, looking for conference hotel bookings, and then through his email inbox, looking for online flight confirmation. Nothing, it must be on his work email.

Who else was going? George and Anita probably went; she turns to their number in the address book then hesitates. If anything bad had happened she would have heard. What if Conrad never went to the conference?

The doubt only enters her head for a moment, teasingly. Of course he went. It's likely that one of the kids at least knows where he is. She phones the other three in turn. Paul doesn't answer his mobile. Megan is on a bus going home from a rehearsal and thought he was coming back on Monday. Daniel is in his room with a very loud TV on and all he knows is Dad was going somewhere last week.

She turns again to George and Anita's number. It is 10pm; if she doesn't ring now it'll get too late. How stupid, what's she fretting about? He's a grown man; if he's too rude or incompetent to tell her when he's coming home why should she chase after him like a mother hen? She makes coffee and settles down to proofread her *British Medical Journal* paper. Paul rings back, he's surprised Dad's not home, he thought the conference ended on Sunday. 'I was going to come round tomorrow night.'

She starts to say, 'Well, you still can—' then remembers she's giving an evening lecture, but Paul wanted to see Con anyway about some new computer program Con is using at work. Eleanor puts the slight fractiousness of the conversation down to Paul's having been drinking, and says goodbye without further chat; in his answering 'Goodnight then' she detects plainly that he is offended.

There is nothing for it but to phone George and Anita. Louis texts her back as she starts to dial. 'Can talk at 10.30?' Her whole being is resistant to phoning George and Anita. Cosy marital double act, George-n-ita. Who each know how many times that day the other went for a piss. Who will be politely astounded that she has no idea where her husband is, and are the last people she wishes to share that information with.

'Hello George? It's Eleanor—'

'Sorry love, wrong number.' The voice is male, impatient, slightly contemptuous. She slams the receiver down and dials again.

'Hello?'

'Anita, hello, Eleanor here – yes thanks, fine. And you? – Good. I was ringing about the conference last weekend – yes – did you by any chance take the same flight home as Con?'

'We didn't fly together – no – I don't know when his flight was. George and I got a lunchtime flight back from Hanover on

Sunday, it was my niece's twenty-first—'

'Oh.'

'Why? Is anything the—'

'Did you talk to him at the conference, Anita? How did he seem?'

'Has anything happened? What's the matter?'

'Nothing – nothing, I just wondered.'

'He was quiet. George and I both noticed that; we asked him if he wanted to have dinner with us on Saturday night but he said there was someone he needed to talk to and I said to George, poor Conrad does look a bit—'

'I see. Thank you, Anita.'

'But what's the trouble? Is he ill?'

'No. No. I – he didn't say anything about meeting anyone – going on anywhere?'

'But why don't you ask—'

'He hasn't come home.' In the brief silence she is amused by the vision of the cogs going round in Anita's head.

'Oh El! Where on earth can he be?'

'He's almost certainly stopped off with friends – he may even have told me before he left and it's slipped my mind, that's why I'm asking.'

'Oh. Well, I'm really sorry, I don't think I can shed any light – let me just ask George.'

Eleanor hears her palm clamp over the mouthpiece, the solidity of her flesh sealing up her conversation with her husband. Eleanor is ready when the hand lifts.

'Never mind, thanks awfully, Anita, I'm sorry to have bothered you—'

'If we think of anything we'll—'

'Yes, there's nothing to worry about, I'm quite sure. Love to George. Bye now!'

OK, where is he? What has he done, the idiot? He was at the conference, he hasn't come back. Tina was expecting him at work today. Eleanor leaves Con's office and heads back to the kitchen, pacing the length of the room. He's missed his flight, that's the most likely – missed his flight and not got onto another and can't cope, sitting in a heap somewhere like a sulky child. He will need rescuing. He was barely functioning at home – the complications of airports and shuttle buses have been too much for him. When she thinks of him she has that familiar sinking of the heart; he has gone downhill. Is this how Con will get old? Depressed, dysfunctional? Why oh why didn't she leave him while the going was good? A little flare of excitement: what if something really has happened to him, and he doesn't come back? It is the dutiful teacherly El who rounds up the sparkles from this firework and brushes them into a corner. For shame. Have you no heart? No no no! she laughs to herself, and her child-self kicks up her heels and cavorts. To be free of Con! To be free of Con without being the bad guy, without dragging them both through separation, without carving up the house, without the children's recriminations (which would all of course be aimed at her) – a get-out-of-jail-free card, how good would that be?

At the expense of his safety, his health, maybe his life? chides teacher-El. For shame.

Then El suddenly remembers Con. She remembers him running along the beach towards her with toddler Cara perched on his shoulders, he's a bull charging the matador, he's ducking his head and shoulders and Cara is screaming with delight and El is laughing and dodging and her skin is tingling with anticipation for the moment he will catch her. It's Con, who she loves. She slumps against the kitchen counter. What if he's with someone else?

She's already thought it of course but now concentrates. Who would want him? Bitch. Because he's dumb and sullen with you that doesn't mean he can't be charm itself to another woman. So: he's with someone else. Who reflects back to him a charming, funny, clever Con, instead of a depressing failure. The familiar clamour of exculpation starts up – OK, she tells herself, OK it's not your fault but that doesn't change the facts. He *is* a failure. If he thinks he is, he is. With someone else he won't be. Of course he's with someone else.

The punch lands. She crouches, back against the cupboard, arms clasped around herself, holding herself together. Con laughing with someone else, lightly touching her arm. Con alive and happy and funny and competent and not with her.

Slowly she pushes herself to standing again, ashen with self-disgust. What's sauce for the goose is sauce for the gander. As her mother used to say.

The phone rings. Paul again. 'I've been thinking, when did you last speak to him?'

El can't remember. 'Last week sometime?'

'But he's phoned you since he went?'

'No. Why should he?'

'You haven't spoken to him for a week, Mum? Or texted?'

'No.'

There's a pause. 'Shall I come round?'

'What can you do?'

'I'm coming round.'

It's getting late now. She remembers tomorrow. It's the

deadline for her grant application and there are still several questions outstanding. She hasn't practised her evening lecture; there's a research committee meeting. She'll have to go in at 7am to prepare. What's to be done about Con? Nothing. She'll get her freedom because he's found someone better, and it will serve her right.

She tidies the dishes, puts the kettle on, and turns on the outside light for Paul. She wishes he wasn't coming. But then he arrives on a waft of cold air and alcohol.

'Should you have driven? Aren't you over the—'

'Mother, stop.' He peels off his coat and they head to the kitchen where El makes them tea. 'Did you have a fight?'

'No.'

'He didn't say anything about—'

'Nothing.'

'So where d'you think he is?'

'I have no idea.'

'So what you gonna do?'

'He's a grown man. If he's choosing, for whatever reason, not to come home, presumably in the fullness of time he'll let me know why.'

Paul puts his mug on the table and paces the kitchen.

'Look, Paul, if something was wrong I'd have heard. He's got his passport, his mobile, his laptop—'

'How long you gonna leave it?'

'Till what?'

'Till you try to find him?'

El laughs. 'How can I try to find him? He's in Germany. Or could be further afield by now, if he likes. How can I find one man, in the world, if he doesn't want to be found?'

'But why would he go and not tell anyone? What's he done?'

'I'm assuming he's with someone else.'

Paul stops. 'Do you know?'

She shakes her head.

'Did you guess? Did he act like—'

'No.'

There's a silence. 'But why shouldn't he, eh?' says Paul. 'You make me sick, you two.'

El drains her tea and stands up. 'Me too. We make me sick too. But there we are. I've put clean sheets on Dan's bed if you want to stay.'

'What about the police?'

'The police?'

'They trace people who're missing, don't they?'

'Not if someone has gone off on his own volition.'

'Why wouldn't he tell one of us? Why wouldn't he tell Cara?'

'Because he's punishing me, I suppose.'

'We can all keep a secret from you,' says Paul drily. 'I promise you, none of us knows where he is.'

'Well, it would be a waste of police time. You ring the police if a ten-year-old doesn't come home, not an independent adult.'

Paul is staring into the grain of the table.

'Paul? I'm going to bed.'

He doesn't answer. As El undresses she remembers she forgot to phone Louis.

El is asleep when her phone rings. She leaps up, knocking over her water glass as she grabs for the phone. This will be it. But the phone twinkles CARA at her.

'Hello?'

'You've bolted the door. I can't get in.'

El pulls on her dressing gown. Paul appears in Dan's doorway. 'Is it—?'

'Cara.'

'Fuck's sake.' He retreats and slams the door.

Cara is dragging a wheelie case. She stands in the hall looking tragically at El as she locks up again. 'You haven't heard anything, have you?'

'No.'

Cara's eyes are welling up; El wonders if she has been kicked out by her nasty boyfriend. Stiffly she holds out her arms and after a moment Cara leans against her and lets herself be enfolded. It is like hugging an empty coat on a hanger. El remembers sickeningly that she has forgotten to worry about Cara for quite a long time. Why didn't Con tell her Cara was bad again? 'It's very late,' she murmurs.

'I can't sleep.'

'I think he's fine, love. I think we'll hear from him tomorrow.'

Cara steps back, shaking her head, raking a sleeve across her wet face. 'I'm going to Munich.'

'That's silly, that won't—'

Cara moves along the hall to the kitchen. 'I've booked it, 10.15 tomorrow, but I need to borrow some money.'

El trails after her. 'I'll make us a milky drink.'

'I don't want one. I feel sick.'

'Cara, you're in no shape to go haring off—'

'He's still there, I can feel it, he's in a hospital or prison or – or kidnapped, he's there, he needs help.'

Paul barges into the kitchen. 'Thanks for waking us up.' He opens the fridge and glares at the contents then slams it shut.

'What are you looking for?' asks El.

'Something to drink.'

'I'm making cocoa.'

'Not that kind of drink.'

Cara persists. 'If it was one of us he'd already be there, he'd be the first—'

If it was one of the kids, he would. He'd be at it like a terrier digging up the dirt. If it was Eleanor herself? She thinks not. 'You can't even speak German.'

'I can go to the hotel. The conference centre. They'll speak English.'

'I'm going to ring them in the morning, there's no point—'

'He's there. I can sense it, OK? And when I arrive I'll know what to do. I've got to follow my instincts.'

'With her supernatural powers, Cara Evanson confounds—'

'Shut up, Paul.'

'Shut up yourself, you loony.'

'Don't tell me to shut up, you bastard.'

'Please,' says Eleanor automatically. They fall silent. 'Why did you say *kidnap*?'

'He could be kidnapped for money.'

'Or by animal rights people,' offers Paul. 'They might have been targeting the conference.'

'He's not important enough,' says El. 'Anyway, there's no ransom demand.'

'Yet,' says Cara. 'You don't know.'

'We should tell the police.' Paul's contribution.

'You shouldn't go on your own. And it doesn't make sense for me to—'

'I want to go on my own.'

'Where are you staying?'

'His hotel, if I can. Or somewhere near.'

'We'll book you a hotel in the morning. One missing person is enough.'

'Can you drive me to the airport?'

This is pure Conrad. The children are grown up but they still rely on him to ferry them to station and airport. 'I'll pay the taxi.'

Paul has unearthed a bottle of brandy last used to light a Christmas pudding. He's filling a tumbler. 'I'll have some, please,' says El. If only to stop him drinking the lot.

Eventually El heads upstairs, and sets her alarm for 6, by now four and a half hours away. She needs to sleep. But finds herself pulling open Con's drawers in the big chest they share. His clothes are all there; he can't have taken more than a couple of pairs of underpants and socks, maybe a T shirt. In the wardrobe his shirts hang in an accusing row. He's got too many, so certainly two or three could be missing. But he's not taken enough clothes to last five days. All his underpants look strangely new. She thinks of him as wearing black Marks and Sparks, but these are blue and green, there's even red – Calvin Klein. Why d'you get new underwear? She closes the drawer carefully, silently.

If the woman was pregnant. She'll be younger, obviously. If she was pregnant, he'd leave.

This time contempt – for both Con and herself – tempers the pain. She needs to feel the pain, to bite down on it like an aching tooth, to remind herself of its reality; but it is wearisome, really. He will try a re-run with another woman, because having young children makes him happy. He will try to repeat. Which only men can do, of course. And she will be the stereotypical abandoned wife. All their shiny hope and this is what it comes to – clichés, staggering through their Punch and Judy roles. Pathetic. Contemptible.

El realises she won't sleep, and creeps downstairs to her office again in search of her glasses. But the kitchen door is ajar, and when she hears Paul's words it is impossible not to stop and listen.

'You know she's having an affair?'

'Louis?' asks Cara.

'Yes.'

'I sort of knew. I tried not to. But does Dad know?' asks Cara.

'I have no idea.'

'You think he's left her?'

'Why won't she call the police?'

'You think she doesn't want him to be found?' Cara sounds incredulous.

'Look – look at the facts. She's in love with someone else.'

'Is she really? Do you know that?'

'All right, she's having an affair with someone she doesn't even love.'

'Paul—'

'She hasn't got time for Dad. Say he won't give her a divorce.'

'She could leave him, if she really wanted to,' Cara offers.

'But where would she go? They own this house jointly.'

'Louis is married! This is ridiculous, he lives with his wife.'

'Right. So neither of them has anywhere to go. If Mum could get Dad out of the house—'

'Then she and her lover could live here? What about us?'

'None of us lives here, my dear little sister, it's not our house.'

'It doesn't make sense. You think Mum has kicked Dad out and is pretending he's missing – why would she do that?'

'If she'd kicked him out, he could still contact us. No. Maybe something worse.'

Eleanor wants to move, she wants to go back to bed and block her ears. But she is frozen to the spot.

'Like what? Like she murdered him? Is that what you're saying?' demands Cara.

'Don't shout. It could have been an accident. What if they had a row and things just went from bad to worse? What if accidentally something happened to him, because of her?'

'Like what?'

'I don't know. But I can imagine, can't you?'

'No, I can't imagine. I think you're mad.'

'Cara, listen to me. People don't just vanish. And when someone does, nine times out of ten it's the spouse.'

'Why would she say he was missing?'

Paul laughs incredulously. 'He *is* missing. The only thing she's pretending is that she doesn't know where he is.'

'And where do you imagine? The garden? The freezer? This is stupid. He's in Munich and I'm going there tomorrow to find him.'

'I can imagine it,' persists Paul. 'It needn't even have been deliberate on her part.'

Paul isn't the only one who can imagine it. El forces herself to move away and on up the stairs. Paul has no sympathy for her in this situation: well, why should he? She has no sympathy for herself. But still her son's harshness brings stinging tears to her eyes; tears for him, for Paul, that he can think so badly of her. What has she done to him? What kind of a mother is she? Lying in bed staring at the darkness, with the distant murmur of Paul and Cara's voices in the kitchen, El allows herself to fully re-enter the wretchedness of her and Con's recent dealings.

She is remembering a night a couple of weeks ago; she has spent the evening with Louis, and come home shockingly late. She lets herself in quietly. It is 2.15 in the morning. The night is cold and clear with stars, and she almost can't bear to step into the stuffy house, with its coagulated smells of old food and un-vacuumed carpets and the sour odour of Con's depression. It closes in on her, how can she breathe? If he won't clean they'll have to get a cleaner, she will have to have that fight again. It is disgusting to have to walk into this. She has a glimpse of them in old age, in their stinking pen. No wonder the children don't visit.

Louis' wife is away looking after her mother, so Eleanor and Louis have been at his place. His clean and tasteful, childless, housewifed house. She meant to come home at 11 but she fell asleep. Now she's wide awake. She makes her way to the kitchen and closes the door silently before switching on the light. Con's dishes are in the sink, no wonder it stinks; since when was he too low to even put them in the dishwasher? She puts a pan of milk on the greasy hob and surveys the kitchen, feeding her own irritation. The paper is spread open on the table. Con's coat and scarf are slung over a chair, his shoes in the middle of the floor, the bin is overflowing. He has not even pulled down the blinds. She does so. Silently she tidies, pressing down the contents of the bin, scraping his dirty plate into it, loading the dishwasher.

Why is he like this? It is his job. His work with monkeys is going nowhere; all the work on transgenic transplant monkeys is stalling. He has been marking time for months. She has given up trying to persuade him to get out. She stands by the table thinking about this house; the big family home, the attic, the empty children's bedrooms, and how Con wants to stick to it like a snail in his shell, and how dead a space it is. She has been pushing for them to sell it and move on. And then she thinks, I should have tried to get him away. Found somewhere else where we could get out of what we are in this house, where we could sit for whole evenings with nothing to do but talk. There have not been any proper holidays for a long time. It has seemed hard to see the point; she has dragged him on the odd weekend city break, where they have done galleries and concerts. But they have not been somewhere with empty time, time to allow the place to change them. She has been too busy for that. And in her own defence, he has never suggested it.

She has automatically taken the brush and dustpan from under the sink and is sweeping up the spillages from the bin. Suddenly he opens the kitchen door. He's wearing the multi-coloured dressing gown Cara got him from a charity shop, for a joke. It is miserably inappropriate. 'What are you doing?'

'Clearing up your mess, as you can see.'

'What are you doing at this time of night?' he persists.

'I couldn't sleep.'

'I heard you come in from outside.'

'OK, I came in.'

'Where were you?'

'You know where I was.'

He pulls out the chair she has just pushed under the table, and sits. She turns to her milk. 'D'you want a drink?'

'No.'

'Did I wake you? I'm sorry.'

'I was awake.'

She mixes her cocoa, noting the tea-encrusted edge of the sugar bowl, the lidless marmalade. 'How are you sleeping, generally?'

He shrugs.

'You ought to go to the doctor.'

'For insomnia?'

'For depression.'

He does not reply, and she glances at him, stirring. 'Con? I know how you feel, but the tablets work. You know they do. You need something to give you a lift—'

'Don't tidy up after me,' he says. 'It's insulting.'

'It's dirty in here. It smells.'

'Because of me.'

'If you leave dirty plates overnight they're bound to—'

'I wash them in the morning.'

She is unwilling to sit. She wants to take her cocoa to bed.

'Why d'you come back?' he says.

'Con, it's late. Let's talk tomorrow.'

'Why d'you come back?'

'For God's sake. Because I live here.'

He shakes his head, running his fingers along the underside of the table. He's like an ox, she thinks, a dumb ox stubbornly refusing something it doesn't even know. 'Why do you want me to go to the doctor?'

'So you'll feel better, Conrad.'

'So I'll put my plate in the dishwasher.'

'For fuck's sake. You're depressed. You're creeping about like an old man. You don't need to be like this.'

'Well, if you left it wouldn't affect you.'

'I'm not leaving. If you want to talk, let's talk tomorrow.'

'When? Before you go to work at 7? After you get home at 2am?'

'I'll come back early. We can have dinner together.' They can't because she's meeting Li, her Chinese Ph.D. student at 7, and has promised Li they'll grab a bite together while El gives Li her feedback. There was no other time this week to slot her in. But he doesn't need to know that now.

He is shaking his head. 'You don't want to talk to me. I'm depressed. Everything I say is stupid.'

'Con, stop it.'

'Why don't you get a place of your own? Then you wouldn't have to deal with me being smelly.'

'I didn't say you were smelly.'

'I probably am. I haven't had a shower for a while.'

'For God's sake.'

'For God's sake indeed. *Sauve qui peut.*'

'I don't want—'

'But *why*?' he says insistently. 'That's what I don't understand. Why? The children? You think you're going to turn Dan around by staying in the same house as his smelly father?'

'Dan doesn't need turning around. Dan is perfectly self-sufficient.'

'Right. By which you mean, Cara isn't.'

'Are we going to go through every old argument you can rake up?'

'You think I indulge her.'

She strains for a conciliatory tone. 'Each of our children is different. They are fine. Paul is fine. Megan is fine. Cara is fine. Dan is fine.'

24

'Don't patronise me. And Dan is not fine. He hasn't got a friend in the world.'

Like you, she thinks. 'We both know what's wrong with Dan. For God's sake, shut up!' Why doesn't she leave him? It is true her heart sinks every time she opens the front door.

'It is possible to talk in the night, you know. Don't you talk to Louis?'

Cradling her mug, she moves away from the sink. 'Dan still needs to be able to come home. The others are in and out. We still have a life here—'

But he rises to his feet, heavily. Like an ox. He is standing in the doorway.

And now El allows the memory to blur, to waver into dreaming, to imagining whatever it is that Paul may imagine. So Conrad does not step aside to let her pass, as he did in reality.

'Let me go to bed, please,' she says.

'No, we don't have a life. I'm here. On my own. Night after night…'

'If you saw your friends, joined something, *did* something, for God's sake – it's a vicious circle, can't you see?'

'You have a life,' he says in the same heavy, bewildered voice, 'but it isn't here.'

'Please move. I'm going to bed.'

'No.'

'Con, move!' She makes a grab for the door handle but he bats her arm away and the cocoa spills down her new wool trousers, scalding her leg.

'No!' she shouts. 'Bastard!' Hopping about in pain she flings the mug at him and it hits him smack on the side of the head and he dodges heavily, too late, and bumps the other side of his head

25

against the corner of the bookshelf behind the door, the corner she has told him about a dozen times. He crashes to the floor.

El rips off her boots and trousers and holds a tea towel under the cold tap then wraps it round her scalded thigh. Pressing her legs together to hold it in place, she runs a bowl of tepid water and puts the pale grey trousers in to soak. They are probably ruined.

When she turns back to Con he is lying blocking the door-way. 'For fuck's sake.' She picks her barefoot way across the shards of mug and crouches beside his head. He's bleeding where the mug hit him but it isn't deep. He's out cold, though. She staunches the wound with her tea towel and scrapes away the broken china so she can pull him out to full length. His head lolls to the other side. Now she can see. The injury to the other temple is serious. It's deep and white and livid. The tissue around it is already swollen. How has he—?

She looks up in panic. The old iron shoe-scraper which they use as a doorstop when the kitchen door needs holding open – the old iron doorstop lies, toppled on its side underneath the bookshelf. It has an edge like a cleaver. She snatches a clean tea towel, runs more cold water, presses it to the swelling. His body twitches convulsively and his bowels open. His eyes roll up in his head.

'Con! Con! Conrad, listen to me.' She leans into his face, searching for breath – grabs his wrist and fumbles the stupid multi-coloured sleeve out of the way. She can't feel a pulse.

Is this what Paul imagines? Or worse, that she attacked him with intent to kill him, with a knife or a brick? What is she supposed to have done with the body? Con is six foot four. Does Paul imagine her sawing his father into chunks on the kitchen floor, then secreting them round the garden? Or dragging his weight into the boot of the car (she wouldn't have the strength, though, so again she'd have to dissect him first) and unloading him at some conveniently isolated landfill site, or popping him in a sack with stones and dropping him in a river?

Eleanor is sweating. She opens her eyes. It seems entirely plausible; if she were Paul she would probably think it too. But I didn't do that, she reminds herself. I didn't do it. It could have happened but it didn't.

There is not much comfort in the thought. She wonders if Conrad too has imagined such a scene. No wonder he has left her. No wonder.

Chapter 2

CONRAD HAS NOT been murdered by Eleanor. He has gone to the conference in Munich. Where he has been greeted with friendliness by colleagues from universities around the world, and where he has slipped into his work persona as easily and comfortably as a man sliding his feet into a well-worn pair of slippers.

It is a short walk from the conference centre in Munich to Conrad's hotel. His Korean colleague, Park, is staying with friends a tram ride away. After the Sunday night dinner, Con walks with him to the tram stop then turns the corner towards his own hotel, away from the brightly lit main thoroughfare.

This is a quiet residential street; on the corner there's a building site enclosed by hoardings, then well-to-do houses, with brass nameplates of dentists and lawyers, shuttered windows, small coiffured shrubs in planters. The streetlamps are heritage, resembling gas lamps and giving as little light. As he moves towards the end of the empty street Conrad hears a lighter step behind him. He glances back. There's a squat tree between him and the nearest streetlamp, and the shadows of the branches reach across the street. A woman is coming towards him through the shadows. Her.

He's running before he knows it. Running for the corner, running past the dark shopfronts, running up the steps, through the open door, into the lobby of his hotel. He slows to a walk, and nods to the receptionist while moving quickly towards the stairs. Once out of the receptionist's view he's running again. Up the stairs, round and round to the third floor. Along the quiet corridor, fumbling his key card, and into his room. Where he manages to not-quite slam his door, and leans against it, breathing hard.

How did she know he was here?

Leaving the lights off he moves to the window and looks down. A few cars pass, but no pedestrians. What is she doing? Why is she waiting in the street, what is she planning? Something moves at the pavement edge and he cranes to see. A cat.

Eventually he turns from the window and moves to sit on the bed. It is neatly made; his washbag on the bedside table has been tidied and straightened. Anyone could have been in here. He runs his fingers over his face, as if the softness of his eyelids, the slight friction of the day's growth of stubble, are new; his face, his head, his whole body feels fragile as an egg. He will have to go to bed. But his bowels have turned to water.

He can't bring himself to switch on the bathroom light. The fan comes on automatically; he won't be able to hear someone at the door. There's nothing he can do if someone does come to the door, beyond not answering it. But he needs to know. He lifts the lid and lowers himself gingerly onto the toilet in the dark. When the hot liquid has shot out of him he wipes himself, pulls up his trousers, and moves towards the door so he's grasping the handle with one outstretched hand, and reaching for the toilet flush with the other. He has to force himself to press the flush and get out of the bathroom on the roar of sound, pulling the door closed behind him. Outside the bathroom door he waits, listens: nothing.

She knows where he is. He can't go back to the conference tomorrow. He undresses in the dark, keeping his underwear on, and crawls into bed. He can listen better when he is lying flat. He can see the shape of the windows, he can see the crack of corridor light under the door. He is keeping an eye on the entrances and exits. Maybe he'll get some sleep.

It is two hours later, after he has lain quietly breathing, staring at the passing illumination of headlights across his ceiling, marking the sounds of the hotel and its inhabitants, including two sets of feet moving along the corridor to a door beyond his own, which duly opens and closes; it is after this that he realises what she is doing. Keeping him dangling. It is her intention that he will lie awake, jumping at every shadow; that the drip drip drip of what she *might* do will slowly unhinge him.

He has already given himself up to it. So why didn't he simply turn and face her in the street? The answer is a spasm of nausea; fear and self-disgust conjoined. The idea of facing her cannot, itself, be faced.

He thinks about going home. He thinks about Eleanor. She sometimes accuses him of playing the victim. She has accused him of that when she has done something which makes him unhappy. 'Don't play the victim, please.' There is no reply, because he is the victim, or has been, of what El has done, and she knows it. He understands her to mean, 'Don't ask me for sympathy' or 'You are as bad to me as I am to you', or simply, 'Don't feel sorry for yourself.' He understands her to mean that his response to her behaviour is tiresome.

He is playing the victim now. He is the victim. He should go to the police. But he is embarrassed by his own naivety. Also he doesn't speak German. And he doesn't believe they would protect him anyway. 'Don't play the victim,' he tells himself. Don't go back to the conference. Don't go home. Don't lie here in the hotel where she knows you are. Go somewhere else, give her the slip.

He imagines leaving the hotel, dragging his wheelie case, crossing the road to the tram stop. No. He imagines asking the receptionist to call a taxi. Skulking in the lobby till the driver calls him. Hurling himself into the passenger street and shouting, 'The station, quick!' The *bahnhof*. All he needs to do is get on a train before she can get on. That's all he needs to do, leave on the soonest train.

He sees himself vanishing down the line, diminishing to a dot. He sees himself gone. He can't make himself be *in* that dot, to know where he is. But he sees himself gone. It might work; it would at least be active rather than passive. Ever since the evening in Malmaison, she has been in control. At least if he vanishes, it is not playing the victim.

The sludge of his responsibilities stirs and clouds up around him, muddying the view. If he disappears, how will it affect the children? Cara especially, on the point of splitting up with her pig of a boyfriend – who can she turn to? If he disappears, what will happen at work? If he disappears, who will take the car for its MOT next Tuesday, who will be there to let the plumber in? Who will know where he has put the key to the shed? If he disappears...

If he disappears, where will he be? There is a click outside his door. He holds his breath. No further sound. He exhales. He remembers how he felt on the plane coming here; the lightening, the relief. Escape.

He gets up at 6 and moves silently round his room, gathering his things into the case. When he looks out the street is still. She can't have waited outside all night, it was freezing. But if she has, he will handle it. A kind of calmness has seeped into him. Something has been set in motion and now he can follow it. Or maybe it's just the animal lifting of the spirits at the passing of the night. He splashes water on his face and cleans his teeth, though he still doesn't turn on the light. He opens his door carefully and steps out, case in hand, into the silent corridor.

His taxi takes him past the conference centre. Its front doors are closed, its interior dark. She will be expecting him to be there today. Maybe whatever she is planning will happen there today. The speed of the taxi through near-empty streets is like flying, winging his way above trouble. He has his case, his phone, his laptop, he is self-contained, extricating himself from the scene. What can she do when he's gone?

He knows, of course. She can target El and the children, and blackmail him with the threat of that. He should close his email account. Then her emails would bounce back, wouldn't they? Close his phone and email contracts, render himself incommunicado. It would be part of vanishing. He cannot put himself out of the reach of the children, he thinks, but simultaneously knows that he can and will. They are adults, all they need of parents now is cash and Eleanor has plenty. They don't need him. It's over, he tells himself. It's over. So what are the choices? To huddle in the shell of his own life, playing the victim, or to strike out into the distance. His fear, his concern for his own safety, is nothing. There are many other things which are more important and which should now direct his movements. The monkeys, the animal house – despite all this sound and fury he has done nothing yet, nothing has changed. His work, El, the children, the house, all still wrong, all unresolved, all in need of – in need of— a figure outside the station snags his attention, as the taxi slows and pulls in. The up-and-down gait, the forward angle of her head… but then the movement of the taxi allows him a glimpse of profile; of course it is not her, it's a young girl. And how will he ever resolve El, the children, the house, work? This ludicrous crowd of impossible things, this unending list of his failures, of his 'playing the victim', of his being at the receiving end of undeserved random events which buffet him from one buffoon-like position of imbalance to the next, which knock him down like the wobbly man the children used to play with, bobbing back up idiotically ready for the next blow. Of course he must disappear. Or the painted smile will be battered right off his face and he will be nothing but a scarred plug of wood tottering into and out of balance, taking longer each time to regain the upright, a kicking stool, a whipping boy, a victim.

This as he pays the driver with the note ready folded in his clasped palm, as he hefts his case and runs into the cavernous noise of the station, as he scans for her, for the destinations board, for the ticket office, for the exits, as he gauges the 08.04 departure for Paris against the time, 7.59, against the size of the queue at the ticket office, against the next departure, 08.07 to Rome, and the next, 08.09 to Berlin. He won't make the Paris train, and anyway Paris is too close to home. He scuttles to the ticket hatch, waits with his head sunk between his shoulders, pays cash for a ticket to Rome, forces himself not to run to

Bahnsteig 12, validates his ticket, moves swiftly down the platform. All the time he's on the platform he is visible. He should get on immediately. But he hurries past carriage after carriage, hunting for an empty one. As he mounts the steps he permits himself one quick glance back. On the other side of the rails which lie between this platform and the next there is a woman facing his train. As he looks she starts to run, up towards the ticket barrier. He dodges into the carriage and peers through the window, holding his body sideways out of sight, but a train is pulling in on the neighbouring rails, she is already obscured. He's lost her. If it's her. If it's her and she's running for this train – he checks his watch. 8.06. If it's her she has time, if she has a ticket. But why would she have a ticket? She was on the wrong platform. She thought he was getting a different train. Or was she just there on spec? It wasn't her. It's nothing, he tells himself furiously, moving down the carriage, aware of other passengers' glances. It's nothing. Even if it is her, even if she gets on this train – what? What is the worst she can do? And why wouldn't he welcome the worst? If he is tired of playing the victim, if he is vanishing into a dot, then what? Why not embrace the consummation of these two? Allow her to vanish him, her victim.

This is not the point. This is white noise, nonsense, gabbling, all he needs to do is find a seat and conceal himself in it. But there are no empty doubles. He can't sit beside someone, he can't sit exposed in the aisle seat, he needs a corner, the end corner of a carriage. People stand in his way, rifling through their open bags for tickets, books, spectacles, shoving luggage into overhead racks, stowing and settling, blocking up the aisles. There are people at his back, he can't move. The train will stop, he thinks. He can get off anywhere, suddenly, just before it pulls out. If she's on the train, she can't know where he will get off. She can't, she's not superhuman, she can't know.

He is in the last carriage: the last carriage is bad, nowhere to run, but finally there is an empty double, he ducks into it and heaves his suitcase onto the seat beside him, blocking himself in. He lowers the tray table, buries his head in his arms on the table and feigns sleep. Which is of course idiotic because he has to know who it is now coming down the aisle in his direction, who it is now hesitating beside his seats, shuffling tickets and seat reservations – he opens his eyes, he raises his head. A querulous elderly man holds out his seat reservation, obliging Con to move. The train pulls out at the same time. He staggers on down the carriage with his bag, finally stowing it in the end-of-carriage luggage rack and slumping beside a skinny youth with headphones, who appears not to notice him. He has a clear view down the aisle, at least. He can see anyone approaching. And everyone is seated now. The train gathers speed; he lays his head back against the seat and allows his burning eyes to close.

He is in the monkey house. He recognises the nightmare before it even materialises, recognises the lurch in consciousness, the fall. He knows what's coming; it should be possible to turn, to wake, but he is powerless, limbs weak as trailing underwater weeds. The first cage swims up at him, the small grey inert body, the yellow vomit. He is holding his breath against the stench of the place, the filthy oranges, he can feel the air sticky on his skin, penetrating every orifice and pore, inhabiting him, staining him. With a gasping cough he is awake and sucking in a breath – the comforting recycled still slightly chilly air of the carriage, with its smell of carpets and burnt dust, its decent anonymity. The youth beside him stares ahead, jerking his feet to the sounds in his ears.

So, to Rome. Conrad has once been to Rome. He has a memory of El with Paul and Megan, laughing beside some towering ancient column, then realises he is remembering a photo. The real Rome is unimaginable. He will be nothing. A wraith, a ghost, a negative. With no reason to be there, no work, no children, no family, no friends, no holiday. Why should he be there? Why should he be anywhere?

Now the panic over being pursued has receded (irrational – she could still be on this train) his own insubstantiality looms. What will he do? For money, accommodation, food? And what is his purpose? He realises he is in free fall. He is making this journey as a result of a perfect storm of negatives. He is on the run from his wife, whose life is as remote from his as that of the twitching boy in the next seat. But what is he running towards?

The vanishing point he imagined earlier now induces giddiness. He's hungry, that's the thing. He counts the money in his wallet: 112 euros. He makes his way to the buffet car, glancing through the passengers as he goes, but there are too many of them, and of those who are facing the wrong way, several have brown hair the same length as hers, so it is impossible and he can only keep going mechanically putting one foot in front of the other, propelling himself forward. He pays for coffee and a mozzarella and tomato panini which needs heating so he has to wait, exposed, leaning against the bar, while the barman serves other customers. He is bewildered by their confidence, by their questions and comments about the food, and the way the barman responds, smiling or shaking his head.

Con stays in the buffet car to eat, staring out towards the flat winter countryside. There is an air of normality here – conjured perhaps by the barman, whose engagement with his work suggests that it is real, that the difference between a cappuccino and an Americano matters to him. As Con chews the comfortingly tasteless cheese, the starchy dough of the bread, he is momentarily oblivious to all other concerns.

None of this is new. Apart from Maddy, the threat of Maddy. None of the rest is new, and what seems at this precise moment to be the central thing – the key, though it will shift again, he's well aware of that – is Eleanor. His marriage, which has already transformed so many times that no one could see it straight. Hasn't he gone from loving her to hating her and back again so many times that the path between them is worn out? There is no love. There is no hate. There is only exhausted and exhausting familiarity, stalemate, they ignore and do not know each other because they have known each other too well for too long, invested too much, watched each other become incomprehensibly different and still the same, dealt each other the most deadly wounds, they have flayed each other alive and who cares about the rest, who cares what happens next? All that could conceivably remain might be kindness, a form of respect. But that's gone too, of course.

The present does not erase the past. The present does not erase the past. The mantra aligns itself with some rhythmic sound in the train's motion – he can almost empty his head. The present does not erase the past. Cara.

No, try not to think of Cara. But why should he not think of Cara? Of Paul, Megan, Cara, Daniel? Why shouldn't a man think of his children, his own flesh and blood? Of Cara. Of Cara's blood.

Not of her blood. Of Cara. Cara in the snow. How many times over she is his. Oh the comfort of family myth; the time Cara got lost in the snow.

He can see her chubby baby face. The fine golden down on her head, still not quite hair, an ethereal promise of hair, transparent, translucent; her ecstatic smile. Now she wears the purple snowsuit that used to be Megan's, with the hood pulled tight over her naked head, and she toddles through the snow in her wellies like a spaceman in different gravity, tottering, tilting, tumbling, laughing in amazement at the cold. She is flickering with life.

He's leaving her with El for the day – leaving them all, fourth day of the group holiday, leaving the women and children together while he goes off for a day's serious skiing with the men. He doesn't want to, but Ian's booked their holiday and he'll be offended if Con doesn't come on one of his macho expeditions. Con doesn't want to leave the kids, he doesn't want to leave El. She's twelve weeks pregnant with Dan and she's tired and not quite herself; her timing's a fraction slow, her focus isn't sharp. All his protective urges, his big-hearted territorial instincts. (Don't – don't sneer at this. Do not destroy the innocent past.) His instincts tell him to stay and protect his family. Which is ridiculous, because what harm can they come to, in the company of two other mothers with their children, in a cosy farmhouse surrounded by a splendour of snowy Swedish countryside? The low sun gilds the slopes, the sky is violet blue, Ian and Morris are calling him. He goes.

But after a couple of hours his arms are aching, his knees are locking, and he seems to have wrenched an ankle in one of his falls. The other two are better than him, he's never done cross-country before – all he's done is downhill skiing holidays with school. Ian wants to press on along a firebreak through woods, to a village with a hotel that serves food. It's 11.30 and Con has given it his best shot.

'I'm heading back, I think I've twisted my ankle.'

They tease him for not being able to take the pace, but he senses the lightness they feel at streaming away from him. He has been slowing them down.

And he heads back slowly, enjoying it. Pausing to watch a single lingering yellow birch leaf twirl inexplicably on a twig end; to photograph a tracery of black branches against the grey cloud which is trundling across the sky like a stage set; to take off his skis and enjoy stamping his feet through the snow crust and feeling stable again. On a holiday like this you're never alone. And now the white land is unrolled all around him and he's at the centre of it. He remembers making tracks in the snow when he was a kid, making the footprints of a creature that would puzzle scientists, the prints of a three-toed dinosaur, by carefully laying one footprint over another. He's smiling and trudging up the last slope before the farm comes into view, when it hits him.

Something's wrong. He has to get back. Skis under one arm, poles in the other hand, he tries to run up the hillside, pushing himself to speed, his heart hammering. Danger. Danger.

From the crest of the hill he sees the farm lying tranquil in the valley under the low grey sky. Little figures are milling around on the opposite slope, they are out with the sledges. There's a good shallow run on the other side, they've taken the kids out on it every day. Nothing is untoward. But his thumping heart tells him different and he's pitching down the hillside like a drunken giant, too rushed and stupid to put on the skis which would have flown him there, striding and gasping and falling and dragging himself up again, keep going keep going keep going. Snow starts to fall as he careers down, big soft heavy flakes that blot the distance, now he can't see them on the hill opposite, now all he can see is the flakes up against his face, huge on his lashes, cold in his eyes.

Suddenly there are dark figures, a large and a small, El and Paul. He realises they are on the farmhouse track. She looks up astonished to see him.

'Con! Where are the others? Are you all right?'

'Yes—' He's breathless. 'I couldn't keep up.'

'Paul needs a poo, I'm taking him back. The others are with Marie.'

'I'll – OK.' It's not here. He needs to get up that hill. He's dumped his skis and poles on the track, he's plunging away from them, El's surprised voice curving after him – 'Con?' – but already they're behind him and he's penetrating the whiteness ahead, it's closing in, the sky is snowing down to meet the ground and he's charging up the hill with his freed and flailing arms for balance, he's powering up to the top. Where one of the other mothers appears dragging her twins on the big sledge. She gives the sledge a shove that sends it flying down towards the farm, the two boys squealing with joy.

'They're coming up now—' She waves her hand at the hill-side behind, and plunges after her boys.

And then Con sees Marie with her Charlotte, and Megan, halfway down the hill. Where's Cara? He's galumphing down towards them and Megan's crying and he's snagged by that but Cara, where's Cara? And Marie is shouting, 'Megan fell off but

Cara—' and he's galloping and slithering down the hill and there's the sledge below him but Cara's not on it. His mind can see and scan and calculate it all in a still glassy moment while his ungainly heavy body stumbles and heaves and falls impossibly slowly towards where he needs to be like the powerless body of his nightmares. The sledge is a funny shape, it's half buried in snow – no, it's broken, the front has snapped off. He's staring through the dizzying snow – the sledge has hit something, a rock or a post, it has snapped, it's ricocheted back. Cara will be up ahead, she's light enough, surely, to have sailed over – he plunges on he plunges on there's no knowing which direction but he plunges on in this one noticing that the snow is deeper down here, harder to walk in, there's no crust it must be sheltered by the next slope. If he doesn't find her soon— He's going to find her he's going to find her. There's a dark thing there a kind of – what is it? Her feet! Her feet sticking out of the snow and he grabs her wellies her little ankles inside them he tightens his grip and pulls her out. She's flown into the snow bank head first, she's been posted into the snow by her momentum, and there's no blood no damage. As he wipes the snow from her face she stares at him, amazed, and he waits for her to cry, but she focuses and a grin spreads across her face. 'Dadda!'

She is unharmed. They work out later that she can only have been in the snow for a minute; Megan had just tumbled off when he saw her. Marie was waiting to catch them halfway down but she missed and Cara sailed on. But if he had not been there – how quickly could the falling snow have hidden her? Would she have been able to make herself heard, buried head first in the snow? Could she have dragged herself out? How quickly could anyone else have been down there to look for her? The new snow fell relentlessly all afternoon. Did he pull her from her grave?

The present does not erase the past. The present does not erase the past. He is surfacing. Eleanor shouldn't have left her, she knew it, Eleanor was irresponsible. He saved Cara. He was honoured for it by El, then and after. She called it his sixth sense. There's irony with affection and irony without. Back then, when she called it his sixth sense, it was all right. They smiled together. Only later has she made it into an insult.

Something's changed and his eyes snap open. The bass chatter of the headset on the boy beside him. It's stopped; the boy is looking at him, wanting to get out. Con rises and steps into the aisle; the boy brushes past leaving his coat nested into his seat. Con checks himself in a stretch and glances furtively at his watch. Five more hours to go. People seem to be… he glances around. They are looking at him. As he meets a man's eyes the fellow looks away, but his wife is staring, and the woman behind is staring – what is it, what has he done? Is there something behind him? He turns – nothing. Heads tilt, eyes are averted. He must be attracting their attention by his movements. They're looking at him because he's looking at them. He slots himself into the seat and makes himself small. All these people. The solidity of their flesh and purposes, the way they look. They look at him as if he is up to no good. They look at him with certainty, as if his lack of certainty is a disorderliness which offends them. They know where they are going and why. They eat sandwiches they have prepared earlier and wrapped in cling film; from plastic bags they extricate crisps and chocolate. They unscrew their bottles of water and flasks of coffee. They peel fruit.

The smell when he identifies it makes sweat prickle in his armpits. Someone is eating an orange.

His stomach convulses and he tastes the acidity at the back of his throat. Orange. It is the reek of the monkey house, of every monkey house he's known, that sharp bitter brassy tang with undertones of piss and shit, it dries his tongue and constricts his throat. He crouches low in his seat, nose half an inch from the fabric of the seat in front, taking little shallow breaths. It is possible to ignore a smell. You get used to it. When he used to visit his nan in the home, the old woman stale pissy used up air would slug him, but after ten minutes he'd forgotten it. It is possible to ignore anything. He sits, head bowed, wrists resting inert on his thighs, holding himself very still. This is your response, he chides himself. To El. To everything. Keep very still, withhold yourself. He has spent months now, waiting, as if hiding, like a stupid creature who imagines it is camouflaged. Waiting for the danger to pass.

Instead of getting up and dealing with it.

Has he been imagining that there is some virtue in stoicism? That his patient endurance might move or soften her? He sees clearly now that it never would; it maddens her. How must it be for her, coming home from work, from her day of lectures and meetings and cram-packed appointments, making the effort (the sacrifice) to come home rather than going for a drink with Louis; how must it be to find him, Conrad, sitting there in the dark in the corner of the kitchen with the day's dishes in the sink and no food prepared, staring into space? A giant reproach. A lump of self-pity. Yet – a tendril of orange stink creeps around the seat back and he jerks his head aside – yet he was not self-pitying, when he sat like that. He was simply blank.

There was nothing for him to do. But she would only have been able to interpret it from her own point of view: him sitting there, offering nothing, like a plug hole, a drain into which energy and affection must be poured.

She has never poured energy and affection into him.

But that's not true either. He wouldn't have known how to deal with it if she did. He didn't *want* that. The boy returns to his seat, Con rises and sits again automatically. It's not true. The strangeness of the dynamic… the strangeness of the dynamic surely is that he imagined he would look after El. Her brightness, her cleverness, her speediness: he would protect and insulate her, with careful thoroughness, from all the dangers she was too hot and hasty to espy in advance. That was the team they had laughingly characterised themselves as – the tortoise and the hare. But the tortoise is supposed to win, not to stop halfway, frozen, pretending to be a stone. While the hare careers off, past the end post, into trackless freedom.

He wanted to look after her. Knowing from the start it would be impossible, since she was quicker and more competent. It was in the impossibility of the role that its attraction lay. That's why the time after Cara… that's why the time after Cara's birth was the best. Because El was vulnerable, softened, uncertain. It was possible to look after her.

Everything is tarnished now. He wonders how other people deal with this. The shame. The shamefulness of the past, the expeditiousness of it, the complacent ignorance in which one lived it, the continual and self-perpetuated delusions. He is ashamed of it all, from start to finish; of his pathetic protective male act, of his stoic refusal to react to injury and insult, of his conviction that he was necessary to the children. All the old clichés are there; no one is indispensable. El has always been honestly selfish. Which has left him the role of dishonestly selfless; the martyr, the victim. Until, with the stubborn perversity of flowing water, which must find a way through, he has come to find his satisfaction in her cruelty, in self-abasement.

Is this true? It is true that he has negated himself, all but rubbed himself out. He has no desires. He cannot think of a single thing he wants to do. Contemptible. No wonder El can't stand him. He can't stand himself. Only sit here, passively, awaiting transformation. Death will come. What other change might possibly arise? That El might suddenly fling her arms around him and apologise for everything she did and was, and devote her days to cherishing and amusing him?

Not only is it unimaginable, it is absolutely horrible. It would entail the removal of El's personality.

His limbs ache. He wants to shift position but won't let himself. If he keeps staring at it. If he keeps boring at it, even though it's solid rock – eventually he must come through to something, surely? This is of course a ridiculous thought. He will sit with his face pressed to a rock wall, and then being mortal he will die, and the rock, immovable and unmarked, will remain. He is pitting himself against something that cannot be altered.

Stupid. The smell persists. Are they peeling more? A bag full – he visualises the circles of peel, the sticky little penknife, the row of sucked pips. Revolting. If this is a battle between him and a smell, the smell wins if he stays. If he goes away, the smell loses, it ceases to exist in his nostrils.

He sees himself. His posture, his defeated shoulders, his empty hands. A monkey hunched at the back of its cage, staring balefully out of its prison. This is the problem. Not the anthropomorphism of animals, not the personification of cuddly kittens with diamante collars and little coats; the problem is the animal-ness of humans. The monkey is not like him, *he* is like the monkey. The monkey exists. The conditions of its existence (imprisoned, at the mercy of others whose priorities do not include the happiness of the monkey) are painful. And so by extrapolation…

It is doubtful if the monkey would venture out, if you left the cage door open. It has become what it is, a bundle of miserable defeated resentment. Like him.

By a monstrous effort of will he forces himself to his feet; drags his coat from the seat, makes one foot move in front of the other step step step along the foetid carriage way, past the faces and the eyes, through the intensifying stink to the sliding door at the end. He pushes the handle, watches it open, steps through into cleaner air. He leans against the partition facing outwards, watching the sodden countryside streaming past. He has left his case in the luggage rack at the other end. But it can stay there till he gets off. It would be good to wait here, instead of ploughing through another carriage-full of upturned, inquisitive faces. Instead of helpfully walking towards her, wherever she is sitting, waiting with the sinister knowledge that he will be unable to prevent himself from offering himself up to her.

There is no seat here and he will attract attention if he sits on the floor. The carriage door shushes and thunks open, someone passes behind his back. That's the problem: if she walks through the train, he is easier to find here than tucked away in a seat.

Nevertheless he stays; there is something compelling in the rain that streams diagonally across the window, in the authenticity of the dull grey light outside. There is a normality to daylight which restores sense at the most basic level, he thinks. Paul's incredulous rage: 'The monkeys never even see daylight in their whole lives!' Why couldn't he listen to Paul earlier? He did listen, but what he heard was a betrayed child, who has discovered that his parent is imperfect. Not a serious argument for the monkeys. Maddy is punishment for that. But Paul. Might Paul even be connected? A new thought, paranoid but plausible. Paul is politically active, he is capable of joining a group campaigning against the use of animals in research. In fact he is highly likely to. And to set someone like Maddy onto his father? Con is unsure if this is plausible or not. Everything is fluid, things which were unlikely even a day ago are now developing, and Con's own previous view of Paul as distant, contemptuous, absorbed in the intricacies of his own life shifts now into a view of Paul as potentially aggressive; determined to make a stand against the old man. Paul is committed to his principles; why shouldn't he try to make Con denounce the cruelties inflicted by his own research? Suddenly Con sees that it is crazy not to have told Paul about Maddy. Either he is a moving force behind her action, in which case Con can work out with him precisely how to do the right thing about the animal house, and ask him to call off Maddy's reign of terror. Or, if he's not involved, Con can at least ask his advice. Paul will understand.

Con has no sooner articulated this thought than he dismisses it. Understanding necessarily entails a desire to do so. Why should Paul desire to understand his father? His biological need, as older son, is to reject and replace his father. This is what is happening, thinks Con. All I need to do is let nature take its course. Which it will do anyway, with or without my permission.

He presses his forehead against the cold window and watches

it mist up with his breath. Is this an agreement to allow himself to play the victim? Is he back to square one? He can twist, he can turn, but there's nothing to be done.

When his back starts to ache he moves into the next carriage in search of a seat. But the few empty seats are beside people who are now properly entrenched in their journey, with bags and books and chattels wedged around them. His arrival in search of a seat when the train has not stopped to admit new passengers will reveal him as a malcontent, a seat-swapper. He pauses again at a carriage end, looking at the same view of diagonally teeming rain. He could go back to the buffet car. He could wait until the train stops and then look for a seat as if he is a new passenger. But the train never stops. Does it? Is it non-stop to Rome? Non-stop for nine hours? Surely not. That would make it a travelling prison, intolerable. He presses close to the window again, and sees the wavering semi-molten shapes of grey industrial units, decomposing and reforming in the streaming tears of rain.

He's being stupid. Flights last longer – twelve hours, sometimes more – why get wound up about a non-stop train? But he needs to get off. He needs to get off, to walk, to be in the daylight, in the rain, in a street, in charge of his own speed and direction. He must get off the train.

When the shapes of warehouses and factories are transformed into houses and blocks of flats; when the train slows its pace, to pass through what is clearly the centre of a city, when there is a tower like Pisa and red stone arches, then he is tight against the door, willing it to stop. It's too soon for Rome. His geography of Italy is scrambled. Milan? Modena? Somewhere in northern Italy, but will it stop? There's a rattle of Italian over the PA system, his brain sifts the words for meaning. Stazione Bologna Centrale. Bologna. Thank God.

Con is on the platform, sucking in lungfuls of cold wet air, checking the signs for *Uscita*, when he remembers his case. Doors are slamming. He makes a start back for the carriage but it's too late. With a silent glide before the noise of motion kicks in, the train is off, at walking pace, slow enough to stop, but unstoppable. The train's next stop is Rome.

He checks his pockets. Passport, wallet, glasses, phone. OK. What's in the case? Laptop, papers, clothes, toilet bag. They can send it back from Rome. He can go to the ticket office now and ask.

He walks through the station, empty-handed and light. The case is not important. Better without it. Newborn. Which is garbage, not least for the cost of replacing stuff; where is money going to come from? How long is he going to last like this? It would be the ultimate defeat to go crawling back to El because he's run out of money. How much is in his account? He doesn't even know. His salary comes in on the 20th, so there's that. But for how long will they continue to pay him, if he doesn't supply a sick note or explanation? How long does a missing person stay on a payroll?

It's been one day. He is not exactly missing. Part of his mind, a treacherous part of his mind, sees himself back at home and at work next week. Sees this as a shameful episode known only to himself – and indeed who else is likely to notice? El? She probably doesn't know when he is due home. The kids? Ditto. People at work might wonder, since George and the others will be there. But a few days' absence, that's nothing unusual. He could stay a couple of nights, do the sights of Bologna and pretend he's a free man, then go back as if nothing ever was. Dip his toe in the water then run away up the beach.

There is a faulty switch somewhere in his circuitry. There is something wrong with the wanting and intending circuit. It flickers. He does not know what he wants or what he will do. I am a feather for each wind that blows, he thinks, and the well-wrought, well-thought words comfort him.

The case will go into Lost Property. They'll keep it there a few weeks at least. Maybe he'll go to Rome next week anyway, and pick it up in person. He walks out of the station empty-handed, into a gentle drizzle. Already it seems the mid-afternoon winter darkness is closing in. Lights shine in the windows of Bologna.

Chapter 3

EL CATCHES HER alarm on the first beep at 6am. She has not really slept, but she must have dozed, because once she is showered and dressed she feels clear-headed. The helpless fear of the night has vanished. She clears the kitchen table – Paul has drained the brandy, naturally – and sits cradling a mug of tea and making a list. She needs to phone Con's sister Ailsa. Not that Ailsa will have any idea where he is, but it would be very poor family politics not to have told her, if he really is missing. Also, El wants an ally in not telling Con and Ailsa's mother. She can't see any point in telling the old lady; Con only visits her a couple of times a year, it will be quite a while before she misses him. Anyway, he'll be back. El adds phoning Dan and Megan to her list; she must be sure they are both up to speed on what is happening, now Cara is going to Munich. All four children are hypersensitive to being left out of any information known to their siblings. El thinks about Dan, in his nasty little box of a room in student accommodation. Not that Dan seems to mind a nasty little box. He has his bed, his desk and his computer; Con reported him isolated but perfectly content, last time he visited.

Dan has been extremely calm over Con's disappearance so far – is that likely to change? El hasn't seen him really upset for a long time; he's grown out of the inconsolable rages he suffered as a child. Those rages were about frustration, El was sure – about not being able to do or have something he'd set his heart on. Now he's seventeen he's got more control, and a better grasp of what is possible; also he's good at something. He's applying his mind to computer programming, with excellent results, and excelling is always good for the spirits. El knows she has always been right about Dan. It is Con who has been wrong, demanding tests and visits to specialists, bandying words like autism and Asperger's, looking for nameless psychological woes. El has always maintained that Dan is fine, and so he is; look at him now, flourishing in his first year at university despite his youth. If it was down to Con he'd have been languishing in some special school, rather than finding his own path through the jungle of the comprehensive, leaping ahead a year and learning how to protect himself from bullies and idiots. Yes, Dan is different. Yes, he's a loner. But there is nothing at all wrong with his brain; he's the brightest of the four. So far he has reacted to Con's absence with his usual blankness. Hopefully that will continue, but if he seems upset she will have to tell him to come home. She wonders whether Paul has talked to him. If so, she really must ring him, because Paul will have wound him up. She underlines Dan on her list. Megan, on the other hand, will be easy. How much better it would be if Megan could come home. El imagines her efficient thoughtfulness; *she* would not have left the table littered with dirty glasses and biscuit crumbs, *she* would not be treating her mother as prime suspect. She would probably be coming up with very sensible avenues of search to pursue. But Megan is on stage in London every night this week. She keeps more or less nocturnal hours, El can't phone her before lunchtime. El has a pang for her older daughter's level-headedness; how much more practical than Cara's weepy hysteria and Paul's hateful anger.

Abruptly she refocuses on work, and lists the most vital things she needs to do today; pours herself a bowl of muesli and chops an apple into it, and consumes her breakfast rapidly. Conrad's driving glasses are on the table. She stares at the navy blue case for a while before checking its contents. If you were leaving for good, you would certainly take your driving glasses. Those glasses have been there for a long time, she thinks. For days, maybe weeks. Has he got a new pair? Come to think of it, has he actually been driving? His car is always in the garage with the door shut when she gets home from work, and there's nothing unusual in that because she leaves before he does and gets home after him. But the little heap of car keys, garage keys and glasses that always used to irritate her on the dusty flower stand in the hall hasn't been there for a long time. She rises quickly to check – no, not there.

He must have been going to work by train. Has he even been going to work? Would she know if he didn't? Yes, of course, George-n-ita would have said something. And there was the Ph.D. student. Of course he's been going to work.

Though it might be better if he hadn't. The work is bad for him, she's sure of that – despite the fact that it was her prompting that led him into it. Oh, it was innocent then, it was hopeful, it was still possible for them to talk; it was before this awful shutter had come down between them.

They had a holiday in Ireland, the summer after Dan's first birthday. Rented an old farmhouse in West Cork, she can still smell the smoky, peaty dampness of the place. There were niggles between them; she had got them a new au pair and gone back to work when Dan was three months, and Con was putting in more time with the kids than he should have been doing. He was already fretting about Dan, who was late to smile, late to sit up, late to crawl. He was on three years' funding looking at immunosuppressants and the treatment of tumours in rats; it was slow, predictable work. El believed he was sublimating his own stasis onto Dan. And both of them were tired – four children were turning out to be significantly more work than three.

But the Irish farm was a good place, and they fell back into their old easy way of getting on that went back to before Dan was born, sitting outside in the overgrown garden in the long summer evenings, while Paul and Megan played hide and seek under the rhododendron bushes. Once Dan was settled and three-year-old Cara in bed, they could leave the older two to play until they dropped. They sat in dilapidated deckchairs with a bottle of wine on a wobbly cane table between them, watching as the sky slowly deepened and bats began to carve the air.

'Tell me something you'd really like,' she said to him.

'First star.' He pointed high above the farmhouse roof. In the bushes all around them the little birds were twittering and fluttering and falling away.

'Tell me.'

'I'd like to never see the inside of that bloody lab again.'

'Well, Con – you must leave.'

'And do what? It's secure, there's funding – I'm working for a megalomaniac and the research is like watching paint dry, but so what?'

'So *that*. It's soul-destroying. Listen, I had an idea. It was just a conversation I barged in on, one lunchtime – they were talking about transplants.'

'Transplants?'

'Heart, kidney, lung, whatever. Saul and Brock have got money for a slab of research on monkeys.'

'I'm not interested in butchery.'

'Of course. But apart from the surgery, what's the main thing that's all about?'

'Rejection.'

'Precisely. Finding ways to stop rejection. Immunosuppressants.'

'I don't know anything about monkeys.'

'Duh. No. But you know a hell of a lot about immune systems. About how they break down. About ways of blocking them.'

'In rats, and humans.'

'Wouldn't there be cross over?'

'El, there are people who've been working on monkeys for years. Saul and Brock for a start.'

'But work on immune markers in cancer might well be relevant for damping down rejection in transplanted organs – they're all parts of the same system.'

There was a silence, and they listened to Megan's clear shrill voice calling out, 'Ninety-eight, ninety-nine, one *hundred*. Coming, ready or not.'

'There must be people who already know about this.'

'I'm not sure there are. Why don't you give Saul a ring?'

'Give him a ring and say what?'

'Oh Con! Say you've heard he's got money to work on transplants, and where's he up to on immunosuppressants. Say—'

'All right, all right. Listen.'

An owl was calling from the stand of beech trees the other side of the lane; into the silence that followed its call came an answering 'tu-whit, tu-whoo' from Paul, and giggles.

'We ought to chivvy those two to bed.'

'I'll make their cocoa. You drag them in.'

They said no more about it that night, but Con himself raised it the next evening. The fine weather had turned to drizzle, and they'd attempted their first peat fire in the wide sooty kitchen fireplace. It was making a wonderful smell and plenty of smoke but not much in the way of heat. El knelt beside it feeding it dry twigs, trying to conjure a blaze.

'That research must have already been done, El, it must have been. Christian Barnard and the heart transplants, the drugs they used must have been tested on animals before people—'

'If they have money to research with monkeys there must be a reason.'

'But they've already moved on to drugs they're prepared to try on people – why go backwards?'

'I don't know. Maybe there's some other factor?'

'OK. If we're both speaking from equal positions of ignorance, then I shall speculate. And I think you should leave that fire to smoulder, that's what peat does.'

'But it's not warm.'

'Come and sit on my knee. I'll keep you warm.'

She remembers the quiet pleasure of that moment, both mental – he was interested, she'd got him hooked, he was starting to chip at the idea – and physical, his long limbs folding her in, warming and holding her, taking charge of her, which was a rare thing now for him to do. She loved it when he was expansive; since Dan, it seemed all energy and initiative must come from her. But now here at last was Con again, chewing on an idea that engaged him, ordering her around, lifting the responsibility of the pair of them off her shoulders.

'Here, move round a bit. I never met a woman with such a sharp pointy bum.'

'You'd prefer me fat?'

'Can't have too much of a good thing. Now look. The biggest problem the transplant people have is not even rejection, is it?'

'Shortage of donors.'

'Exactly. How can they build any kind of success rate, how can they hope to sort out what works from what doesn't when they're reliant for their supply of organs on accidents? You never know what's coming in, what blood group, age, size.'

'OK. So?' She could already see where he was going.

'So are Saul and Brock actually looking at monkey hearts for humans?'

'I don't know. Could it work?'

'It could work in the sense that you could breed them specifically for that; you could prepare the recipient, take the organ from the donor at the most opportune moment – but whether you could make a match I have no idea. Chimps are closest, aren't they, but I have no idea even how big their hearts are. And I've a feeling they're an endangered species.'

'If humans reject other human hearts, a monkey heart is even more alien.'

'Yes, but like I said, you could prepare it; breed it specifically for that purpose. I don't know anything about monkeys but you could treat the donor heart in advance with drugs that would make its less antigenic to the new host.'

Eleanor suddenly remembers the funny clicking noise that interrupted him. A tap followed by a rattling click, coming from upstairs. She uncurled from his lap and they both crept up the steep creaky staircase. The door to Paul and Megan's room, left open when they'd gone to bed, was closed. In the feeble glare of the forty-watt bulb that hung from the landing ceiling, they could see the latch on the door wobbling up and down, clicking, as if manipulated by invisible fingers. When Con opened the door there was an exclamation and a clatter. And there was little Megan in her pyjamas, with the cricket bat she had been using to try to push up the latch. They took her downstairs for a cuddle. All the doors had those old iron latches that need lifting with a finger, so high up the doors that only Paul could reach them; Megan and Cara were trapped if a door was closed on them. She remembers Con praising Megan for trying the bat rather than waking Paul. 'Good lateral thinking, little lass.' And how then, with a drowsy Megan curled between them on the battered sofa, and the sounds of her desperate thumb-sucking gradually relaxing into nothing more than gentle breathing, he had quietly returned to his speculations about transplanting monkey hearts to humans.

They kicked the ideas back and forth between them for the rest of the holiday, and the optimism which reanimated Con is linked in El's mind with the physical attributes of that creaky old house, its stubborn functionality: the big cold stone slabs on the kitchen floor that could be swept or sluiced down when farm muck got trodden in; the booby trap of a door sill on the back door to the yard that each of the children tripped over repeatedly, put there, she assumes, to keep flooding mud out of the kitchen; the noisy, uncarpeted wooden stairs, black and slippery with use, that they had to keep Cara away from, but that they all managed to avoid falling down. That old unyielding house sheltered them and imbued their holiday with its character; regrounded them in a physical setting that demanded their attention and was so old it did not need excuses; making them aware every time they clanked open a door or set a bare foot on the cold kitchen floor or drew in a breath of peat-smoky air, aware of being alive and able and in motion, aware of their own lightness and warmth and mutability.

Would Con have generated the enthusiasm to contact Saul, if these conversations had happened at home? El doubts it. That strange old house brought out the best in him – in them – and fostered a new kind of energy.

The sound of Cara in the shower brings El back to this kitchen. Cara will not eat anything El offers her for breakfast, so better not to be in the kitchen when she comes down. She may just pick at something she fancies, if left to her own devices. El takes a new mug of tea and her list into her office. She can polish off some work emails before it's time for Cara to leave.

Chapter 4

CONRAD PASSES LITTLE hotels by the station but feels the need to identify the centre of the town, to locate himself geographically in this dot on the map where the train has deposited him. It is a real city. He swings into a rhythm of walking, enjoying the exercise and the fresh air in his lungs – feeling himself physically present in the place. The drizzle stinging his face is real. In the diminishing light it is so real it transports him, effortlessly, back to the night when, like this, the drizzle was a blessed relief. To the farmyard, in the rain. The night his father died.

Con's father hanged himself from a beam in the barn, at the age of sixty-seven. Con's mother found him, and rang Con at work with the news.

There is no one else (well, there is Con's sister Ailsa, who will of course have to be told, but she is unlikely to be much use). Con rings El to tell her, then drives straight to the farm, arriving as darkness falls. His mother is in the kitchen, peeling potatoes. Con kisses her. She is grey but seems composed. 'I can't get him down so he's still there.'

'You haven't rung—'

'Who? Bit late for the doctor, isn't it.'

'I think we need a doctor for a death certificate. Maybe the police as well.' Con makes the necessary phone calls while his mother stolidly peels carrots and parsnips. Going out to the barn is unavoidable. The dog, which has been lying under the table with its ears flat, gets up and follows him to the door.

'You'll need the torch,' she tells Con. 'The light's gone out there.' He picks up the big flashlight from the shelf above the coats and makes his way across the uneven yard. It has started to drizzle, the fine rain stings his cheeks. He looks down to the dog for solidarity, but it has disappeared. He unlatches the barn door then shoves it open with his foot and waits on the threshold until he can bring himself to raise the torch and direct its beam into the dark interior. For a moment he can't see anything but the barn, the shape-shifting arena of his and Ailsa's childhood dramas, and can't smell anything but its familiar straw, damp earth and creosote. Then his nose catches an ugly whiff of human excrement. The light hits the body; unnaturally large, swinging slightly, the face made hideous either by the exaggerated light and shadow or by its own interior workings. Before Conrad can stop himself, he is outside again, leaning against the barn wall for balance. He bends to rest his hands on his knees, trying to breathe evenly, feeling the welcome drizzle on his burning neck and head. How can he go in there?

But why should he expect strangers to deal with it? Then he realises that he can and must leave it to strangers, so the police can verify that it is suicide. He straightens, staring into the darkness of the yard and the yellow light of the kitchen window. Puddles glint treacherously. His open pores are drinking the rain, and he upturns his face and opens his mouth too, receiving the clean water gratefully. He waits in the yard until the dog gives a cursory bark and the first vehicle arrives. The doctor. Made capable by the shocked presence of a stranger who clearly knows his parents, Con enters the barn with him and positions the upended flashlight on a bale to give them some light. The doctor takes Ethan's wrist and feels for a pulse. 'He's cold,' he says. 'He's been dead a while. I'm sorry.'

Con thinks he should touch his father's hand but he can't make himself do it. The smell is awful. 'We can't cut him down, can we?'

'The police will do it.' The doctor is heading for the barn door and Conrad follows him out into the blessed rain again.

'Can you write a death certificate?'

'It's one for the coroner, suicide. He'll probably call a post-mortem.'

Con's ignorance embarrasses him. 'I'm sorry. I've called you out for nothing.' The kitchen door opens, spilling light across the muddy yard, and his mother appears in the doorway. 'Go back in, Mum. There's nothing for you to do here. Stay in the warm.'

She hesitates, then slams the door. From somewhere the dog begins to howl.

'Want me to take a look at your mother? Give her something for the shock?'

Con nods. 'I just need to—' He goes back into the barn. But there is nothing he can do out here. He picks up the flashlight, closes the door, follows the doctor into the house.

His mother is sitting at the table and the doctor is taking her pulse. 'I don't want anything,' she says. 'I'm all right.'

When the doctor has finished he offers, 'What about something to help you sleep?' and she shakes her head.

'Well,' says the doctor. 'Well, Nancy, I wish I'd known he was feeling so low. It shouldn't have come to this. I'm very sorry.' He stands for a moment with his bag clasped in his hands, then turns for the door. Conrad follows him out again.

'Thanks. Thanks very much.'

'Let me know if your mother needs anything.'

'Yes. Thank you.' Con stands quietly in the drizzle while the car reverses, raking the sodden yard with its lights, then turns and disappears down the track. When he goes back into the kitchen his mother is standing at the sink staring out into the darkness. 'Mum? You all right?'

She does not reply.

'Do you know…' He hesitates, the question is crass. 'Is there – have you found a note?'

She shakes her head then lifts the pan full of vegetables onto the cooker and fills the pan with hot water from the kettle. 'I've got some chops,' she says. Con is about to say he isn't hungry when he realises that he is, in fact, ravenous. Let her cook; some ancient piece of received wisdom advises him that it's better for her to be busy.

'Have you told Ailsa?'

A quick shake of the head. He dials before giving himself time to think.

'Conrad. And to what do I owe the extraordinary honour of my brother phoning me?'

He tells her. She begins to sob immediately. 'Ailsa, listen. I'm with Mum. She's pretty calm. We're waiting for the police.'

'I'll come.'

'Better to leave it till the morning.'

'You're there. Both his children should be there, what do you think I am?'

'All I meant was, there's nothing to be done tonight, and it's a bit grim, and a long drive in the dark for you—'

'I'll get a taxi, how d'you expect me to drive after this?'

'Ailsa, there's nothing either of us can do until the morning.'

'How could he do that? Why?' Renewed sobbing. 'I can't bear it.'

'I don't know, I really don't know. We'll try and sort some stuff out in the morning.'

She is crying noisily now and he doesn't know if she hears him. His mother cocks an ear at the wailing coming down the phone.

'Ailsa, I'm going now, OK? We'll talk in the morning. Bye. Goodbye.' He puts the phone down gingerly; she will accuse him of hanging up on her but he can't listen to that any more. Leaving his mother in the kitchen, he goes into the sitting room and calls El on the extension in there.

'He's still hanging in the barn, El, it's horrible. Mum seems completely disconnected.'

'Oh Con, I'm so sorry. Why not ring one of the neighbours – the Fieldings are OK, aren't they? Couldn't you ask Joe's wife to sit with your mum a bit?'

She does not understand how much this would offend his mother. Con can hear Cara bossing Dan in the background. 'Now pick up the crayons. You have to tidy up your toys like a good girl.' She likes to pretend Dan is a girl; she had been desperate for a little sister. A few times she has dressed his hair with her own bows and slides, which Dan has accepted blankly, and Con and El have debated the evils of gender stereotyping and whether to intervene or not. The blast of home warms Con and steadies him. 'I'm not sure she'd appreciate Mrs Joe,' he says. 'I suppose I should try and talk to her. I just rang Ailsa. She does my head in.'

'D'you want me to come over? I could ask Lily to stay with the kids. I can't get out of my morning lecture, but after that—'

He wants her desperately but her effect upon the ugly dynamic between his mother and his sister would not be good. 'Thanks, El. It's OK. Just be there at the end of the phone to talk me down.'

Her laugh, close in his ear.

'I don't understand Mum. I don't know if she's even asking herself why—'

'She'll be in shock. How long have they been married?'

'Something like forty years.'

'It'll be like losing a limb, won't it? She won't believe it, she'll have a phantom.'

'Jesus, El. I don't know what to do.'

'Oh love, just make sure she eats and drinks. Maybe ring the police again? Then pour both of you a good slug of whatever alcohol you can find in the place, and get some sleep.'

'I love you,' he whispers.

'You too.' There is an indulgent smile in her voice. He listens to her put the phone down, holding the empty receiver to his ear for the last reverberation of her voice.

The kitchen is full of the steam of overboiling vegetables and the spitting fat of the chops. His mother wrestles with pans, and he makes them both a cup of tea. Still no police. At table his father's seat is conspicuously empty. Con breaks the silence. 'Is there anything I need to do for the sheep? Have you started lambing?'

'Not yet. They'll need looking at in the morning.' She has

piled his plate with food but taken very little herself.

'Mum, can I get you anything else? Are you OK?'

'Why shouldn't I be OK.' It is not a question.

Con eats quickly, greedily; he was empty. And maybe with food inside him he'll be more able... he needs to speak to her before Ailsa comes and ends all possibility of communication. When he puts down his knife and fork his mother makes to rise and take the plates, but he puts his hand on her arm. 'Mum, it's all right, just sit still a minute. D'you have any idea why he did this?'

'To spite me.'

'Mum—'

'He's been doing it all his life. Putting me in the wrong. Getting one over on me.'

A stupid giggle bursts out of him. 'Dad's killed himself to spite you. Did you have a fight?'

She shrugs.

'Mum?'

'No more than usual.'

The back swill of numberless wretched family meals sloshes around Con: his mother slamming down plates, his father chomping through his food with a show of insouciance, hectoring Con and his sister with his excuse for humour. 'Where d'you get that nose, sonny? No one on my side got a schnoz like that.' And 'Eat up that cabbage, Ailsa – put hairs on your chest that will. You can come out and do your strongman act after tea, Connie boy, got a pile of feedbags need shifting, ha ha.' It amused him to find Con weak and effeminate. This became a furious charge when Con made it known that he did not want to be a farmer. Ethan did not address his wife except for the occasional

'Cat got your tongue, Mother?'

Con clears their plates from the table. 'Mum, have you got any whisky?'

She indicates the bottom cupboard of the dresser, and he locates a half bottle of Bell's and pours them both a dose. 'Well, if it was no more than usual, why's he chosen to do it now?'

She sips at her whisky and coughs. 'There's plenty of reasons.'

'Tell me.'

'His children for one. He's not stupid. He knows neither of you want to give him the time of day.'

Con suppresses his first impulse, which is to correct her use of the present tense. 'I think it was more the other way round, Mum. He wasn't very interested in my life, he never once asked about my work.'

'Oh your work!' she says contemptuously. 'How often did you ask him about his work?'

'But I know his work—'

'Do you? Do you? Did you know he's been losing money? Do you know the price of feed for the lambs he raised last year?'

Con does not.

'£120 a ton, and it was a wet spring, he had to bring them all under cover.'

'Was he worried about money, then?'

'Of course he was. Worried sick.'

It is long enough since Con has talked more than trivia with his mother that he has forgotten her inveterate habit of reviling and criticising her husband both to his face and to anyone who will listen, and then leaping with outrage to his defence if anyone else breathes a word against him. 'I'm sorry. If only he'd asked me, maybe I—'

'When's he supposed to ask you anything? When does he ever see you?'

'Mum, I visit you a damn sight more than you ever visit me. In fact I can tell you how many times you've been to our house – once. The party we had the summer after Cara was born.'

'You can't leave a farm, you know that.'

'He could have taken a day off once in a while. It's not as if you went on holidays, at least you could have a day out.'

'He wouldn't have known what to do with himself on a day out.'

'He could even have picked up the phone.'

Con's mother snorts. 'The phone!'

El has suggested that Dan's possible autism is handed down from Con's father. Con found the way he 'teased' her, when she visited, cringeworthy. 'How's the women's libber?' he'd say to her, and 'D'you see those children often enough to tell 'em apart?' El thought his 'bluff humour', as she called it, was a defence against a distressing sense of social inadequacy, and that Ethan was to be indulged rather than despised. She would tease him back and quiz him about sheep fertility and the mechanics of AI, and tell him she was doing similar things with women. One of Ailsa's bitterest complaints to her parents was, 'You think more of Eleanor than you do of me, even though I am your own flesh and blood.'

'He didn't like getting old,' Con's mother says suddenly.

'What?'

'He didn't like the aches and pains. He didn't like not being able to lift a bale on his own any more, he didn't like to ask for help.'

'I didn't know…'

'There's a lot you don't know. He would have walked bare-foot to China for you two.'

Con pours himself another whisky. His father has killed himself and it is his fault. 'Did he talk to anyone about – his money troubles?'

'Who would he talk to?'

Nobody. He was a friendless man – no social skills. 'D'you think he was depressed?'

'Of course he was depressed. What'd he got to look forward to? His own grandchildren don't know him, the farm's losing money, how long till we get turfed out and dumped in a home?'

'His grandchildren do know him. Did know him.'

Con's mother humphs. 'They saw him twice a year. More interested in the lambs than him, more interested in shrieking and running amok.'

It is true that something gets into the kids when they visit the farm. Maybe it's the space and the dilapidated state of the place, but they do tear about, their calling voices echoing across the yard. And of course they avoid his father; what child wouldn't avoid a man who pinches your cheek too hard and bellows, 'You need to get more pudding down you!'?

'Mum, you know how he was with kids, he wasn't the easiest—'

'You asked.'

'Was he taking anything?'

'Medicine?' She counts off on her fingers. 'For blood pressure, cholesterol, heart—'

'For depression?'

She snorts derisively and gets up to finish clearing the table. Her accusations are all verified by the fact that Con didn't know his father was on any medication at all. He calls the police again and is put on hold while they try to trace what has happened. It transpires that they are very stretched but should be with him any minute now, and indeed as he ends the call the dog starts barking furiously again.

It is quickly done; the dim barn jerked into horror-film brightness by flash photographs, the rope untied by gloved hands and slipped into a plastic bag. Paramedics stretcher the body to the ambulance, there is a brief spattering of questions and platitudes for his mother and himself, and then the yard is filled with the throb of engines and the sweeping lights, and they are gone. His father's awful presence is gone. Con stands in the empty darkness. He would rather be here in the drizzle than inside with his mum. He thinks about the person whose job it is to clean the bodies, in the mortuary. To peel off the clothes and wash the dead flesh. A part of him is surprised his mother didn't want to do it. He wonders if she thought of it. Would it help with the grief?

She does not appear to be grieving, though. She is simply apportioning blame, which Ailsa will also want to do when she pitches up in the morning. They will have to organise a funeral together; they will have to sort out what happens with the farm; they will have to sort out their mother (not that she will let them). His limbs are heavy and his head a dull stone. How is he going to deal with all this?

His mother is not in the kitchen. He follows the sound of movement upstairs and finds her in his old bedroom putting sheets on the bed. 'It's all right, Mum, I can do that.'

She brushes past him, shaking out the sheet, and he bends to help her tuck it in. When the bed is made he wants nothing but to crawl into it and bury his head, but he offers to make his mother her Horlicks and she nods. Down in the kitchen he makes up the fire. Maybe she will want to sit up and talk. Putting off going to bed alone. He wonders if his parents have ever slept apart. Many a time on opposite sides of the bed, no doubt, unspeaking, clenched and angry. But not actually in separate beds. They have lived together in a state of hostility more closely entwined than all the loving couples Con knows. Mutual dislike has bound them together. They didn't talk, they didn't go anywhere; they didn't see anyone. Just followed the repetitive pattern of their respective duties, his outdoors, hers in. Any suggestion of change would have been regarded as criticism: any criticism would make them angry.

The only line of thought worth following now is practical. When his mother comes down her drink is on the table and Con has an old envelope and a pen and is starting a list. 'What we need to do,' he explains. 'Fire away.'

'Funeral.'

'Yes. And the farm, the running of the farm? I mean now's not the time of course but we will need to put something in place quickly—'

'Sell it.'

Con looks at her.

'Sell it. I'm not going to run it, am I?'

'OK, Mum, let's talk in the morning. I was just going to make a list of things we need to think about in the short term, not try to decide big things tonight.'

'What are we going to decide with Ailsa putting her oar in?'

He realises his mother is old enough and tough enough to need to pay no heed to the niceties of grief. Does she feel anything? He indulges for a moment in the shameful fantasy of his

71

own death, of El's stricken face; of her striding blindly from the house, refusing to speak to anyone, until she can contain her sorrow. He knows this is true. She would have to wrestle with it on her own, she wouldn't want people to see, and inside she would be an open wound. As would he, if she died. They will never ever be like his parents.

His mother is staring at him. 'I don't know,' he admits. 'But it's a big decision, selling the farm.'

'I've thought about it before. I'll buy a house in the village. There's one opposite the co-op been on the market eighteen months.'

'But—'

'We could have sold up years ago, for me. It was that awkward old sod hanging on to the place like a drowning man with a log.'

'Did he know you wanted to move?'

'Of course he did. Why would anybody want to be mopping mud off a stone floor twice a day for the rest of her life? Dragging in buckets of coal, and keeping three empty bedrooms clean and aired? You think this is a good place to grow old?'

Of course he doesn't; he and El have discussed a hundred times the problem of his parents, and concluded helplessly each time that they could never be persuaded to leave the farm.

'Women live longer than men,' she says. 'I thought I'd get a little village house in the end.'

Con has abandoned his list. His mother is in full flow. 'We'll sell the farm at auction, that's the only way to shift it quick. Break up the land – Fieldings will be after everything their side of the river. And you might get planning permission for the paddock and lambing pens. If they knock down the farm and barn as well, there's a good-sized plot.'

She is looking at him so he nods. 'Right.' His father is an obstacle disposed of. If Con is honest, that is precisely what he feels; why should he be such a hypocrite as to expect his mother to feel differently? But something is churning inside him, and he has to bank up the fire and bid her goodnight. He has to sit on the edge of his saggy boyhood bed and examine the memory which has threatened to unhinge him, which comes with a bittersweet wash of relief, as at impending tears, which due must be paid by someone on this day, someone other than Ailsa whose tears are crocodile-easy and only ever about herself.

His father picked him up from school one day when he'd been in a fight. Christopher Boyle had taken his dinner money twice, and had made a grab for his new calculator. Con had lashed out and, amazingly, given Chris a bloody nose before Chris hammered him. Con was blamed for starting the fight. The teacher phoned his parents and his dad came to get him. Con eased himself into the car. He hurt all over and his lip was oozing metallic blood into his mouth, which he wanted to spit out and had to force himself to swallow, though it rose in his throat like sick. His father didn't say anything to the teacher, which was a mercy. He never hit Con, there was no fear of violence, just the horror of embarrassment and misery at the impending lecture. Ethan drove them to the top field and left Con sitting in the car while he walked across and opened the gate to the next pasture for grazing. Con sat catching his breath, surreptitiously holding the door open and spitting blood onto the grass, running his tongue around his teeth and finding them all present. When his father came back he just sat in the driver's seat without turning the ignition.

'All right then?' he said eventually.

'Yes, Dad.'

The two of them sat there, side by side, staring into the field of sheep which began to raise their heads and stare about and make their way, in gathering speed and numbers, towards the open gateway. They were like iron filings, Con thought, drawn together by a magnet underneath the grass. When the last one was in his father got out again and shut the gate, and they drove home in silence.

Con can cry for this version of his father. It seems like his only clear memory of him, but there must have been other moments. He was not always that pushy loudmouth. The tears when they come are for the man that Ethan's wife and children did not allow him to be. And now Con's mother is glad his father is dead. And so is Con. Glad the man they knew is dead, while the unknown man they might have had has never even had a chance to live.

When Con thinks of his children – who love him, who run squealing to the door to greet him when he comes home, who bring him gifts of paintings and cooking and crumbling play-dough animals, who run to him with stories or hurt knees to kiss, or for explanations of electricity or rainbows, or with tales of friends' betrayals – when he thinks of his children who create him daily with their hot, needy love, his heart breaks for his father, who could not be loved. No wonder his father killed himself. If Con spends the rest of his life giving thanks for his own life, it will not be enough.

This, he remembers, in the chill drizzle of Bologna. Shame.

He is wet now and realises that he has no clothes to change into. It's 4.30. Get a room. Go shopping. But these are the wrong sort of shops, tiny local supermarkets with boxes of fruit and veg

74

on the pavement. Where are the real shops? Here is a hotel with a modestly small sign. Two stars. The nightly rate is cheap. He is given a key to a room up three narrow flights of stairs. It has been badly partitioned so it gives the appearance of being higher than it is wide, a kind of upended coffin, but there is room for a single bed, a narrow wardrobe, a tiny sink and a red plastic chair. The shared toilet is on the floor below. The window looks out over the street, it's fine. He asks the receptionist where he can buy clothes and tries to explain that his case is lost. The man draws some arrows on a little tourist map, but it seems a distance away. Maybe he should get a taxi? Perhaps he can buy an umbrella at the little supermarket?

The corner supermarket, on closer inspection, turns out to sell many things: toothbrush, toothpaste, razor, soap, deodorant, umbrella, socks and an extra large T shirt with a yellow smiley face on it, which will serve as a nightshirt. He takes the bag of shopping back to the *pensione*, changes his socks and sets out with the umbrella to follow his map.

He is tired now and the street names are high up and difficult to read – he has to peer up through the slanting rain, then down at his quickly sodden map. He tries to dodge his way through the increasing numbers of people on the pavements. All are carrying umbrellas, many holding them in front of their faces so they are unable to see or avoid collisions.

In a row of expensive-looking shops he locates a window featuring three artistically lit sweaters. Inside he finds that nothing has a price tag under 200 euros. Outside again he peers at the other shops but none sell clothes. He sets off again, wet map in one hand, umbrella in the other, into darkness that seems to congeal between each pair of inadequate streetlamps. Cars crawl along the narrow streets, splashing pedestrians, emitting smoking exhaust. Now there are no shops. But a bar, on the opposite side of the road. He waits, dodges through the traffic, and enters a place of blissfully steamy warmth. It is full of men talking; it is easy to slip into a corner table and absorb the heat and amiability. He has a coffee and then a red wine, and then a curling cardboard slice of pizza from a heat cabinet. It is not good but it puts new heart in him. Shops on the Continent stay open late, he reminds himself. He asks the barman for new directions, to a big shop, department store, for clothes, and tries to memorise the route, but once he is out in the dark again there's a small alley off to the right, which may be where he's supposed to turn, or it may be he should continue to the next road on the right. He walks past the alley and takes the road, takes lefts and rights obediently, and finds himself, where he judges the shop should be, outside a school. The crowds on the pavements have thinned. A church bell strikes 8. People are going home to dinner; he won't find the clothes shop now. All he must do is go home to his hotel, put on his big smiley T shirt, and sleep.

Turning a corner off the main thoroughfare (a corner he remembers passing on his way from the bar) a shadow scurries ahead of him. Quite suddenly he remembers Maddy. Is she here? Has she followed him? Did she see him get out at Bologna? He has been traipsing about the streets for hours, on display for all to see. As if he were taunting her, if she's here; flaunting himself. The shadow that reminded him – is she up ahead, lying in wait?

He turns and hurries on down the main street. It will be possible to turn right later; the bar is not even necessarily on his best route back to the hotel. But he could probably retrace his route from the bar. Maybe. In fact he's lost. He moves quickly for a while, putting distance between himself and that shadow. But his feet are wet again, and his trousers too, and the hand holding the umbrella is icy. The name of the hotel is not springing to his mind. He pulls his plastic tagged key from his pocket but it simply bears the room number, 7.

There's nothing to do but keep going in the direction he imagines is the right one, keeping his eyes open for stragglers (hardly anyone out in these wet dark streets now) and hoping to recognise something. Eventually a sign for *Stazione*. He has to get all the way to the station before he can locate the route he took away from it, and follow it through puddle-coated streets, through memories of the farm, back to his starting point. Pensione Arditti. He is here. When he locks his door and strips off his wet things he is shivering uncontrollably and his feet are yellow and bloodless like the feet of a drowned man. He dips them, one at a time, into hot water in the little sink, then curls up on the shelf of a bed and clutches the blankets tight around him. She did not follow him here. There is no reason for her to know where he is.

Chapter 5

THERE IS A string of work emails, many of them expressing sympathy or anxiety about Con. El's eyes glaze over, she has no idea how to reply to them. Why can't they just leave her alone? She needs to think about why Con might have left. It's no good just pretending it hasn't happened. But you do know, she tells herself. You do know why. It's because of Cara, isn't it?

This realisation is shocking. It is so close to her, so enmeshed in the fabric of her life, that it is painful to force herself to see it. To see it as Con sees it. She has never given it its due. She realises it must be working inside Con like a poison. It is almost certainly the reason he has gone. She has handled it terribly badly.

Sitting rigidly in her computer chair she retraces the memory from the start. There was a kind of obliviousness to it, it was part of that shiny protected disengaged life of hers. Glenn was a visiting research fellow from MIT. Cynical and funny, and always working late. While Con was giving the kids their tea and bathing them, El and Glenn were the last two out of the lab one night, and they went for a drink. Glenn was heading back to Chicago at Christmas, back to his girlfriend and his life. That's what made it possible. He complimented El on her chestnut brown eyes (an unthreatening compliment, since it made her think of conkers, hard shiny brown conkers pressed into a doughy face, so that she could laugh and throw that back at him and pretend they were not staring into each other's eyes). He told her she was the most intelligent woman he'd ever met, and she jibed at his sexism.

Glenn laughed. 'OK. Since I can't say the right thing I might as well be hung for a ram as a lamb. You've got a fantastic arse. Come home with me.'

In her own triumphant laughter El identified an element of celebration of Con. She was Con's wife, whom another man was making a play for; it confirmed Con's status. She didn't go home with Glenn that night, and didn't think she would at all. She simply hoarded the compliment. Came within a hair's breadth of telling Con, as she lay luxuriously in the bath that Sunday morning and Con stood shaving at the sink ignoring her. 'Guess who fancies me?' The teasing words were already formed in her brain when Paul ran in crying that Megan had swallowed a Lego man's head.

But after that it was impossible not to be conscious of when Glenn was working late; of his breathtakingly blond head bent to the microscope. Or of which jeans she wore to work. And the evening when they coincided at the lab door with their coats on was unavoidable, as was his, 'D'you have to rush home?'

'No, I've already missed tea.'

'Well,' glancing at his watch, 'I could make you an omelette.' Leading them into the glut of terrible egg jokes that haunted the IVF unit at that time; leading them giddy with excitement to his flat, where they did not get around to cooking food. Leading to her cycling home at breakneck speed from the 9.55pm train, swooping round corners and through traffic lights, more invulnerable and shiny than she had ever been.

She wasn't in love with Glenn. Not at all. She was simply joyous at being desired; revelling in the laughter, high on the excitement. She had to make a conscious effort not to tell Con about it. There was no anxiety, no danger, no subterfuge involved; in two months Glenn would return to the States. This was simply about having fun. And then she got pregnant.

She knew when it had happened, as soon as she missed her period. It was the only time she'd out and out lied to Con about where she was going. Saturday afternoon, she told him she had to check something at the lab, a couple of hours' work. She took the bike on the train and cycled straight round to Glenn's house, at the time they had agreed. She stopped at the kerb outside his house, heart flapping like a pigeon in her chest, waiting to calm her breathing, and looked up to see him opening the front door with such a grin on his face that laughter burst out of her.

They made love twice, and afterwards lay talking and stroking one another until she said she had to go, and Glenn – who'd used his last two condoms – entered her again, 'Just to say goodbye.' And their lovemaking was achingly slow so that she came almost without moving, except for the powerful contractions of her orgasm, which wrung an answering climax from him.

'God! I'm sorry! There can't be more than a drop—'

'Fine, that's just a few thousand sperm then!'

She wondered afterwards if it was because their daily labours were about adding sperm to egg and monitoring progress that they felt such sublime confidence in their own ability to control what would happen. The episode left her amused, cherished, all-powerful. Until she knew she was pregnant. It could have been Con – their contraception certainly wasn't foolproof – but her instincts knew it wasn't. And once she was pregnant there was nothing that could be done about it without Con knowing. She finished with Glenn, which was sad but not traumatic. He would be leaving in a few days anyway, and she told no one she was pregnant till he'd gone. There must be no danger of Glenn ever knowing, and the only way to absolutely keep him from the knowledge was to quarantine it until after his departure. But then, how to tell Con? Creating the right space and time to tell him became vastly important; she didn't need to think about what she would say, didn't need to plan that – just needed to ensure that the setting of the conversation was right. Not at home; there was never enough time or privacy, and she needed to control it, to manage whichever way the conversation went, without the random intrusions of Paul, Megan, or Hélène the au pair. She did not even think she would lie; she didn't have to lie – in the right place and mood they would both find out what she would tell him.

Con didn't much like leaving the kids in the evening, despite the au pair. El had learned that he made excuses, like tiredness, to take them home early; it was often difficult to feel his attention was fully focused on the play or whatever it was they had gone out to do. It would be better, she reasoned, to steal time from work rather than from the kids. That would disarm him.

Four days after Glenn's mid-December departure there was a sharp frost. As El cycled to the station through the dark blue morning she willed the day to be clear, and when she looked out, mid-morning, it was. She went straight to phone him at work. 'Con? It's such a beautiful day. Shall we play hookey? Meet for lunch and a walk, and go home early?' It was carefully calculated.

They agreed he would pick her up from work and they'd go for lunch in Greenfield, so they could collect her bike from the station. As they drove through the bright sunlight she tried to gauge his mood. He was quiet, rather absorbed in himself, not as exultant in escaping work as she had hoped. 'Such a beautiful day. It makes me want to plan holidays. Shall we go away at Easter next year instead of the summer?' She spoke at random. But the baby would be due in July; as soon as she had said this El realised how strange it would seem, when he looked back on it, that she should have suggested this departure from routine without telling him why. And then realised forcibly how strange it would seem, altogether, that she had been hugging the information to herself. Having children made him happy. In the normal run of things she would have told him as soon as she guessed she might be pregnant. This big deal, this afternoon off work, built it up – made it suspicious. Then she realised she was going to tell him the truth. Admit what had happened, tell him she was sorry. She could have an abortion, or not. It would be up to him.

She had not considered saying this, before, and thinking it now as they drove in silence made her nervous. Con would not see infidelity in the same light as she did. He would be upset. He spoke suddenly into silence. 'I want us to get rid of the au pair.'

'Hélène? Why? I thought you liked her.' An argument about the au pair was the last thing they needed.

'She's pleasant enough. But she's…'

'What? Not good with the kids?'

'No, she's OK. But – well, I think we should get someone else.'

El readjusted. So he wasn't reviving the argument against au pairs. He was simply wanting rid of Hélène. 'OK. If you like. What's wrong with her?'

There was a silence as Con slowed for traffic lights, waited, moved off again, seemingly deep in thought. 'Well, to tell the truth, she makes me uncomfortable. I don't want you to say anything to her—'

'Then I won't. But tell me.'

'Oh, you know. Flirting. Flitting about half dressed. She's – you know…'

El realised. It would be better probably if she laughed, but she couldn't quite trust herself to make the right noise. The timing of this felt terribly unfair. 'I see.'

'Nothing's happened.' He glanced at her quickly. El finally located her laugh, and a suitably light tone.

'That's very restrained of you. She's beautiful!'

'It makes me uncomfortable,' he repeated, as if she hadn't spoken. 'I want you to ask her to leave.'

'What can I say to her?'

'Say we've decided to do without an au pair for a bit. Anything, it doesn't matter. We can give her a good reference.'

'OK.' She should have said more, but her mouth was dry. It would be best to laugh it off, to tease him about how fatally attractive he was. But how could she say to him… how could she now…? Con virtuously resists advances of beautiful nineteen-year-old French woman while El falls into bed and gets pregnant by American lover. If only they matched one another in crime, how much easier it would be; tears and forgiveness all round, and on to the next chapter.

'El? You're not upset, are you? I wanted to tell you the truth—' Con negotiates into the pub car park.

'Of course not.' There is nothing to do but plunge on, and rediscover control where she can. They need to have this

conversation in the car, not in the pub. 'Anyway, I've got something more important to tell you. I'm pregnant.' She feels him
turn in his seat to stare at her, and has to force herself to meet
his gaze.

'You're sure?'

'Absolutely.'

His astonished face suddenly cracks, and he is leaning in to
her, arms encircling her. 'Oh El! El!'

His body is shaking, and she realises he is crying. 'Con – it's
OK, it's OK—'

'I'm so glad.' His breath is hot in her ear. 'I'm so, so glad. You
don't know how glad I am.' He draws back far enough to look
at her, his face alight and happy. She knows she must press on,
not let this joyfulness distract her.

'But we weren't planning to have another—'

'It doesn't matter, it doesn't matter. It's like Paul, it's meant
to be. It's exactly what should happen now. I don't know how I
didn't guess. Have you tested?'

'Yes.' She needs to tell him why she didn't mention it before.
'But there's something I must tell—'

'You're wonderful! You're perfect! Come on – we'll have
champagne.' He is out of the car before she can reply, bending
to lock his door. She gets out slowly, and he is looking across the
car roof at her, still grinning from ear to ear. 'When you rang this
morning – I should have guessed! What an idiot!' He takes her
hand as they approach the pub and doesn't drop it even when
they reach the bar. He asks for champagne and they have to wait
while some is found in the cellar and apologies are made about
its not having been in the fridge.

'Celebrating?' asks the barman and Con nods. El is afraid he will tell the man, but he just smiles at her and squeezes her hand.

When all the business of opening it and pouring and toasting and sitting at a table is out of the way, El tries again. 'We need to slow down a bit, Con. There's a reason I didn't tell you before—'

He reaches over and puts his finger against her lip. 'Remember when you wanted to get rid of Paul?'

'It wasn't Paul then, it was a five-week embryo, no bigger than a pin head.'

'Yes. And what a mistake it would have been. Left to ourselves we'll never decide to have another – how can we? You're too busy, I'm too busy, life's too short. And so, like a blessing, it just happens. If you even for a moment imagine us talking about not having it – forget it. It would be the worst and stupidest thing we could ever do.'

'But—'

'No buts. Drink.'

She sips, bites the inside of her cheek, starts again. 'I have—'

But Con is speaking at the same time. 'It's a new beginning. Let's start again, El. Look how we've drifted – I didn't even notice you'd missed a period—' His voice catches and El glances quickly at the barman, afraid Con may be about to cry again. But he gathers himself. 'No wonder you couldn't tell me before. Why should you tell a man who isn't even aware—'

'Con. Stop it. I didn't tell you because… because I didn't believe it myself.' Is she? Is she going to tell him now he's said they must have it, is she going to break his heart? 'I thought my period was just late because I was tired. It didn't dawn on me for ages, I felt stupid when I realised—' El is out of breath. Is she going to lie to him after all? She is astonished at herself. But what can be gained by telling him about Glenn, when it's gone and over and done with? When he will read far more into it than there ever was? What can be gained by souring his joy over this baby which may, for all she knows, even be his? (But she knows it's not.) Wouldn't honesty be self-indulgent?

The turnaround is giddying. But it is clear now: she must lie. Better for Con, better for the baby, better for Paul and Megan, better for Glenn. Better for everyone, to lie. To let life be as Con would like it to be. As Con deserves.

And the lie had taken, and beautiful blonde Cara was born, and Con loved her more than any of the other three. He was her father, a wonderful father, and she was his daughter. And El had hugged her past to herself and imagined herself safe from discovery. As indeed she was for nineteen years. This house was wonderful then – they had bought it the year before, with money El inherited from her grandfather. A big old weaver's house, right on the road, with the back rooms facing south, and sunshine pouring in. A previous owner had installed rather inappropriate French windows, but when they stood open on a summer's day, letting onto the stone-flagged garden area which was bounded by a wide lawn, ending in an overgrown vegetable garden, it was idyllic. Con planted roses and honeysuckle and buddleia, and the children wore little pathways in the flower beds to their favourite hidey-holes behind the bushes. It seems it was always summer, when they were little.

She is dragged from her memories by Paul, who claims he also could not sleep, and says they must call the police today.

'I'll tell them,' he says. 'You don't need to do anything.'

'They'll want to come round and question us all.'

'So?'

'They'll go through his things – his computer.'

'Of course. That's how they'll try and trace him.'

'Paul, I just don't think it's necessary yet.'

'I'm phoning them now, Mum, right now.' He heads for the kitchen.

El has realised she has not scoured Con's computer as thoroughly as she meant to. What if they take it today? She dresses quickly and goes to Con's study. She'll have to call in sick, there's no way she can do the departmental meeting and the lecture. She'll try to go in later and finish the grant application.

Turning on the computer and sitting at his desk, she feels sick with dread. The dread of finding something out, something secret, shameful, something he has chosen to keep hidden from her. The grey box on the desk in front of her is basically an extension of his brain; flicking through its files and folders, its Work, Home, Contacts, is fully as invasive as prying into his mind. She imagines a surgeon peering into an opened skull, delicately probing the dense grey tissue, pressing apart the folds in the living cortex with his blunt pink fingers.

As the computer slowly churns to life and opens its programs, she steels herself. Bad as his disappearance is, to find out the truth of it will be worse. Because then she will have to know. People talk about closure, thinks El. The first time she saw it in the press, she thought it typically American. Part of a culture that talks too much, faking understanding with the glib vocabulary of therapy. In so far as she understands closure, she surely doesn't want it. How can the end of this story be good? As long as it is unknown there is a chance it might be OK. There is a tiny space for hope. With closure, there will be none.

Scanning his emails is not as big a job as she imagined. His desktop is only a year old, and the email traffic is tiny in comparison to hers. His emails are mainly junk and intermittent exchanges with colleagues about research papers. The Deleted box is empty, but to judge from the spam in his Inbox, that is because he has never deleted anything, rather than because he is a scrupulous PC housekeeper. There are storage folders labelled HOUSE, ADMIN and MAD. She clicks on MAD. There are seven emails, the first dated four months ago. *Don't worry, I haven't forgotten you, wanker.* The subject line is empty and there's no signature. The sender's address is mad@me.com.

The second says, *Oh Conrad I have something very special up my sleeve for you.*

The next, *Why so quiet? Squeal piggy squeal. You will.*

Next: *You looked cute on that hotel bed. Shall I send the photo to your wife? Pity about my bra n panties on the bed.*

El pauses, the words dancing before her eyes. OK, she knew. It had to be a woman. But what kind of woman is this? A blackmailer? The following one, sent in December, reads, *What punishment is good enough for what you've done? I should rip your heart out.*

He must have dumped her. What else could it mean? Next: *Long distance torture is easy, eh. What the eye doesn't see. You will see, shitface, trust me.*

Only one left, dated two weeks ago. *See you soon, sweetie.*

El's heart is pounding. She clicks wildly, looking for replies in the SENT folder. There are none. There is not a single email addressed to mad@me.com. She checks the MAD folder again – none of them shows a replied symbol. She becomes aware of a hubbub in the hall. Cara's taxi has arrived. Swiftly she closes the folders and runs out to say goodbye. Should she say anything?

No, not yet. Not till she knows more. But this woman – why has he kept these emails? As evidence? In case she really harms him? Has he left them here for El to find?

Cara's face is white.

'Did you have breakfast?'

'No time, Mum.'

'For God's sake. Have some at the airport. Here – and for the taxi.' El thrusts £60 into Cara's hand. 'Ring me when you get to your hotel. Promise.'

'Yes, Mum.' They hug and Cara is gone. Paul – police-botherer Paul – is mysteriously quiet. Unless he has gone to work. El heads back to Con's office.

I should rip your heart out. Meaning he had ripped out hers? And that last message – a reconciliation? An agreed meeting? Or is the 'sweetie' a threat? El stares at the emails, opening them one after another, and eventually printing each one off. If she gives these to the police, won't the police be able to trace an email address? If anyone has harmed Con it must be her, Mad. But what if he has changed his mind and run away with her? What if he has chosen to be with her? But how could he be with someone so abusive and hateful? A blackmailer, a woman who makes threats?

El is going round in circles. There is something missing here, there is something that doesn't make sense. She will email the woman herself, she thinks. When she has a clear enough head to work out what to say.

She glances at her watch. There's still time to get to the meet-ing, and she might as well go. As she's putting on her coat she calls Paul's name and he appears at the top of the stairs.

'How did you get on with the police?' she asks.

'Someone will call me back.'

'Is that it?'

'Yeah.'

'OK. Are you here all day?'

'Yeah.'

'I've got to go to work. Ring me if—' She hesitates.

'Yeah yeah. Bye.'

Chapter 6

CONRAD IS SITTING on the floor under the window. There is a revolving light outside. The orange glow flashes across the room from left to right, chased by darkness. It must be an ambulance or a police car. But there's no siren. Breakdown truck? Roadworks? It doesn't really matter. But he can't close the curtains because of the suffocating dark, and if he leaves them open the room is filled with this measured flashing. You can count to ten between each turn. On the bed it was going over him. Under the window he is sheltered.

It's 2.30. A long time till daylight. Reaching forward he pulls the pillow and duvet from the bed and curls around it, foetal under the window. He can't remember when he last slept. He tries to imagine the children. But all he can see is Cara, crying; it's an image from a dream, he was willing El to pick her up because he couldn't reach but El raised her eyebrows as if he was stupid. He sits upright again.

The people next door have stopped. That was the other thing that drove him from the bed. The increasingly frenzied knocking of the other bed against the wall; then he thought he heard a woman crying. Maybe it was pleasure; what does he know? Just get through the night. It will feel better after dawn.

A primitive understanding.

The lights in the monkey house go out at 8pm. It's pitch dark in there, apart from the red safety light above the emergency exit. He used to think it must be a relief to the monkeys, when the switch is flicked. In the dark, no humans come to stick needles in you, or carry you away to the knife; no one rams a tube down your throat and force-feeds you drugs; no one peers at you critically through the mesh, weighing up your chances. You are at peace in the dark with your dreams and warm sleep and the fug of other monkey snores all around. But now he thinks of their terror. The recently operated upon, alone in the dark with their pain, fighting waves of nausea. Unable to see either friend or foe, smothered by blackness. And the healthy, on borrowed time, knowing their turn will come; in the dark there's no possibility of the slenderest imagining of escape. At least in daylight the mesh is visible, the lock is visible, the door is visible. At least a way out *exists*; at least on the clothes of rapidly passing humans, there is the scent of outside, the reassurance that another world still exists. In the dark there is only absence.

He considers himself as the subject of an experiment. Watches himself with a note-taking eye. *Subject not sleeping. Huddled by wall. Rejecting food. Irregular bowel movements.* He is here in this box. Surrounded by the noisy lives of strangers. What has he ever done to deserve more? He is alive. That's what he has got. His life, in this box. His fifty-year-old life.

In fact he is hungry. That's a thought. He's hungry and what can he do about that? He struggles to his feet and the revolving light catches him, flooding his retinas and blinding him so that he has to put his hands to the window ledge and rest there a moment, waiting for the dark to re-form. You can't get food at

3am. You have to sleep. You can only get food in the morning. He wraps the duvet round himself and curls up on the floor again. In the morning he must find something to eat. He tries to remember what he last ate. Before this night – before this night – he was walking. There was a train. Yes, a train. The train was stuffy; as it warmed up, the compartment he was in began to stink of orange peel. But he was afraid to go to another compartment, because she might be waiting for him. He hunted for the peel in the luggage rack and in the armrest ashtrays, but it was nowhere to be found.

He sees himself in the kitchen at home. Trying to decide whether to peel one potato or two. Reaching into the cupboard for a plate, a cup. Checking the time although no one will come in, only El, late, after he's gone to bed. Pulling down the blind in order not to see his lone reflection at table, sitting in his same old place as if the ghosts of the children occupy the others. He puts the radio on but it is too brash, and music is too loud at any volume. Music shouldn't be used to fill silence. It should be listened to or not played at all. All he is doing is waiting. Anything else would be false: outings, music, TV, social arrangements. Waiting for the next step to become clear.

In routine, he has discovered, you can have less and less. You need hardly ever touch the sides. You can stay in the empty centre. Drive to work at 8; read the lab reports and mail; adjust drug regimes, whip through research reports, analyse statistics, check some results. Attend a departmental meeting, drive home. Heat something from the freezer. Sit in the empty kitchen letting the evening pass. Sometimes one of them would ring. Or there'd be an email among the junk. Sometimes El would be at home, uneasy and cheery in his presence, hastily trying to cook or make conversation, offering him wine. He was relieved when she went into her study after dinner, to do a couple more hours' work. It was astonishing how little one could do and still get by. Time never stood still, there was no need to invent ways to pass it, it simply passed itself.

His mind turns to Cara. He had to go to Leeds to fetch her back. She had been ringing and crying for three weeks but when he knocked on the door of her room in the hall of residence, he wasn't prepared for how she would look. Deathly pale, her hair lank and unwashed, her eyes brimming with tears. He hated the boy, the stupid callous thoughtless boy, the boy who wasn't worth her grief. He saw that whatever reasoning or persuasion he had imagined offering to her would not be relevant. She was packed and ready; they carried her things in silence to the car.

She cried all the way home, weakly, inconsolably, while he made ineffectual attempts at comforting her, and noticed the stick-thinness of her fingers, hands and arms, and blamed himself and El for not realising sooner. But she was rescued, he reassures himself, swimming up from his doze. He did rescue her. He stayed off work, he made her soups and snacks and treats, he took her out for walks and swims as if she were a little girl again. And palely, sadly, brokenly she obeyed, ate and took exercise, listened and nodded to the mantras he offered: it's all right, there's no pressure, you don't have to go back.

He and Eleanor argued. 'You make her worse, you're pandering to her, encouraging her to wallow—'

'El, can you not see the girl is ill? She's on the verge of breakdown, she's lost over a stone—'

'She's got to learn to cope with life. What on earth has

94

happened that's so traumatic? Her boyfriend's dumped her, OK, it happens every day to thousands of people. They don't all fall apart at the seams.'

'You really don't see, do you—'

'I see she's getting behind with her essays. How much harder is it going to be to go back if she has a mountain of catching up to do?'

'She doesn't want to go back.'

'She's already got enough of a chip on her shoulder about Paul and Megan's A levels. What good will it do her self-confidence to know she couldn't hack university?'

Was El right? Was it right that he looked after Cara and honoured her distress, or should he have packed her off back to Leeds the following weekend? In that she has never returned to university, perhaps so. Con sees there was no right answer. All the questions have been trick questions, and here he has been, all his life, earnestly trying his best while something somewhere snorts with laughter at his attempts – at his naive and credulous life.

Dawn comes slowly, grudgingly. When he hauls himself up to the window there is thick white mist outside, cloud, there's no sky to be seen. There's nothing in the street, the flashing light has gone. In the half-light Con finds his shoes and puts them on. Cautiously opens the door. No one there; no one on the stairs; no one on the desk. He unlocks the heavy front door and slips out, pulling it to behind him. The air is thick and icy cold, like stepping into a freezer. When it hits his lungs he coughs, tugging the lapels of his coat together, turning up the collar. The pavement is dark grey and wet, coils of white mist linger in the street. There's a noise approaching; materialising as a street-sweeping van, its rotating brushes scouring the gutter, its driver's glazed eyes sliding as impersonally over Con as if he were a bin of grit.

Something to eat. He turns right then left, and there is a bright glass front of a café. Its golden window is filled with heaps of croissants and cakes; the aroma of fresh coffee zips across the cold street. People stand at the bar in their coats or sit on high stools along the walls, sipping coffee, absorbed in papers, an extraordinary vision of ordinariness. Con gets a latte and two croissants, finds a vacant stool, joins the ranks of the saved. The regular hiss of the espresso machine rhythmically drowns out the barman's banter; Con is inside a warm sweet engine. When he has finished he orders the same again, relaxing into the slow contentment of being fuelled. There's a long heavy mirror above the ledge where his coffee rests; the bevelled edges remind him of one they had at home, the first mirror they ever owned. El bought it in a junk shop. It stood in their bedroom and its edges caught the morning sun and scattered flakes of brilliant light across the walls and ceiling. He remembers how it used to fascinate Paul when he was toddling – he would reach up to try to grasp the specks of light from the wall. There was no other furniture in that bedroom, only the bed. At night, in the soft glow of the bedside lamp, the mirror reflected their pale bodies intricately and intimately combined.

Staring into the glass Con registers a young couple come in, with a baby. The infant is wrapped in a pouch strapped to the boy's chest. As the girl orders their drinks, the boy smiles and nods at the child, who gazes up at him adoringly. Turning from the bar with a coffee in each hand, the girl leans in and blows a breath of air at the baby. She and the boy laugh.

They had a pouch like that for Paul. Faded blue corduroy, slightly padded, it came up to support his head at the back. They used it when he was very young. In the days of innocence.

Con remembers the feel of the warm weight of the child pressed against his chest. The secure binding of the corduroy straps around his back and over his shoulders. He remembers walking down the street like that, holding hands with El.

'My turn to carry him for nine months now.'

'OK. Just as long as I don't have to carry him again for the nine months after that!'

'I'm serious about looking after him as much as you.'

'Con, it's understood.'

He found her lightness slightly irritating. 'You say it as if it's not even worth discussing, but no couple I know have ever done this.'

'But we agreed from the start! Things have changed – loads of fathers will be looking after their kids from now on.'

'When I took him to baby clinic on Friday I was in a waiting room full of women.'

'You don't need me to praise you for this. You and I are equal; we both *know* what it means.'

'I just want recognition. My father never changed a nappy. Never got up in the night. We're reinventing the roles—'

'OK! I recognise it. Our Experiment; the new model family.'

'Thank you. That's all I wanted. What *he'll* do, of course,' stroking Paul's fluffy head, 'is reject us for a pair of crazed ideologues and find a wife he can treat like a slave.'

Together, they laughed.

But the experiment was serious stuff. Since no one but El could feed Paul, Con did all the rest once he was home from work: bathing, nappy changing, long walks round and round the sitting room at night, gently rubbing the fretful baby's back and waiting for him to burp and settle. Con remembers it as a time of generosity between himself and El; she gave him the baby, in return he gave her time for her work. While she was on maternity leave they passed the child back and forth between them with the elegance of an old-fashioned dance; he remembers leaning in to lift Paul from her arms as she sat in the pool of light cast by the old anglepoise, watching her stretch and smile at him as she buttoned her shirt, watching her reach for her books on the table and pull them into her lap where the suckling child had just lain. He remembers the warm boy against his chest, his wife's glossy head studiously bent in the lamplight.

Once she stopped breastfeeding and returned to work, he was able to take on more. El was finishing her house job at Oldham Royal, and her specialism was Obs and Gynae. Steptoe and Edwards were making history with their attempts at IVF, and like many others at the hospital, she was caught up in the drama of it. It was inevitable that she should end up working in the same field. It was Con who took Paul to Kelly the childminder in the morning, he who was regularly able to leave work earlier than El and pick him up in the afternoon. They made it equal between them then, that was why it was good. The only grounds for bitterness must be that it ended. They were agreed on the great benefits of breast over formula, and from the start, after feeding Paul, El always expressed milk and froze it. So when she returned to work there was a good supply stashed away for bottle-feeding. Though her own milk dwindled once she was on the wards again, she could still manage to feed him herself morning and night; bottle-fed by Con and the childminder with the frozen supplies, he didn't need to go onto formula for a whole extra month. Utterly endearing, to Con, this typical El efficiency applied to her own milk production: cow, farmer and dairy rolled into one. She was decisive about all sorts of practical aspects of their life: they must always use disposable nappies, because of the savings in time and energy; it was more cost-effective to employ a cleaner than for her or Con to do it; cooking stews and soups at the weekend and freezing portions was the most convenient way for them to eat. They argued briefly about clothes, he remembers.

'Con, it's idiotic to dress a growing child in new clothes. The charity shops are full of really good stuff—'

'But I like to see him in new things, things that haven't been washed a thousand times.'

'New for a month. Till he grows out of them.'

'We can keep them for the next one.'

She laughed and teased him at that, and mostly he gave in. But just as for himself he has always loved the feel of a crisp new cotton shirt, so for Paul he coveted Mothercare's bright stretchy babygrows, and would from time to time sneak one into the house.

Con remembers there were evenings when he would be stirring the frozen lumps of stew in the saucepan, with Paul crawling round underfoot, and both of them stopping and turning with big grins at the sound of El's bicycle nudging down the ginnel. Everything they did was purposeful, every moment of their lives was precious, the care of the child passed back and forth between them like a blazing torch.

Trying to linger now, trying to be fair, trying not to throw the baby out with the bathwater, ha ha, Con watches the young couple and their baby leave, with a surge of grief. The fine balance that they had, the working, childcaring, giving-to-each-other balance, was it really El who smashed it?

Yes. He feels his shoulders sag; he doesn't know how to stop blaming her. He wants to reclaim his own life, at least some of it, from her; he wants her not to have been the one who made everything happen.

It isn't right, it isn't plausible, it isn't even possible, he knows; he must have played as much of a part as her in the fiasco that has turned out to be their life. But where… how… when? He's stumbling about like some blundering old fool, and all he can make out is the harm she has done him. But does his own life only exist where it's touched hers? He wonders if she thinks of him as parasitic upon her energy. Maybe that would make him deserve what he has got, if he has been leeching upon her all their married life? If she has acted and he has only reacted. If his darkness has swallowed her light. Still he can't avoid what's coming. Still he can't excuse her.

When Paul was ill he stayed off work. More often than her, longer than her. He had thought there was a satisfaction in it that they shared; a tacit agreement that her work was more import-ant, and so a pleasure in the role reversal. He did it for Paul and for El and for himself, all three of them could gain.

And when they made the decision to have another child, when Paul was two, it seems to Con they both recognised that Con was doing the lion's share – without complaint, since he knew El wouldn't have agreed to a second if it had threatened more disruption to her work. With the decisive and happy calm which had characterised their life together thus far, El became pregnant with and delivered Megan.

And two months after Megan was born, El dropped a bombshell.

'We need to get an au pair.'

'Why?'

'To look after the children. To keep things going at home while we're at work.'

'What's wrong with Kelly?'

'Nothing. She's been great. But it's getting too complicated, Con.' An au pair could take Paul to nursery, which was due to start in September, pushing Megan in the pram. Then she could come home, tidy up, collect Paul, give the children their lunch, take them to the park, do a bit of shopping, make their tea.

'What will Kelly say? She needs the money.'

'She'll get two other kids to mind, you ninny. And she could have them a couple of afternoons a week while the au pair goes to her language classes – it'll work out heaps better.'

'But—'

'Imagine just coming straight home from work, and the kids not needing to be bundled from pillar to post; no bags of nappies and changes of clothing, no dashing away from unfinished work because it's pick-up time—'

'You never have to dash away from unfinished work. I pick them up in the afternoon.'

'Well, *you* won't have to dash away from work. And I won't have to feel guilty about you doing it.'

'There's no need for you to feel guilty. I enjoy it.'

'There is need because you bring it up in conversations like this. It's clearly unfair. You do more childcare than me.'

'I do it because I want to.'

'That's not the point, is it.'

'I don't understand.'

'If you do more than me, it's not fair. And if I spend more time at work – and if my career inches ahead of yours—' It wasn't inching. They both knew that. It was striding. It was leaping and bounding ahead of his. 'Then one day you're going to resent it.'

'El, you don't *want* to spend more time with the kids. And because I do, that liberates you to work all the hours God sends. Which is fine. But you don't like that because you feel you might owe me something. You don't want to think anyone else might have had to make any kind of sacrifice, for Eleanor Evanson to be a name in IVF; so you'd prefer to farm out your kids to some unknown exploited foreigner, and say it's all for my sake—'

'You're twisting—'

'You've never even consulted me. Maybe I prefer cooking my children's food to leaving them to eat shit.'

'That's ridiculous. We can control what they eat whether we're there or not.'

'Fine. But you're saying I'm not allowed to choose being with the kids.'

'You want to be doing Hill's tedious research for the rest of your life?'

'An au pair is not a compromise. It's your wish. A compromise would be you deciding to come home early two nights a week. Or – better – you employing an au pair two nights a week.'

'I *can't* promise to be here early two nights a week. It's not possible. Not while we're working with newly harvested eggs. It doesn't work to a timetable, you know we can't freeze them.'

'You could agree a timetable with Simon. As you know perfectly well. You could take it in turns.'

'The kids don't *need* their parents twenty-four hours a day. They need to be loved and fed but they don't need *us* all the time. In fact they'll be better socialised without us. It's pure emotional blackmail, what you're doing.'

'Because you don't want to come home early, you want to stop me from doing it too.'

'You can still come home early every bloody day if you want. But at least it will be a choice.'

'That makes rather a mockery of paying someone.'

'I'll pay. My guilt, my money.' She was already earning more than him. She had him cornered and they both knew it.

An au pair came from an agency. Con wouldn't have anything to do with it so El interviewed her and took her on. She was a stolid Austrian, wretchedly shy with him, answering his attempts at conversation monosyllabically. The kids seemed to like her. She was thorough. The house was cleaner than it had ever been, the children's clothes neater. When he came in in the evening (having forced himself to stay till 4.30, till 5, till almost half past) they had already had their tea and she was cuddling Megan and reading to Paul, or, if Megan was asleep, playing endless games of Continuo, coloured squares spread across the floor and the eighteen-year-old crawling around them alongside the three-year-old. She was embarrassed by Con's presence and the kids were happy with her. So, more often than not, he'd end up pretending to read the paper in the kitchen, listening to their chatter through the crack in the door.

'I'll give them their bath,' he told her, and she went immediately to her room. She was silent in there and never went out.

It was impossible to banish her to such solitude every evening, but when he asked her to watch TV or stay in the kitchen and eat with him, her embarrassed presence was a strain. El went into action and found the girl an au pairs' social group to go to on Thursday nights, and an English class for a Tuesday. She recommended her to colleagues as a babysitter. Gradually Con reclaimed some evenings at home. But he never stopped resenting it. She stayed with them for two years.

When Gresl left, the children cried. But then the next au pair was Hélène, whom everybody loved. It was different with Hélène; she was happy to sit in the kitchen chatting to him all evening if she wasn't going out. She took it for granted he would want to relieve her of the kids when he came in, and while he bathed them and read stories she would put on the radio and clear up the mess in the kitchen. She rarely ate, claiming she had eaten with the kids, but if she wasn't going out and El was late home, Hélène would sit companionably with Con while he ate, regaling him with the minutiae of the children's day and lurid tales of the other au pairs in her language class. Some were expected to work terrible hours, 6am till midnight, one even had to get up to bottle-feed a new baby in the night. Some had no days off. (Hélène had all weekend.) Some children were so spoilt you would not believe, screaming and pinching their au pairs, threatening to tell their parents bad things if they weren't given sweets or privileges. And the fathers – dreadful, predatory men. Two girls had already left their placements after being cornered by the men of the house; one even came into her friend Natalie's bedroom at night while his wife was sleeping.

She delighted in these scandals and Con knew perfectly well that he was being tested. She was nineteen and devastatingly pretty; he was twenty-nine with a wife who never came home. 'I see more of Hélène than I do of you,' he said, once.

'Lucky you!' laughed Eleanor. Hélène had no particular boyfriend Con could identify, but calls from her friends both male and female monopolised the phone, and her weekends were full of outings and parties. Gradually Con noticed, though, that she rarely went out on a Wednesday or Thursday, always El's later nights at the hospital. On those nights she was almost always in with an evening to spare, helping him down a bottle of wine at the kitchen table. She wanted to be an English teacher when she went back to Marseille, and she was constantly asking him for explanations of different phrases and colloquialisms. There came the inevitable evening when they got on to the subject of sex.

'Natalie says you have more words than us for *baiser*.'

'Kissing?'

'Fucking.'

'I thought it meant to kiss.'

'Both. It means both.'

'Doesn't that get confusing?'

She began to laugh, it was infectious. 'Usually you know – which one you are doing.'

'But can't one thing lead to another?'

It did, after they had drawn up, without the aid of a dictionary, a list of more than thirty euphemisms which all needed explanation and amplification. Shag. Bonk. Bang. Screw. A spot of how's-your-father. (This made her howl with joy.) The old in-out (plus discussion of *Clockwork Orange*, which she had just read). Knee trembler. To know in the Biblical sense. Fornicate. Intercourse. Have relations with. Come together (necessitating a playing of the Beatles song of that title). Lewd act (discounted, after discussion of the range of behaviours to which it could be applied). Give one to. Have it away with. Sleep with. Make the beast with two backs. Mate. Jiggy jiggy. Do the horizontal tango. (She swore he'd made this up. Con couldn't remember where he'd got it from.) Lie with. Give a good seeing to. A quickie. A ride. A little death. To get your oats. To spend the night with. To go all the way with. To tumble in the hay. To make it with. To poke. To pork. In the sack.

When at last he said, 'It's bedtime,' she giggled and pushed her chair back. He determined to sit, nursing his erection, until she had left the room but she came around the table to him and put her hand on his shoulder, and it was impossible not to reach up to her. All the time he was kissing her and running his hands over her warm body he was calculating. Not in the kitchen, one of the kids might wake up. Not in his and El's room, that would be too… It would have to be Hélène's little bed. He pulled away from her.

'Hélène. I don't want to be one of those men – you know, pawing the au pair.'

'*Non. Non.* Please—' Her fingers had found his zip.

'OK, OK. Let's go to your room.' Hastily he locked the front door, leaving the key in the lock in case of a surprise return by El; followed Hélène into her room and wedged a chair against the door. He had no condom and wouldn't risk not using one; after years of married sex it was like being a sixth-former again, frenziedly doing everything but.

In the pounding silence afterwards he felt his heart sink like a stone. She was curling up for sleep: he kissed her lips, nose, eyes, gathered his clothes and went to his own room, where he lay awake all night cursing himself and vowing it wouldn't happen again.

In the morning he busily behaved as if nothing had happened; in the evening rang from work to say goodnight to the kids and that he'd be late home. Then, blessedly, the weekend. He had caught her reproachful glance a couple of times; knew he was behaving like a shit. On Monday night when the kids were in bed and Hélène was silent in her room, he knocked on her door.

'*Oui? Entre.*'

'No, I won't, Hélène. You come out to the kitchen, would you? We need to talk.' It embarrassed him to offer his explanations; her age, his position as her employer, the betrayal of El's trust on both their parts, etc., because she simply smiled.

'It's OK. I know all that. It's just a bit of fun, no? I don't think you exploit me. I don't think you'll leave your wife. But it feels good. You don't think so?'

'It feels wonderful. But it will lead to trouble, Hélène. Better not.'

'OK.' She raised her hands in an 'I will leave it alone' gesture. 'OK. Don't worry about it. Now I must finish getting ready, I am going out for a drink.'

He brooded for a week before buying some condoms just in case. They used them fairly quickly. But all the while he was enjoying it, he was worried sick. Despising himself for a coward, he determined to get El to ask Hélène to leave, dropping just enough of the truth into the conversation to make it plausible – Hélène was flirting with him, he said, she was making him uncomfortable. He was afraid El would laugh it off, but she agreed with surprising ease. Then it turned out she had news of her own.

She was pregnant.

'How late are you?'

'Well, I thought I was late because I was overtired, run down, so I just didn't think of it for ages—'

'How late are you?'

'About two months.'

'So it's due in July?'

'Yes.'

Con was consumed by guilt. Here was his overworked, exhausted wife, carrying his child – from a sexual encounter he couldn't even remember (and he did, they both did, for both Paul and Megan; had pieced together backwards from the day of knowing she was pregnant, the times and ways they'd done it, and isolated the most likely, the most memorable) – while he had spent the last three months oblivious, shagging a young girl under his and Eleanor's roof, with their children sleeping sweetly in the next room. Hélène left without a fuss. 'It's a shame,' said El. 'She was much nicer than that Austrian girl. Let's see if we can get another French one.'

'Please,' said Con. 'Can we just try for a while without?' Astonishingly, Eleanor agreed.

Now he knows his guilt blinded him. Now he knows there was another story. When did Cara become his favourite? Maybe it began right then, when he heard of her presence in El's womb, and thought with shame of her unnoticed conception, of her ignored and uncelebrated first two months in utero, of his distraction from her mother's body.

Chapter 7

By 11PM El is convinced she should have gone to Munich with Cara. A policeman called in the late afternoon and took some details, then kindly explained that tracing someone who is overseas is not easy. The phone has been ringing all evening, as people pick up and respond to Paul's messages, and as the circle of those who know of Con's absence grows. Some make suggestions or reveal confidences; some want to help, but what is there to do? Paul has driven over to Sheffield and brought Daniel back, and gone away again himself. There seems to be some consensus among the children that El is not to be left alone. But there's nothing for Dan to do; she sends him out to choose some videos for the evening, and when he's hooked into the first, excuses herself and goes to Con's study.

Cara has not phoned. The address of her hotel is pinned to the noticeboard but they're one hour ahead, it's too late to phone her now. El is afraid that she has allowed Cara to enter something dangerous; a black hole, which has already swallowed Con and might easily devour Cara too. Why did she let her go alone? She forces herself to look at a map of Germany. Munich is real. It is a place on dry land, linked by roads and rails to the other cities of Germany, less dangerous probably than Manchester. Her fear is irrational. She is not an irrational person. But now she's experiencing physical unease, looseness in the bowels, pressure in the head reminiscent of trying to solve an intellectual problem, for example pulling together all the threads in the concluding paragraph of a paper. But she knows that kind of pressure can be relieved by working on through it: it is pressure which dictates its own release. Whereas the pressure of anxiety, now, is empty – like a balloon blown up inside her head, squashing all other thoughts and knowledge to the sides, and yet containing nothing but dread. She's reminded of something Con once said, about how he felt when he was in America. He claimed he had been slightly short of breath all the time – as if he couldn't draw a full deep lungful of oxygen, as if he was always a little suffocated. 'Haven't you ever felt like that?'

El thought he was neurotic. 'No. I've felt scared – when I hitched a ride with the guy who child-locked me in, for example, but that's different, it's the flight response, isn't it – speeded-up heartbeat, increased rate of breathing—'

'Yes, I'm not talking about that. I'm talking about continuous low-grade anxiety, the kind that dogs you like a smell, so you get used to it, apart from when you're trying to sleep.'

'But what was it about?'

'The kids. I can't believe you've never felt that. When you go away to a conference or something – when you're on a plane heading away from the children – you've never had that awful nagging anxiety about them?'

'Of course not. I'm always leaving them in safe hands.'

'I don't doubt that *your* hands are safe. It's not about me thinking you won't look after them well – it's not rational, it's just anxiety engendered by being far away from them. It's not uncommon. Other people feel it too.'

Eleanor loves going away: strapping herself into her plane seat and waiting for it to lift her from the earth; breaking through clouds and looking down on their rolling whiteness; the sensation of soaring, held back by nothing – she loves that. Her thoughts run ahead to her paper, the city she is visiting, the colleagues she will meet, the excitement and energy of it drawing her like a magnet. It is rare for her to think of the children at all until she is on her way home again.

'Is this symptomatic of my inadequacy as a mother?'

'No, my dear. The opposite, I should think. You've read as much cod psychology as me. Don't a parent's fears transmit themselves to the child and become internalised threats to its confidence?'

'So selfishness is OK?'

'Couldn't needless anxiety be construed as just as selfish as forgetfulness?' She remembers laughing at him then, and both of them laughing together; they could make anything mean anything else, they were not restricted to the petty definitions everyone else was trammelled by.

But now she recognises that she is anxious in the way he described. It wouldn't be irrational if it was about Con, because something must have happened to him. But it is irrational about Cara, and the surprising point is that being able to identify it as irrational does not in any way help to diminish it. Con began using sleeping tablets while he was in America. El saw it as evidence of weakness. Now she goes to the bathroom cupboard to find them. There is a full new packet; he's got them on prescription and the date of issue is only two weeks ago. If you were planning to run away, wouldn't you take your new sleeping tablets? She pops one through the silver foil and gulps at some water. She doesn't know any longer whether it is better or worse if he hasn't planned it. It opens the door to more dangerous and dramatic scenarios – injury, kidnap, act of God – but it does remove perhaps the worst, that he might have cold-bloodedly planned and engineered this disappearance as the culmination of a whole history of lies and double-dealings.

The woman, Mad, Con has had a relationship with her. That much is obvious. But it is also obvious that he had finished with her. And he was alarmed by the nastiness of her threats, that's why he's kept the emails. As evidence. So the last thing he would do is to walk into a situation of danger with her. He has not run away with her, El can't believe that. And the woman – hateful though she seems – is hardly likely to have murdered him. El is mentally filing the MAD emails under 'Red Herring'. She has emailed mad@me.com from her own computer, not wanting to leave any traces on Con's. She settled on a simple *Do you know where Conrad is?* But the email bounced back within minutes, address unknown. She does not believe Mad is anything to do with Con's disappearance. But what it does show is that he has had at least one other relationship, while El has been sailing happily and obliviously along. Having an affair of her own, to be sure. But not suspecting him. And the feeling it gives her is of grief and panic. How could she have drifted so far from him?

The noise from Dan's TV niggles in the background, but better to leave it; nothing is worse than Dan's awkward silence and slightly belligerent confusion over how to behave. She wishes the children would leave her alone, just leave her to get on with it. At least Megan has a life she can't leave, performances every night, at least there is one who won't come mithering.

El picks up a pen and starts a list:

1. tel Cara.

And stops, pen poised. What should she do tomorrow? Louis has offered to look after the visiting American, Michael, and she's agreed. Which means she can't go into work, she'd have to spend the whole day avoiding them. She can't go into work anyway because everyone will be asking about Con… but what can she do at home? Work on the stem cell book? Try to find Con? But how? She should go to bed, she's stupefied by lack of sleep.

The ring of her mobile makes her jump. Louis. 'Can you talk?'

'Yes – yes, I'm in Con's office.'

'Any news?'

'No. I told you Cara's gone to Munich?'

'On her own?'

'Yes. I'm thinking I should have gone with her—'

'If there's any news it'll come to you at home.'

'I guess so.'

'What do you *think* has…?'

'I don't know. Louis, I can't imagine.'

He is silent.

'You're sure you're OK about Michael tomorrow?'

'Of course. Are the kids there?'

'Dan. Paul was, he's coming back tomorrow morning.'

'Anything you want me to do?'

'I—' There is something in his tone that checks her. A formality, a politeness. He would ask a distant colleague or friend in that way, to exhibit necessary human decency. But what can she ask him to do anyway? She has enough trouble finding something for herself to do. There's a pause. He clears his throat.

'D'you want to meet?' He doesn't sound enthusiastic.

'I don't know. Won't you be busy with Michael?'

'Tomorrow, after work. I'll ring you as I'm leaving.'

'Is that OK? Meet at the Hind?'

'Sure. I'll have to get home for dinner, though. Susan—'

'Yeh. It's OK. See you then.' She disconnects before she can hear how he signs off, vividly and physically conscious of his mood, his wariness. He will have rung her from the park opposite his house; he takes the dog out for a pee last thing.

Why should she mind? Wariness is built into the thing, on both sides. It has only ever worked because they are both equally wary. Never making the impetuous phone call, never asking too much, she thinks. Clearly she is in danger now, of asking too much.

She hears the sitting room door open and Dan emerge. She goes out to him. 'Good film?'

'OK.'

'You going to bed now, Dan?'

He looks at her and blinks. 'Are you going to bed?'

'Yes, it's nearly midnight. Want a milky drink?'

He shakes his head and sets off up the stairs, stopping at the fourth. 'Dad—'

'No news yet. I'll tell you when there is.'

He stands there a bit longer, computing, then moves on up without acknowledging her further. El switches off the lights and follows him; her head is aching and her eyes are heavy. Of course: she took that sleeping tablet, must be more than an hour ago now, no wonder she's fuzzy.

El wakes at 6.30, clear and sharp after a deep sleep. She has a quick shower and takes a cup of tea straight to her office, mentally flicking through the items clamouring for her attention. She has a hunch Con may turn up today, and be rather irritated by all the fuss. But even if he doesn't – nothing to be done there beyond ringing Cara. The April conference: there are enough speakers committed now for her to arrange them in some sort of order and consider where the gaps are; and people must be invited for those gaps as soon as possible – it's only two months away. She must pursue funding for the Africans. Cape Town is the only African university willing to pay their delegates' fares. She can find a way of fudging accommodation costs at this end, but fares from Lusaka, Nairobi and Lagos – who can she get to sponsor them? Might the British Council? There must be no drug company connections. Think laterally, move outside medicine, what charities promote exchange of knowledge and understanding between First and Third Worlds? She could do with £15,000, or a bit more, realistically, then it would cover accommodation as well. Who stands to gain from this? She jots down her publishers, and makes a note to list all the main speakers' publishers.

She's glancing through her emails now; good, finally, the most recalcitrant contributor to the *Viability* book has sent in his chapter. She clicks on the attachment to print. It would be good to plough through this straight away and ask for whatever changes by return; the rest of the book has been ready to go for nearly a month. The index will need his additions, though; she emails her own editor to see if they can speed things up by getting someone at the publishers to do that. A stupidly officious complaint from Karen about certain colleagues over-running in the big lecture theatre. El taps an acerbic reply and freezes with the cursor hovering over *Send*. She is off work because Con has gone; if she's lobbing petty work emails into their midst mightn't they think it odd? She glances impatiently at the time – 7.19. She could go into work today, frankly. There's nothing to be gained by being in purdah here, and a thousand things to do at work. Louis will be good with Michael but really she needs to speak to Michael herself; for a start she wants him to do the key-note for the conference, and cast his eye over the delegates to see if she's missed anyone vital. Can be done by email, she counters.

Two research students want references. Mechanically she calls up their details and slots them into her standard letter, adding an extra sentence of enthusiasm for Maya, who has been a delight to work with. There are four requests for her to speak; she quickly rejects and deletes three, and stares at the fourth. Toronto in June. A guest lecture at the medical school. The academic year will be dying down by then, and this Con nonsense will be over; maybe she could even persuade him to go with her? Either way, it's a lovely month, and she doesn't know Anita Mistry, the new ethics person there, so it would be useful. The name rings a bell; she leafs through the last couple of editions of the *BMJ* and is pleased to find A. Mistry, Toronto, contributor to the November issue. She folds it open to read and puts it under her phone, saves the invitation and moves on. Proposal for a book, request for a chapter. Invitation to submit papers. Change in the university regulations regarding extensions. Change in procedure for obtaining parking permits. Ph.D. student submitting a draft for El's comments. Request from Bristol for her to be an external examiner. She fires off replies and deletes until the backlog is dealt with. Switches off the computer and takes Carlo's chapter on 'Financial and human costs of the premature baby' to read with her breakfast.

It's a good piece of work. The introduction needs tweaking slightly, and El adds a cross reference and cuts the two paragraphs on grief counselling, because Niamh's chapter covers it in more detail; beyond that and a few typos, nothing needs doing. She can get back to Carlo now.

El stands up and stretches. With the morning, her thinking on Con has changed. Those emails are from a lunatic. He'll come back. She can trust him. What reason has he ever given her to believe otherwise? And all the hanging about in the world will not make Con come home any faster. She should go into work.

She feels a gathering sense of impatience with the kids' anxiety, the police, people's questions and sympathy, Louis' caution; impatience and a desire to brush it all aside and get on. She's not impatient with Con; no, at this moment Con is even an ally, a person who has taken action and will also be impatient at the fuss. She can leap to understand the change he has embraced, she won't need to burden him with demands for explanation, she simply wants to get on with their lives. Energy, movement, that's what's needed; to fare forward and outpace bad things. To leave dullness and stasis behind.

Feeling this impatience connects her with her life again, with the surge which has propelled her ever since childhood. She visualises herself as a teenager, a blur of movement. Hurling herself past the marker posts, racing out of childhood towards life as fast as she could go, brushing off the irritating strands her mother tried to hold her with. Packing her rucksack the day after her last O level exam. Brilliant June sunshine falling in bright blocks through the windows, the whole world outside was glowing and throbbing with light, drumming her out of the nest as surely as the rhythm of the first contractions begins to squeeze the ripe foetus out of the dark womb. Her mother coming into her room.

'You're going to London today?'

'Yes, Mum.'

'You're not even waiting till the end of the week?'

'What for?'

'Well, apart from anything else, you could have given me a hand painting Minnie's room. All the time you've been doing your exams you've not lifted a finger in the house—'

'I had to revise.'

'Fair enough, but I did think that afterwards there might be a bit of give after all that take take take.'

'*Mum.*'

'What?'

'I'll help some other time. I just need to get away.'

'To what? What's so special in London? That long-haired streak of pump water—'

'His name's John.'

'Why doesn't he come and see you here, if he's so keen on you? His term must have ended.'

'He's got a summer job.' A lie.

'Doing what?'

'Swimming-pool attendant.' An inspired lie.

'And where are you going to stay?'

'In a spare room at his house. One of the guys he shares with has gone home for the summer.' Another lie.

'And what are you going to do with yourself all day?'

'I'll try and get a job.'

'You could get a job here.'

'Yes, but this isn't London.'

Somewhere in her mother's cluttered head a penny drops. 'I know what you're going to do.' Her tone is outraged.

Eleanor doesn't reply.

'I know what you're going to do,' her mother repeats aggressively.

Too right, Mother. Lose my virginity as fast as I possibly can. 'What?'

'And you're making a big mistake. You're going to end up in all sorts of mess. Girls always think it won't happen to them.'

'What?'

'Getting pregnant. Why d'you think you know better than—'

'Mum, I'm not going to—'

'I wasn't born yesterday, I'm not that stupid, I've seen girls your age throwing away their chances.'

'I'm not going to mess up my life.' Eleanor wants her mother to leave the room, so she can have a last proper look round, and get her cigarettes from under her mattress. But her mother stands there, stubbornly belligerent, a dark lump blocking her path.

'Mum, trust me. I can look after myself.'

'How are you going to get there?'

'I'll take the coach.'

'I don't want you hitching. You never know what kind of person might stop.'

'Right.'

Her mother knows as well as she does that she's going to hitch. But these rituals must all be observed, before she can step out into her freedom.

'Well.'

It seems to El that her mother is obstinate stupidity incarnate. It will take a bulldozer to shift her bulk out of El's path.

'Well?' she risks.

'I said, well. I've got to sort the washing.' Grudgingly, she turns in the doorway and El can feel her heart and lungs expanding as the constricting presence is removed. Light and quick as a swallow, she slips the last few things in her bag, darts to the bathroom, grabs her toothbrush, swoops down the stairs, listens for the sudden hush as her mother lifts the lid of the washing machine, and timing it perfectly, sings out, 'Bye, Mum! I'll give you a ring on Saturday!' before, in a single balletic movement, hoisting the rucksack onto one shoulder and twisting the Yale lock and swinging open the front door with the other hand, stepping out into the light, pulling it closed with a locking thud behind her.

The lane is a blaze of light. But nothing can harm Eleanor. And nothing ever has. She ticked off a whole list of experiences that summer: sex, getting drunk, bumming cigarettes (and twice, money) off total strangers, LSD, learning her way around central London, art (working her way systematically round the National Gallery, memorising names, styles, movements).

It seems to her, looking back, that she was efficient yet not mechanical. Her memory of that summer holds snapshots of happiness. Lying on John's dishevelled bed after sex, naked and light as a feather in the afternoon sunlight, his fingers tracing a tickling line around her breasts and down her belly. Catching his eye as his spaced-out housemate rambles on over tea, and choking on her laughter. Emerging out of Charing Cross tube and climbing up onto Hungerford Bridge, staring down the gleaming river to St Paul's and Tower Bridge and relishing both her own joy in being there, and the cliché of that. Maybe that was the note of the whole summer. Her discovery of a world of things the world already knows – common experience, old things all bursting with new juicy pleasures. Sitting in a smoke-filled room at 2am with a bunch of people whose names she'd forgotten but who all loved and understood one another better than anyone in the whole idiotic world outside – that was new, and to be gathered in and savoured, as much as the strange beauty of the Italian Renaissance section in the National. She stood before Piero della Francesca's *Nativity* with tears in her eyes. Yes, other people liked it and thought it good. But her own response was more real, more rich, more special, than anyone else's.

Going home after that summer made her giddy with impatience. Her mother was a dull weight seeking to attach itself to her rising star and drag her down with leaden fears. Eleanor was working hard at her A levels and getting top grades. She was dumping John and moving on through a succession of boys who amused and interested and pleasured her without ever hurting her feelings or breaking her heart. She was encased in her own bright bubble of confidence, her own spell of innocence, as secure as a babe in the amniotic sac, or as a young sleeping beauty in her eleven fairy godmothers' spells, and there was never any sign of a puncturing needle. Launching herself on adult life, she did exactly what she wanted as fast as she possibly could, and always got away with it. Con loved that. She knew he loved it in her, which made her even shinier. It was part of their myth; Con thorough and deliberate, El brilliant and fast – a perfect partnership, each counterbalancing the other, the tortoise and the hare. Acknowledging that was one of the early pleasures of the relationship. El remembers an evening soon after Paul was born; she was sitting at the kitchen table making notes, and Con was reading the Sunday paper with Paul dozing off over his shoulder. Con began to scoff over some mention of 'female intuition' which he found patronising.

'Why is it patronising?' El put her pencil in her book. He looked across at her suspiciously.

'You know perfectly well why it's patronising.'

'No I don't,' she laughed. 'Tell me.'

'For heaven's sake, El. Instead of having rational minds like men, poor little women have to make do with "intuition"?'

'Oh, I see. I've always thought it was a good thing.'

Con raised his eyebrows.

'But I guess I didn't see it as *instead of* a rational mind. I think of intuition as the highest action of the rational mind.'

'Go on.'

'Well, for me it is. When I make a decision—'

'What sort of decision? Should this woman have a caesarean? Or, should I scratch my bum?'

'A serious decision.'

'OK.'

'I make it by intuition.'

'That's ridiculous.'

'No. It's how I make my best decisions.'

'In an instant, on a whim?'

'Fast yes, but not on a whim. Everything feeds into it, your mind speeds up; your mind scans all the options and alternatives, but quickly, almost in a blur, so you can hold them all together at once in your head; you don't go, if *a* then blah blah blah, on the other hand if *b* then blah blah blah – you have the whole problem, and all possible outcomes on view like – like—'

'An aerial photograph?' Con offered.

'OK. I was going to say like all-round vision, so much the same. And then with all that in your head you leap to the best possible conclusion.'

'Right. This is where it's silly. You do all this rational stuff and then you "leap". You jump to a conclusion. That's not rational.'

'It's not rational, it's better than rational. Because it involves some other form of knowledge as well.'

'*Some other form of knowledge?* Like what? Primitive instinct?'

'There isn't a term for it. OK, I'll tell you what it is. It's the knowledge that a trapeze artist has in letting go of one rope in mid-air and flying to the next, or the knowledge a researcher has in looking at the first batch of results and leaping to a conclusion. It's the knowledge that a fighter pilot has in suddenly swooping out of range of an enemy he's scarcely glimpsed.'

'What's the good of a researcher leaping to a conclusion? You've shot your own argument down in flames.'

After he had put Paul to bed, they spent the rest of the evening dissecting how each of them individually had come to the decision that this was the house they should buy – which El had decided after fifteen minutes (intuitively) and Con after four days (rationally).

'So intuition beats rational thought?' he asked slyly.

'You know I'm not saying that, I'm saying it *incorporates* rational thought.'

'And beats it. By three days, twenty-three hours and forty-five minutes.'

'Oh rubbish.'

He smilingly kissed her forehead.

Later her speed became a stick to beat her with. He accused her of bulldozing people at work, of riding roughshod over Cara's depression, of never stopping to think. She wonders if being with Conrad, over the years of his appreciation of her speed, and later, his opposition to it, have combined to make her more speedy; firstly by encouraging it, and then by forcing her into defiance. She thinks of the impatience he now fills her with, a physical pressure. Not just Con, most people. People are so slow. She always has to make allowances, to wait for them to catch up.

Blearily the present surfaces through the past, the thick grey back of a whale humping out of the waves. The bad thing is now, El realises. Con's vanishing is the puncture wound which will let it all slip out, all her bright success, all her confidence and certainty. This is how her finger gets pricked, this is where the bubble bursts.

It is possible to wander round this notion and examine it from different angles: she is still anaesthetised by the glow of the past. Last night's painful anxiety has not yet returned although she senses now it will. There is a kind of superstition which is attached to speed and success and happiness. It is to do with never letting the bad things in. Energy and movement have been her protection, and have all her life kept her immune from psychological harm. Con slowed down, and so made himself susceptible. She has had this argument with him more than once. About his work, last year. 'If it's not going anywhere, if it's stopped engaging you – for heaven's sake, Con, get out.'

'Out and into what?'

'There are other areas of research you could move into. Look at some of the cancer treatment work that's being done with immunosuppressants.'

'I've spent half my career on the transplant programme.'

'It's not so different – you know that as well as I do.'

'There isn't anything.'

'How do you know if you don't look?'

'I know.'

'The only thing that's stopping you getting out of the monkey house is your own depression. If you told yourself it was possible—'

'Your mind has this wonderful ability, my dear, to sprinkle gold dust everywhere you tread, but—'

'You don't even try. You're just completely negative.'

'But for some of us, our minds sprinkle shit, and we see it coming and then we tread in it.' He let the bad thing in. It is like any other imbalance. Once a person starts eating too much, even if they diet later, they have destroyed their natural balance. Once fear and gloom and despair are allowed in, you are contaminated.

On cue the doorbell rings. She hurries to get it before they ring again and wake Dan. A policeman and woman ask to come in.

'Have you found – have you got some news?'

But they haven't. They've come to take away Con's computer and personal papers.

'People often leave clues on computers,' says the man, as if she were stupid. 'They think they can delete things but we have ways—'

'Yes, I know.' She has already decided not to tell them about the MAD emails; let's see how long they take to find them, she tells herself, and let's see what they do about them when they do find them. It probably won't be these two anyway, it will be a special computer nerd in a garret somewhere. If they find something she's missed – well, good.

Within minutes they are gone, the full drawers of Con's desk piled in the arms of the man, the woman clutching the computer tower, its lead dangling pathetically. El is left surveying the gaping absences in Con's room. Her eyes fill with tears. It is ridiculous to howl about his room when she hasn't cried for him. But she shouldn't have let them take his computer. God knows how long they'll be, and his work is on it. In Con's recent state of mind, how good is he likely to have been at backing things up? What if they accidentally wipe it? She should have made copies, she should have told them she needed copies.

She puts on smart clothes, leaves sleeping Dan a note, and drives to the police station, where a flustered and overworked desk sergeant is trying to deal with a queue. El gives him the name of the policeman she spoke to yesterday, shows him the receipt she was given for Con's papers and computer, asks to speak to whoever is in charge of the case. The desk sergeant takes down all her details painstakingly (Name? Address? Phone number? Date the crime was notified?) then vanishes to an inner office for a full five minutes, only to re-emerge with the news that no one can help her at the moment, but someone will phone her later today. He cannot even give her a name.

Chapter 8

CONRAD BECOMES AWARE of his two hands gripping the ledge where his coffee cup rests. His own long bony fingers; pianists' fingers, Eleanor used to say, kissing them and pressing her palms against his, laughingly comparing sizes. Such lovely, clever hands, you should have been a surgeon. He sees that the finger ends, beneath his close-bitten nails, are yellowish white with pressure; that the joints, bent like the splayed legs of a spider, are arthritically bulbous; that his chapped skin pulls and creases across the knobbly bones and protruding sinews like an ill-fitting stretch cover draped over an old sofa. He can see his swollen veins, purple worms beneath the skin.

Quickly he releases the ledge, and buries the hands in his pockets like the shameful things they are. People must be staring at him, a madman gripping a shelf like it's the edge of a cliff, reflected in the mirror for all to see. He pushes himself up from the stool and out into the cold air. There's a queue of cars all pumping exhaust into the clinging white fog, making a choking mix that catches in his throat. He retraces his steps to the hotel. Now it's light, perhaps he'll sleep. He needs to think what to do, but he can't think until he's slept. Dull heavy hammer blows are pounding the back of his head, low down, just above the nape of his neck, as if a dogged executioner is trying to chop off his head with the wrong implement. He curls into a foetal position and closes his eyes.

But it's no good. Closed eyes make the pounding feel louder, like he's shut inside a box with it, and his heart, beating to a different rhythm, is speeding up. Of course, all that coffee. He shoves the pillows against the wall and sits up in bed, his mis-shapen head lolling back against the wall. Every time he moves it now, lumpy pain rolls across like thunder from one side to the other. He needs to hold still. Perhaps there's something wrong. There is the momentary possibility of a smile at this. Perhaps there's something wrong, eh. That'll be beyond being holed up in some distant Italian city on the run from an animal rights fanatic and from his treacherous wife and his children (his and not his) and the howling mess of the research and the whole useless shooting match of his life with no inkling where to go or what to do – that'll be something wrong *besides* that, will it? And what did you have in mind? Meningitis? Brain tumour? Blessing in disguise, if you ask me.

How ignominious to be ill. To be lying here incapacitated; clucked over by hotel staff, his passport flicked through, a doctor summoned. How pitiful, to have Eleanor sweeping into his room, exasperated and in a rush, arranging for him to be shipped home like some malingering pet.

No. He's not going to be ill. He holds his neck and head still, gingerly reaching down to pull the blankets higher up his chest. Slowly he closes his left eye. Opens it, closes the right. Watches the way the end of the bed jumps from one side to the other with each blink. What he thought was here – is there. Here. There. What he thought was good is bad. Is it possible to revision it? (To see it again, to re-vision, re-envision perhaps, to have a different vision of it?) What he thought was good is bad. The truth he loved was lies.

But isn't this a lie too, this reinterpretation of history? This Stalinist revisionism? In each single eye's opening, each lurch of vision to left or right, good, bad, good, bad, isn't there simplification?

Of course, dummy, that's why you have two eyes. Two in one. Both good and bad… 'Time that tries all, both good and bad'… The shadow of a quote hovers in his mind, some long-ago school-learned quote, 'both joy and terror / Of good and bad; that makes and unfolds error…'

He knows all this. The good within the bad, the bad within the good. At work: the drugs are good, stop rejection, enable the host to accept the transplant. The drugs are bad, destroying the host's defences, making him susceptible to every infection going; necessitating killer doses of antibiotics. Take away the good, he dies. Take away the bad, he can't accept the good and dies. Simply yet intricately knotted together as the two ends of a shoelace in a bow.

Without experience, there's no innocence. This must be true too: experience doesn't obliterate innocence. Innocence was once as real as experience now is. Making different assertions, offering an opposite interpretation. Experience can't wipe it from the record.

Is it that he wishes it could? Those innocent visions: El in the sunlit garden with golden-haired Cara in her arms? His wife and daughter in his bed, milky sweet to wake up to, warm and white and soft as dreams, as melting happiness right there within his grasp – Oh, he would prefer to surgically excise it.

Slice the nerves, sew up their ends, lop off the pain.

Yes, tell that to an amputee with a phantom limb. Tell the brain that what can't be seen isn't real and can't be felt. Good plan, Conrad. And the hospital beds – the hospital beds on that paediatric heart ward – the small flotilla of hospital beds with their frail cargo, they can't be excised either; and since they were good – or rather, *he* was good, if innocence and ignorance are good – then that element too, that goodness, that innocence, must be compounded into the bitter mix with experience and self-hatred, allowing both conflicting sets of qualities their due.

He was a different person then. He reaches with disbelief for that young man's conviction. He thought he knew what was right. He had an interview with Saul and Brock. He was tempted by their research. Excited by the challenge they were offering him, and the autonomy he would have in the research. He didn't like the monkey house, though; he'd never liked the monkey house. (Let that be a warning to you, lanky young man, innocent ignorant cocky young man, who thinks he can, at no cost, re-program his own visceral responses.) He didn't like its rank cloying smell, he didn't like the way their eyes followed you, their raised eyebrows, their grimaces. He wanted to make the move, but he dithered.

And El, impatient that he wasn't making up his mind, said, 'Why don't you go to the hospital? Go to the heart ward, children's surgical. I'll give Keith a ring, he'll brief you. Go and see who's waiting for a transplant.'

Keith suggested he join him on his ward round, took him through the notes in the sister's office before they started out. 'There's four on this ward with chronic heart defects. The little chap in the end bed – Ryan – he's only recently been picked up, Barth syndrome, you remember that one? Dilated cardio-myopathy. He should have been diagnosed years ago, he's got all the symptoms – short stature, constant stream of bacterial infections, neutropenia. I've got him on anticoagulants and anti-arrhythmic drugs but as he gets older the effects'll become more severe. A transplant is the only option that could offer him a decent quality of life. The little girl in the next bed's post-op. Hypoplastic left heart syndrome. We've just done a Norwood—'

'Keith, I'm not up to date on this stuff—'

'Sorry. Norwood procedure, to create communication between the right ventricle and the aorta, and enlarge the ascending aorta – temporary measure, it'll keep her going for a while, but she needs a new heart. Then Amanda in the end bed, she's fifteen. Hypertrophic obstructive cardiomyopathy. She's been in and out, classic symptoms, enlarged septum, shortness of breath, dizziness, fainting, angina pectoris, there's a murmur. She's had one op for the obstructive form but it wasn't wildly successful. All I can do now is keep her on propranolol and hope for a heart. She's hit the wall, basically, she's becoming more lethargic day by day.'

'Does she know?'

Keith shrugged. 'The parents know. Their decision to tell her or not. I don't think she'll go home again.'

'How long—?'

'Two – three weeks? They degenerate rapidly at the end. And the other, Sally, she's heading the same way. She's nine. She's been one of mine since she was born. She was born with tetral-ogy of Fallot and pulmonary atresia, blue baby syndrome. So we did surgery at six days to improve blood flow to the lungs, then open-heart surgery when she was twelve months – basically, reconstruction work. She's had every respiratory disease going, pneumonia, you name it – we had to put her on ECMO for a while. I told the parents she'd need a new valve at some point, but now she's back in, to be honest it's not worth opening the poor kid up again just for a new valve. The heart's worn out, if she doesn't get a new one… I've got her on intravenous milrinone to strengthen heart function but basically we urgently need a match. And to add insult to injury, she's rhesus negative, so we're that much less likely to find one.'

'When did you last do a transplant?'

'About six weeks ago. We were able to send him home last week.'

'So you might get one for her—'

Keith shrugged again. 'If we're lucky. If someone else is unlucky.'

And then they went out on the ward. The little boy seemed normal enough, sitting up in bed with a pack of felt pens and a big pad, painstakingly completing an intricate drawing of a spacecraft, grinning shyly up at Conrad. The post-operative child was asleep, as was Amanda. She had a pale, slightly podgy face, and her lips were bluish. Sally was propped up on her pillows, engrossed with a handful of finger puppets. She was the size of a four-year-old. Her fine blonde hair stood on end in little tufts.

'Morning, Sal,' said Keith. 'How's the family?'

Her skin was doughy and her lips also had a purplish tinge, but her eyes were bright. 'The baby's been naughty again, and the twins're fighting.' She gasped for breath. 'They're a shower, a proper shower!' She wriggled her puppet fingers at them and laughed breathlessly. Keith bent to take her pulse.

'And how about you?'

'Running around after these children – I'm at my wits' end.' Though light and whispery, her voice mimicked perfectly the cadences of an exasperated woman. 'A holiday in the sun, that's what I need.'

'Maybe you should have a little snooze.'

She looked at Keith. 'Can I get up today?'

'I'm afraid not, Sally. Not today.'

She turned her attention away from him immediately, waggling a puppet on her right index finger at the tribe on her left hand. 'I told you not to fight! Now get up to your room and stay there.' A gasp for air. 'I don't want another peep out of you.'

Staring at the tiny pink and green puppet Con realised it was familiar; Cara had a set of these at home, a last year's Christmas present. She had played with them obsessively for a couple of weeks then one of them had been lost, feared swallowed by the vacuum, and after tears and recriminations the others had been put to bed in match boxes.

The girl's voice became tiny. 'Oh please, Mummy, we'll be good.' 'Please pretty please, can't we help you sweep the floor?' She had to gasp for breath but didn't look up, blanking Keith completely. 'Get along with you now, no sweets today!'

Keith patted her gently on the head and turned away, but Sal did not acknowledge him. Afterwards Con couldn't shift her image, her fierce concentration, her breathless energetic voice, the sweetness of her laughter, her blue lips. Or perhaps what he really couldn't shift was the notion of another child in her place. Another little girl who was equally intent upon her puppet-babies, another little girl whose golden hair and sweet smile caught at his throat. How could you bear it, how could you live, if it was your own child in that hospital bed? 'There's nothing else you can do for her?' he asked Keith, back in the ward office.

Keith rubbed his eyes. 'Short of going out and murdering a donor, no. I'm going to have to watch her die. Rubbish, isn't it?'

So Con went to join Saul and Brock, because one day a monkey heart would save a girl like Sally. Blessed in his innocence. A torturer of dumb beasts. Blanking out all he didn't need to see.

When Con gets up to piss and have a swig of water, he realises the headache has diminished. There's the sound of a maid vacuuming, which he finds comforting, that sense of order, the day's routine under way. He hangs out his *Non disturbare* sign and gets back into bed, pulls the covers up to his ears, and falls into black sleep.

Banging. The glare of fluorescent lights, and banging. Don't let it be... banging. Banging. It's hurling itself against the bars, battering, demented, over and over again. And he can't move. He's willing it to die, to be over, how can the creature take any more? A moth, thank God for moths, a moth would be dust by now. But this well-constructed vertebrate, this parcel of nerves and bones and tough sinews and tendons and muscle, encased in hard-wearing leather, cushioned by protective fur, this takes a long time to batter itself to death, a good long time, despite the blood oozing and then pumping from its neck. Only when Con's own face is dripping with its blood does the animal stagger back and slump, to lie twitching on its side. And now all the others are screaming. Screaming, screaming; his head can't contain so much noise.

Con wakes, unsure how much time has passed, slick with sweat. Six years he worked on the monkey transplant programme with Saul and Brock. Six years of optimism and hard work and terrible futility, punctuated by his wretched visit to the States. By the early nineties funding was drying up, and the in-house monkey-breeding programme was increasingly unsuccessful, so they were having to source monkeys from other research centres and even from overseas, with all the attendant uncertainties about how pathogen-free they might be. Worst of all was the sense that the monkey–human transplant programme might not really be going anywhere anyway; even if they cracked it, even if hyperacute rejection could be stamped out, and the median survival rates increased, there would never be a big enough supply of monkey organs to meet demand, given how slowly and erratically they reproduced in captivity. Brock started talking about moving on in spring '93. If he went, that would certainly be the end of their funding. When he asked Con to come for a drink to discuss plans, Con assumed he had decided to make the obvious move to the States.

Brock had selected the Square Albert, a big ugly pub in the centre of town – Con understood that it was in order to avoid anyone else from work, and allowed himself to feel flattered. They took their beers to the upper level, and sank back into an alcove. 'Cheers.'

'Cheers.'

An appraising stare from under Brock's sprouting eyebrows, and then a sudden grin. 'You know what this is about.'

'Yup.'

'You know where I'm going?'

'Boston?' The most interesting research Con was aware of was happening at New England Deaconess hospital there; they had made a breakthrough with an enzyme that blocked some of the immediate immune reaction. If there was any mileage in it, it would become treatment of choice because it would considerably lessen the dosages of immunosuppressants needed after transplant.

But Brock was shaking his head. 'I'm going over to the other side. I'm staying right here and I'm going over to the other side.'

'The other side?'

'Taking the drug company shilling.'

'You've lost me.'

'Have you heard of a company called Corastra?'

'I've seen the name – involved in transgenics?'

'OK. Small UK company founded by a guy I was at school with, very bright man, Christopher Farrell. He trained as a surgeon and went to work in Bristol. Decided the work he was doing – the publicly funded research – had good commercial application and formed himself a company before he told anyone what he was up to. And now he's made a killing.'

'How?'

'Sold it on to Kneiper.'

'It sounds a bit unethical.'

Brock shrugged. 'You want ethics? With no funding and no monkeys and no investment in the future of research in this country, and anyone with an IQ over a hundred decamping to the States? At least Corastra is a British company. At least it's based here. Kneiper are paying the bills but he's keeping the Corastra ID.'

'What's the work?'

'Pigs.'

'You don't know anything about pigs.'

'Pig to primate transplants. With the ultimate aim of pig to human xenografts.'

'It's mad. The hyperacute rejection across a species divide that wide is instant.'

'They're genetically modifying the pigs. They've been breeding pigs which are transgenic. They believe they'll be able to prevent HAR.'

'They've already bred the pigs?'

'They've done trials. And now they're going for it.'

'What's the programme?'

'Transplant the pig hearts into primates, cynomolgous monkeys. Without HAR it should be possible to use a standard immunosuppressive therapy, cyclosporine, cyclophosphamide and steroids.'

'And Kneiper picks up the profit on the immunosuppressants?'

'I don't know if they've patented the transgenic hearts. If they have, that's where they'll make their fortunes.'

'And pigs breed quickly.'

'Precisely. Two to three litters a year, ten or so per litter. Enough hearts to supply the transplant wants of the world. They're envisaging a two-year research programme of testing on monkeys, moving on to clinical trials soon after that.'

'Good grief.'

'Yes. And they're doubling my salary. Are you interested?'

'What do they want?'

'It's a small team, they want another immunologist with primate experience, and when they approached me I recommended you.'

'Where is it?'

'We stay here, use our own lab facilities: Kneiper will pay the university, and we become Corastra research fellows. The only big change is that the animal work is farmed out – which, given the state of our monkey house, is a consummation devoutly to be wished.'

'Farmed out to where?'

'A group called Carrington Bio-Life, all the surgical and routine stuff is contracted out to them. They have a dedicated staff who send us reports and samples for analysis, and we tell them how to adjust dosages. It's a much more streamlined, efficient use of manpower.'

Con remembers the particular draw of the distant, professionally run animal house; the delightful and utterly unrealistic vision it conjured of contented animals in surroundings rather like a zoo, tended and monitored by kindly keepers who knew each animal individually and had no other concerns or claims upon their time than the welfare of the monkeys.

He remembers it now, less delightfully, as the attraction of not having to get his own hands dirty.

When Con discussed the idea with El she was less hostile to it than he had expected. For her, as for him, having Kneiper for his paymaster was the sticking point. 'It's the privatisation of knowledge, isn't it? Research not to increase the sum of human knowledge, but to increase shareholders' profits.'

'Yes,' he agreed. 'But it's hard to know which way to turn. Brock's right, we're not going to get any more government funding for monkey transplants. In the absence of public funding, the choices are pretty stark.'

'They'll make their profits out of knowledge and expertise like yours and Brock's that only exists because of years of public funding.'

'Yup. Like hospital consultants with their private patients.'

'True.'

'The thing about the level of funding they're prepared to put in is that things will move quickly. There should be a break-through within a couple of years. And if that happens – if we can move to clinical trials – then whoever's making the profits, it is lives saved, at the end of the day. It's lives saved more quickly than they would have been without Kneiper.'

'If it becomes standard practice, they can't actually keep a grip on the world supply of transgenic hearts, can they?'

'I don't see how they could. They'll rake it in to begin with, but someone else'll soon catch up, make some slight modifi-cation, slither around the patent laws – it'll enter the public domain, won't it. Like generic drugs. You'll be able to get a Boots own-brand pig heart, one tenth the price of a Kneiper one.'

El laughed. 'Kneiper will be keeping the lid on it as long as they can. Bet you have to sign some sort of loyalty oath.'

He hadn't thought of that, of course. Loyalty to Big Pharma. It was one thing to be paid by them to move swiftly on ground-breaking research. It was another to be their creature, his silence bought with their silver, his tongue shackled by chains of their clinking coins. He hadn't thought seriously of what yielding up his freedom of speech might mean.

Which reminds him of his last visit to a monkey house. His last visit: the day he first met Maddy.

The day he meets her – nearly a year ago, only a year – is ever-present in his memory. The day when the nightmare breaks through and confirms itself as real. He finally visits the Carrington Bio-Life animal facility, where his research animals are housed. They have all been outsourced from the university animal house, which is where they were always kept in the early days of his research. Now other people – technicians, vets – dose them and operate and make notes on them; all he has to do is make sense of their reports. It is a two-hour drive, but it is something he has known he must do for a very long time. To be honest, since he started working for Corastra. But there has always been a good reason for putting it off. Now, longevity has apparently improved, and he has to check at what point they are sacrificing moribund animals, to ensure that this really is good news.

He knows it is not, the minute he is let into the building. There is no good news here. The smell is enough to tell him that; the smell of sickness and old faeces and urine, strong enough almost to block out the stink of oranges. The security guard who checks him in takes him as far as the glass-panelled office, where a youth sits with his feet on the desk, stabbing at his mobile. Con gives his name and lab address and the youth ticks a list and carries on stabbing.

Con goes into the changing room to remove his shoes and put on the biohazard suit, then heads to the primate section. Monkeys awaiting surgery scream and chatter from their perches. He lets himself through the final door into the sterile room, and finds the three surviving monkeys from his own tests. The new hearts have been grafted onto their necks, a quicker and simpler way of testing rejection, and all three look poorly. F20 is huddled in the corner of her cage, eyes closed, breathing rapid and light; the bigger of the two males, M17, is reeling against the bars, retching up small amounts of pale yellow fluid. The other has his eyes open but is lying on the floor of his cage and makes no move as Conrad approaches. Con glances at F20's notes. She has been quiet and huddled for two days. He can see immediately that all three of them are suffering from too-high dosages of immunosuppressants. But there is no way out of this. Their bodies won't accept the hearts unless their immune systems are utterly suppressed, and the suppression of their immune systems causes vomiting and renal failure. But there have been so many adjustments to the drug regime over the last year – he had hoped to have a couple of longer-term survivors out of this batch; he had hoped they might regain at least some quality of life for a short while. He reaches for M17's notes. There is nothing written against today's date; for yesterday, 'Quiet but alert.' How long has he been vomiting? He moves over to M20's notes. They are in the same hand, up to and including today: 'Quiet, unsteady.' So have they just forgotten to make a note for M17? Or have these been filled in yesterday for today's date as well? His sudden conviction that this is what has happened fuses with his earlier concern about the death rate in surgery.

He straightens up quickly and goes through to the room labelled Technicians' Office. It is empty. Why is the place so deserted? He rifles through the filing cabinets until he finds 'Monkeys, surgical'. He takes out a handful of folders; the first one he glances through electrifies him. *Piglet heart found to be unsuitably large at 10.75 oz. Subject died on the table.* How could they have a 10.75 oz heart? The heart sizes are specified, nothing over 6 oz. The piglet itself must have looked large, and they must have known as soon as they opened it up – did they have no piglets in reserve? And why should the monkey die? Could they not repair the neck surgery?

For an enraged moment he simply tots up the costs: £3,000

for the monkey, then the drug regime it has been on, the cost of the transgenic piglet, the man hours of planning and preparation…

He thumbs quickly through the other notes. They lack detail. One states simply, 'Technical error', and another, 'Failed to recover from anaesthetic.'

Con makes himself put the files back carefully. He is trembling with rage. As he heads back out of the primate house he forces himself to look, to not allow his eyes to close. There are numerous comatose animals, who should have been sacrificed days ago. Cages have not been cleaned out, old vomit and excreta and spilt food litter the floors. He reminds himself that monkey houses are always bad, but this is intolerable. When he has changed he strides back to the office. 'What time do they do the rounds?'

The lad glances up at him and shrugs.

'What time do they come round to check the animals?'

'Afternoon? Yeah, sometime in the afternoon, I think.'

'I need to talk to them. What time will they be here?'

The lad scrabbles through a few papers on his desk but does not seem to find anything. 'Around 2-ish?' he offers.

'Have you been round yourself this morning? Some of them need water.'

'Cleaners see to that first thing.'

'Well, what's your job?'

'Keeping an eye on things,' he mutters, restoring his attention to his phone.

Conrad realises there is no point, though he'd like to slap the lout off his chair. There's no point, it's not his fault, they're probably paying him all of £5 an hour. 'I'm coming back at 2,' he says. 'Please make a note.' He stands over the youth while he scrawls Conrad's name in the slot beside 2pm. Con can see now that all the other time slots are empty.

When he gets out he goes to the car but can't face getting in. He tells the guy on the gate he'll be back, and slips through as soon as the gap is wide enough.

'Two miles into town, mate!' the man calls out, and Con raises his hand in acknowledgement. Two miles is what he needs, walking fast, breathing clean air, eyes staring blankly through leafless March hedges to newly ploughed fields beyond. He can't think who he can safely talk to about this. Brock was the one: but Brock died last year of a heart attack. And after his death, Saul decamped to the States. Con is the only Corastra fellow left in the department. Maybe he can sort it out on his own? Maybe if he tells someone at Corastra? He thinks of the loyalty clause, of the hunger for results, of the increasing sense of futility. Maybe they would pull the plug on the whole thing. Maybe that would be a good idea. More likely, he thinks, they would tell him to keep it quiet. And if they told him they had dealt with it, would he believe them? Isn't it perfectly likely they already know? They are spending an awful lot of money – presumably Carrington Bio-Life come cheap.

By the time he arrives at streets with houses and gardens he is able to focus on his surroundings again, and when the smell of coffee wafts at him from an open café door, he turns in and orders a drink. He sits by the window, cradling his mug between his hands.

'May I join you?' A woman's voice. He's so startled he slops coffee across the table. She apologises, slipping into the other seat, and mops up the spill with paper napkins. There are several tables empty but she is already sitting opposite him, smiling timidly. 'Sorry,' she says. 'It's so nice to sit by the window. Do you live here?'

Con feels he is staring wildly. What is this? Why can't she leave him in peace? But she is inoffensive enough; mouse-brown hair, pale and serious and devoid of make-up. She looks like a librarian. She looks like someone he might already know. 'No,' he says.

She nods. 'It's all right,' she says. 'Apart from one thing. There's one big skeleton in this town's cupboard.'

'Really?' He sees her clocking that he's afraid she's a nutter; she adjusts, and gives a little laugh.

'Sorry. It's my obsession, but there's no need for me to bore you with it. You probably came here for some peace and quiet.' She half-turns her chair, so that she's facing the window, and stares fixedly into the street.

Why did she sit by him? Is she trying to pick him up? The thought almost makes him smile, but why not? 'What is this skeleton? You can't leave me in suspense like that.'

'You'd be surprised how many people don't even know. There's a vivisection laboratory. Where they do experiments on living animals.'

As soon as she says it he realises he knew she would. She is part of the same nightmare, but at this stage he does not realise her role. 'Do you work there?'

'God forbid! I love animals. I'm a pacifist. I don't believe we should ever hurt animals, or people.'

Why is she telling him this? And what's the reply? He sips at his coffee. 'My son's a vegetarian,' he offers.

'That's good. So am I.'

They sit in a brief silence; the librarian takes small bites of her sandwich and quickly chews them. 'I've joined a protest group,' she tells Con. 'Against animal testing. They test make-up, you know. They put the chemicals in dogs' eyes. And sweeteners, they feed them artificial sweeteners till they die of poisoning.'

'Better poison an animal than a human,' says Con automatically.

'Oh no, they force-feed them huge doses of the stuff, more than a human would ever consume, and that's why they die. From the overdose.'

'I see.' The woman has soft downy hairs on her upper lip; when she turns they catch the light. He has a sudden pang of – what? Jealousy? – for her complacency. Her cleanliness. He knows he is still contaminated by the stench of the animal house. 'You haven't been inside?' he says.

'No. No. I don't think I could bear it.'

'So how do you––?'

'PECA. Prevent Experiments and Cruelty to Animals. The protest group. Sometimes they manage to get information, or pictures. Photos really help because anyone who sees them knows they want this to stop. Even a small blurry picture, it turns your stomach.'

'So how do you protest?'

She smiles at him gratefully and he finds himself smiling back. She looks younger when she smiles. 'The main thing is to let people know. Education. Because people don't imagine such things can be done in a civilised society. Nearly everyone loves animals, don't they?'

He visualises the motley assortment of Evanson family pets: the short-lived funfair goldfish, the escaping budgie, Megan's rats, Paul's hens. El's constant opposition, 'Haven't we got enough to look after with four kids, never mind a menagerie?' Yes, nearly everyone loves animals. El never stops to stroke a cat or pat a dog. Hard-hearted, practical, busy El. Yet it is Con who tortures monkeys. The woman is looking at him. 'Yes. Of course. But how do you educate people?'

'Posters. Articles. Protests. We hold monthly vigils outside the gates, and we advertise them in the town, sometimes new people join us. And online, of course; if we get any information we put it on the website. That's the way to reach people.'

'But does it have any effect?'

'What d'you mean?'

'Does it make any difference to what – what they are doing in the labs?'

'Don't you think it would?'

Why is she asking him? 'I suppose if someone who worked there saw it from a protestor's point of view…'

'Exactly! Cruelty becomes routine – well, look at the Nazis – and then if you step outside the routine a moment you realise how awful it is.'

'I'm sure they aren't Nazis.'

'No, but I often wonder, do you think they have pets? D'you think they go home after a day of inflicting pain on their fellow creatures, and take the dog for a walk?'

Con drains his coffee. It is enough. He needs to find his own thoughts again before it's time to go back. 'I expect they do,' he says, pushing back his chair.

'I believe in the power of love,' she says. 'Sometimes I go and sit outside the fence and will love and strength to the animals.'

'On your own?'

'Yes. I want to give them hope.'

He imagines her, in her mousey grey coat, sitting on a plaid rug beside the prison-high fencing, her serious gaze fixed on the animal house roof, goodness radiating from her. 'That's – well,' he gives a laugh and shakes his head, 'that's impressive.' He is on his feet, threading his arms into his coat.

'You're a scientist, aren't you.'

'Why d'you say that?'

'I saw you. I was by the fence. I followed you.'

When Con replays the scene this is the moment of pause. Why doesn't he walk away? She reveals her hand; she has already lied to him and manipulated him, she is far more serious than she has led him to believe. Why doesn't he walk away?

He doesn't walk away because she is his creature and he must collude with her. She is his, conjured out of his visit to that hell hole and his own guilt, spawned by his queasily churning stomach. She is his own distress made manifest. This must be how God got Jesus, he thinks. His own distress made flesh. What He saw in his great experiment, Earth, was so wicked, so unendurable, that He conjured a human being to go deal with it; He externalised the simplest part of the argument. The good part.

He doesn't walk away because he thinks she is good. Conrad sits down on his chair again.

'I'm sorry,' she says. 'I had no right.'

'No, you didn't.'

'But your face looked so kind and I could tell you were upset by the way you hurried out. I just thought, he's my chance, maybe he's my one chance to try and save those poor innocent creatures.' She takes an instamatic camera from her bag and places it on the table.

So much for her fancying him. 'How did you think I could help you?'

'I thought you might tell me what you've seen, and I could put it online. Or you might be going back, you could take some photos for me.'

'My research is based on some of these experiments.'

'But you've seen what they're doing. You know it's evil. Don't you?'

'It's not that simple. Experiments are done for a reason. To try to save human lives. I can't – this is a really long argument. Discussion.'

She bobs her head. 'I know. I know. But there must be ways for you to find out what you need to know without hurting animals.'

'If there were, don't you think I wouldn't choose an alternative?'

'You would, you would. You're a good man. But some of it is so pointless – the cosmetics, the sweeteners – so unnecessary.'

He checks his watch: 1.15, time to head back to the animal house. 'Look,' he says. 'I have to… I have an important meeting now. I'm afraid I have to go.'

'But you will help.'

'I don't see how I—'

'Oh, you can. Take my camera. I'll wait for you here.'

'That's ridiculous.'

'No. I know you can help, I knew it the moment I saw you.'

'I don't know when I'll finish, and then I have a long drive home, I have to get back for my children—' Yes, he even told her he had children.

'But just pop in,' she says. 'You have to drive back through town. A quick cup of tea. I promise I won't keep you longer than that.'

He can't imagine how he will feel after he has been back in there. He'll tell them they're breaking the law, he'll have to threaten them with inspectors – whatever he has to do, a cup of tea with her afterwards will be easy in comparison. 'OK.' He pockets the camera reluctantly.

This is the second pause. Why, after he has braced himself and been admitted to the wretched prison again, and waited in vain for anyone in a position of responsibility to appear, and walked about the place like a tourist of sadism, snapping pictures of the worst cases and finally realised that no one is coming and that anyway a carefully worded email from his desk would be more efficient and less liable to end in physical confrontation – why, after all this, does he return to the café? Why doesn't he just put his foot down and head for home? Because he has already committed himself by taking the camera.

Because she is what he deserves.

When he opens the café door she is there with a pot of tea and two cups. 'It's just fresh,' she says. 'I must be telepathic.'

He is shaking with pent-up anger and frustration, with all the unsaid things he has rehearsed for the animal house managers. It doesn't take much of her candid questioning for him to spill the beans, and for him to admit he took photos, though he draws the line at her seeing them. He winds the film on to its end, extracts it from the camera and pockets it. 'I can't let you use any of this now. I have to try to get change within the animal labs first; I need to retain the threat of making the pictures public as a second line of attack.' He hands her back her camera.

She understands. She clasps his hand in gratitude and he

finds himself strangely moved by the contact. Her skin is cool and dry, contained, like her quietly confident face. He finds himself thinking, she does not often touch other people. This is an important day for her. Balm to his own distress.

By the time he is ready to leave they have exchanged names (Maddy) and email addresses and he has promised to keep her informed about how he gets on. She in turn promises to keep what he has told her a secret. When they stand to leave he almost hugs her. It is only on the drive home that he has doubts, and wonders why he has told her quite so much.

If he is honest, it was always bad going into an animal house. Even when he was dealing with his own animals at the university. Treating the monkeys was always bad. He remembers steeling himself against their pretty faces, resolutely not giving them names. Occasionally in extreme grogginess they would submit to his syringe almost willingly, allowing him to feel for a tender self-deceiving moment that he could minister to them, help them, heal them. Instead of making them more sick. Sitting up and folding his knees up to his chest, Con rocks on the bed. There was a reason. Good in bad. Bad in good. It runs through all things. The best time was the worst. Think of it. The year after Cara's birth. Its random-seeming contentment. Its surprising satisfactions. Its joy. Were *because* of the bad. Would not have existed without the bad. And what is he to make of that?

There was something very strange about the year after Cara was born. There was more time. How could there be more time, when they had three children instead of two, and no au pair to help out? There was more time, Con supposes, because Eleanor was at home. She took a full six months' maternity leave. She was reading and working at home, of course, she never stopped thinking and working, but she was there – there when he left in the morning, there when he came in at night. They were a team, functioning perfectly together. She would pass Cara to him when he came in, and Cara's round wondering face would slowly fix on him and blossom into a smile. He'd run the tepid bath and swoosh her in it so she gasped with delighted laughter, Paul and Megan leaning over either side of him to brandish bath toys at her, a hippo that spouted water, a fish-shaped sponge, and Cara like a plump pink starfish herself beaming up at the three of them, waving her arms and legs. When Cara was done they poured in their own bubble bath and hot water and shrieked and giggled and piled each other's heads with froth while he dried and powdered Cara, and El cooked. After they'd eaten, El gave Cara her evening feed while Con cleared up. And all the time, they talked. He loved having no au pair, having the whole house to themselves; would have been happy never to go out. He was dismayed when her sister asked to come and stay that autumn.

El's younger sister Minnie had been living in Italy for six years; Con hardly knew her. Now she was in crisis – her boyfriend had broken her heart, she wanted to move back to England, and she had no base, no job, no friends.

'Why does she have to come to us? Why can't she go home to your mum?'

'Because my mum would drive her nuts, you know that. It'll be nice for the kids anyway, an aunty.'

'It'll be as bad as having another au pair cluttering the place up.'

'Con, we've got two spare bedrooms. And anyway, she's looking for a job. She'll go out – she'll do stuff – it'll be OK.'

Minnie arrived pale and tragic, and monopolised El for two days of low, urgent confidences. Con's worst fears were being realised; after he'd put the children to bed he sat grimly in front of the TV while the sisters' continuous murmur ran on in the kitchen, with only the most random and infrequent accompaniment of chopping or stirring to indicate that dinner might ever arrive. When he cracked and went in to join them and open a bottle of wine, he was hurt to see they were already halfway through one and El had not even thought to offer him a glass.

But after a few days, alliances shifted. Coming to bed early for the first time since Min's arrival, El rolled her eyes at Con and shook her head. 'She's slurping up sympathy like a great sheet of blotting paper.'

'She's slurping up *wine* like a great sheet of blotting paper.' They cackled, together.

'But she has had a horrid time.'

'Go on.'

'Oh, he's been seeing someone else for months and stringing her along with stuff about it being a brief passion he needs to get out of his system, 'cos he loves her really.'

'He's told her?'

'Asked her permission. He's been bringing this female back to where they live.'

'So has he got it out of his system?'

'Well, the other woman's pregnant.'

'Ah.'

'He's a foul old thing anyway, he's about forty, and there's a first wife somewhere in the background too. Min's better off without him. But she's really upset about the sex—'

'Upset about it?'

El bounced gleefully on the edge of the bed. 'She thinks she'll never find anyone to have such good sex with again.'

'Blimey. What does he do?'

'I shouldn't tell you.'

'Oh yes you should. You get in bed, I'll nip down and fetch up the rest of the wine.'

'What rest of the wine?'

'You're joking! Has she found the whisky?' Con crept down to the dining room and took Grouse and glasses from the sideboard. A crack of light still showed under the kitchen door; there was the sound of running water, and of Min singing softly to herself. 'Alas my love, you do me wrong, to cast me off discourteously…' When he got back to the bedroom El took one look at him and shrieked with laughter.

'Hush! Hush!'

'Your face! What is it?'

'She's in the kitchen, singing "Greensleeves".' Neither of them could stop giggling.

'Ssh!'

He poured them each a slug. 'Tell me about the sex.'

'It's just all so – elaborate. Apparently he's got this thing about doing it outside.'

'All Italians do.'

'How d'you know that?'

'Stick around, honey. I know some things.'

'Right. Well, they both go out with nothing on under their coats—'

'Nothing?'

'Not a stitch. Just shoes. And then they go to a restaurant where the waiter offers to hang up their coats so they dither and say they'll keep them just for now, thanks.' El choked on her whisky and had to be thumped on the back. 'We're making so much noise!'

'She's downstairs, she won't hear.'

'And while they eat they're exposing themselves through the buttons, or sticking their feet up each other's coats—'

'With shoes on?'

'You're ruining it.'

'Sorry.'

'And drinking delicious wine, and pouring the odd dribble down the inside of their coats to lick off later—'

'Mmmm.'

'When they've finished their meal in a nice, slow, decorous fashion, they leave the restaurant and find the nearest dark alley, open up the coats and have a good long fuck against the wall.'

'Sounds wonderful.'

'Or climb over the fence and do it in the park.'

'Climb over the fence?'

'Apparently. So they can sit on the edge of a bench. That's her favourite—'

'Sitting on a bench?'

'Well, you know, sitting on him on a bench—'

Con imagined large pale lugubrious Min wobbling on a park bench on top of her elderly lover, who would be a rather frail, skinny gent. 'Stop it, I can't breathe!'

El's face was pink with laughter. 'Oh God, I shouldn't tell you this!'

'What did you tell *her* about us?'

'Nothing.'

'Liar.'

'Nothing.'

'Liar!'

'What would you like me to have told her?'

'Well, I just hope you made it exotic enough.'

'Nothing true, then?'

'Baggage!' They rolled and rocked together on the bed.

Min, whose mental age, Con suggested to El, was very close to Paul's, encouraged Paul and Megan in elaborate games of dressing up, making extravagant headgear out of cereal boxes, tinfoil, feathers and plastic bottles. She took them out to the Oxfam shop to buy long skirts for robes and trains. Paul's incipient hostility to the new baby ('I would of liked it if it was a boy') was totally deflected. Con and El found themselves with delicious giggly afternoons alone with Cara, who learned to crawl backwards at great speed before discovering the other direction. When Min was tipsy (most nights) she was lugubriously funny, relating the woeful tales of her attempts to find a job. She didn't get one in a bookshop because they asked her maths questions about how much change she'd give, and she was thinking in lira and said three thousand instead of three pounds. She didn't get one in a travel agent's because the woman who ran it wanted to know if she was married, and when she said she wasn't, told her she didn't think she was suitable, because some of the men who came in made difficult requests.

'Sounds right up your street!' laughed El.

'Are you sure it was a travel agent's?' Con wanted to know.

'I haven't told you the filing one yet. You know that one you found in the local paper, El? Filing and light reception duties?'

'Yup, it's really near—'

'Builders' merchants. It's in a kind of garage, no heating. The entire place is plastered with pornographic posters, and there are these cardboard boxes – I kid you not – a pile of about fifteen cardboard boxes completely full of damp scraps of paper – letters, bills, receipts, final demands, old fag packets, snotty tissues and chip wrappers—'

'You're making it up.'

'I am not. And this monster-man with a beer gut the size of your fridge goes, "All you gotta do is transfer that lot into the new filing cabinet, darling." And there isn't even a *desk*—' Her dramatic arm swing sent a new bottle of wine flying. El's glance at Con as she mopped up reduced him to silent hysteria.

'Sorry. As for the reception bit, well, the only furniture in the entire place was a camp bed. I suppose I was meant to *receive* callers on that.'

'Why don't you go to the tech, or ring up the WEA? See if you can teach some Italian?'

'But I don't teach Italian, I teach English.'

'I know, dimwit, but you could do conversation, couldn't you? You could do *basic* Italian.'

'But I want to get away from all that, I want to put it behind me—'

'Min, you can't start anything without money.'

'No need to think about it again till Monday now. We're going to cook you a fantastic tea tomorrow. Me and Paul and Megan, we're making a five-course feast, starting with quails' eggs and ending with chocolate mousse, with mead to drink, and everyone has to dress up like kings and queens…'

Her room became a treasure trove of jumbled bargains, chocolate biscuits, dirty towels, rejection letters, half-empty glasses, and all the household scissors, pens and Sellotape. Paul and Megan foraged through it in amazed delight. El and Con discussed Min as they walked around the reservoir next afternoon, with sleeping Cara strapped to Con's chest.

'Has she always been like this?'

'Pretty much.'

'She's a complete fantasist.'

'You like her, don't you?'

'I think she's great. But she needs to sort herself out.'

'I know. There must be a job that'll suit her, if only we could think—'

'She doesn't seem to feel any urgency about it.'

'D'you think we should ask her for food money?'

'It would focus her on the need to earn. How's she financing the quails' eggs and mead?'

'Well—'

'El, you're not giving her money.'

'Think what we're saving on an au pair.'

'Yeah, but it's not helping her, is it? She's twenty-six, she needs to be a bit more responsible.'

'You don't think we could employ her as an au pair for a bit?'

'It would be mad. For a start she creates chaos wherever she goes. Also she needs to learn to stand on her own two feet.'

'You're right. Well, I'm going to find out which of the local schools offer Italian.'

Min made them co-conspirators: plotting to find her a suitable job; managing her shameless requests for loans. She was the perfect foil to the whole family; even Megan would burst out joyously, 'Look what silly Minnie done!' pointing out the latest outrage of burnt cake, coffee-stained carpet, or disastrous use of hair dye. (She escaped a whole week of job hunting after dyeing her light-brown hair deep red, with a corresponding immovable stain across her forehead, ears and neck, so she looked as if she'd been dipped head first in red wine.)

'It's like having another child!' El confided to Con, and it was, making them amused and exasperated allies. But she also gave them time together to enjoy it. Leaving the kids with Min was much simpler than leaving them with an au pair, since the kids loved it, and it was a way for Min to pay them back. They spent a couple of evenings a week in the pub, relishing each other's company, and once attempting, with some hilarity, to enact Min's favourite sexual fantasy. Mostly they just talked, making plans for the kids and for Min, and arguing over the chapter headings for El's IVF book, which at that stage they seriously thought they might co-write. And through that whole laughing giddy time, Cara grew sweet and round and golden-haired, everybody's darling, the sun that warmed the whole family.

He must have drifted off to sleep because he wakes with a memory of that sun, and with a chill of dread upon him. It's gone. All gone. Now the dark is stretching its fingers towards him, and warmth and laughter are as unrecoverable – as unattainable – as sweet midsummer sunshine in the midst of winter's frost.

He gets up quickly and reaches for his shoes. The late afternoon daylight is already failing. When he turns on the light, outside the window becomes dark blue. The memory of his previous night spent huddled beneath the window, and of his hunger, comes back to him. He will go out and buy supplies of food, and a bottle of wine, to see him through the night. He will prepare himself against the dread which already seems to be taking him by the throat… How stupid to have slept in daylight, wasted the day in sleep. When darkness is the thing he wants to blot out. When darkness is what he really fears…

In the dark street Con doesn't know which way. The cold mist that has hovered all day is low again, blurring and haloing streetlights, making an icy wetness that trails against his face like thick cold cobwebs, muffling sound so that passing vehicles loom, blare, then suddenly fade. Footsteps come from nowhere, volume distorts.

End of the road and a sudden stream of traffic, he jiggles from foot to foot trying not to glance behind, keep moving, keep moving, steps into a gap in the traffic and is wrong-footed by a dark shape that scuttles after him and cuts in front – almost loses his balance. Close behind him a man shouts and there's a streak of pressure against his calf. He blunders on to the opposite pavement and the scuttling dog is waiting, its lead stretched taut past his leg to its owner somewhere behind Con. In the light of a shop window Con sees the little dog's ratty trails of hair and nasty bat-face snarling up at him. He stumbles on.

The shops are still open, despite the dark; here in the awful cold a florist's shop brims with garish colour; scarlet and yellow roses in tight buds that will never open, dyed blue daisy-like flowers, unnaturally turquoise. He hurries on, blinking the clashing colours from his eyes. A lit hairdresser's clear as a goldfish bowl; an oblivious young man with sandy-golden hair, tawny lion hair, is being trimmed. Fair hair like Cara's. Cara hair.

They are a family of dark hair. Thick, glossy, choking black is Eleanor's, Paul's, Megan's, Dan's, and dark brown was Con's, before the grey. And tawny golden lion-haired Cara. 'Must be the milkman's,' he had said. Joke.

He knows the slightly wiry texture of Cara's hair, he knows the shape and curl of it, how she has to keep it long so the weight of it makes waves – if it's too short it curls around itself like a lamb's thick fleece. He has been combing Cara's hair ever since there was enough of it to comb. From the first year of her life. Because he knows it better than his own there is a sense in which it belongs to him. Although, of course, it is nothing of his. Between a father and his adopted child form emotional bonds of closeness over years. Proximity and habit, the habit of love, turn strangers into family. For the adoptive father, it is all gain; he turns a random little girl into his very own.

But played the other way, all loss. Turning his blue-eyed daughter, his laughing infant, lasting product of the transient pleasure of numberless unions between Eleanor and himself, gold currency coined by the hammering of their flesh on flesh, astonishing reward for what they did together for their own delight – into a fraud. Counterfeit, an impostor. Turning his daughter into his not-daughter, and his pleasure, retrospectively, into another man's. Of course dogs chase him. The severed nerves and sinews of love that bound her to him trail behind him down the street like a string of intestines. He is gutted.

That the year of Cara's birth was the happiest of their marriage was Con's myth, in which Eleanor so skilfully conspired that he fully thought it a joint myth; enjoying, thanks to there being more than one believer, the status of objective truth. Instead of the defiant efficiency El displayed after the births of Paul and Megan – instead of rushing back to work, programming meetings, slotting breastfeeds into the tea breaks in her sched-ule – she hesitated. She waited. She failed to organise. She was gentler, softer, than her old self. Con was moved to see in her a more consuming maternal affection than she had displayed with either of the first two. She would change her mind and not go out, because Cara cried. He would find her sometimes standing over the cot watching the child sleeping – a habit he himself had had from the first. She had grown up, joined him, on an emotional plane which she had briskly discounted with their first two children. Sometimes, as she fed Cara, she was blinking back tears, which filled Con himself with a primitive desire to protect her. He remembers one afternoon when Min had taken the other two out, sitting on the arm of the chair and putting his arm around El, drawing her head in to rest against his chest. The vision of himself, stern with love, perched on the chair arm protectively embracing his damp-eyed wife and baby, revolts him. He is disgusted at the creature that he was, at his culpably innocent pomposity, at his assumption that he is understood, his pitiful desire to play the man. It is disgust and shame, as if he had found a picture of himself masturbating in public. Eleanor was weeping for her lover, her baby's father. And so blinding was Con's own arrogance that he welcomed her grief as a sign of dependence, and used it to bolster his own self-importance. Calling it all 'love'.

Lacerating incidents from that year. The belated celebration they had nearly a year after Cara's birth, a summer party in the garden on a cloudless June day; they had been in the new house two years and he had battled with the garden. There was a bank of delphiniums and smoke-blue lupins. On that after-noon there must have been sixty of their friends and relatives eating and drinking and laughing in the sunshine, and Eleanor and Cara running like a gold thread through the shifting groups and conversations; even as it unfolded the afternoon was in his mind a still moment of perfection, a richly woven tapestry, with jewel-bright daisies and buttercups underfoot, Eleanor in her long blue dress with the gold-haloed child in her arms, the children's echoing laughter as they played hide and seek in the bushes, a wisp of sound like smoke lingering in the air and mingling with the scent of the heavy old-fashioned chalk-pink roses that dropped their soft petals across the path. His picture, he had composed it; the figures and the background were his. His picture of happiness. He never noticed the death's head in the corner.

He remembers comforting Eleanor over Cara's skin; the eruptions of eczema that plagued her soon after her first birthday. He remembers telling her, every child is different, and the other two are probably prone to some illness that Cara will escape. He remembers Eleanor's grateful smile and nod.

He remembers the night after El's six-week check-up, her sitting in bed grinning at him as he undressed, and him grinning back, knowing what she meant. Knowing and acting upon that knowledge. But what had that grin really meant? She'd got away with it.

There are photos of Con and Cara. More than of him with any of the others. More than of him at any time, for that matter. El takes up the camera only occasionally, almost absentmindedly, fires off a few shots. But there are lots of him and baby Cara; him bathing her, dressing her, feeding her, playing with her on the floor. El must have done that deliberately; pictures of her husband bonding with Cara. To reassure herself. Or him.

And why did she invite Min? She and Min weren't close; they hardly ever saw her after she moved out. Her stay was a lovely, silly, isolated incident. Why invite her when there was a new baby and so much to do and El already knew what a chaotic creature Minnie was? She can't have known how well it would all work out. To convince herself, by contrast with poor Min, that the life she had with Con and the kids was worth hanging on to? Was Min a confidante? Is that the information El bartered, in exchange for Min's outlandish tales? Was Min there so that El could save herself from temptation to phone the man? She's told Con she broke it off before the birth, that the real father never knew she was pregnant. She must have found that hard. Enough to be afraid she couldn't sustain it? He doesn't know. It's not in his experience of Eleanor. The Eleanor he knows is not afraid of herself, is not anxious, is not impulsive, or guilty, or at the mercy of her emotions. Another man knew that Eleanor; he only knew the Eleanor his own limitations allowed him to observe. A four-square Eleanor, an ambitious, decisive, efficient woman, with no mysteries or hidden depths. As the eye, so the object; among the many distresses he feels this is perhaps the greatest, that he has created for himself (of her) so dislikeable a woman. What help can there be for either of them?

Chapter 9

WHEN ELEANOR GETS home from the police station Dan tells her Cara has rung and will ring again later.

'What did she say?' asks El.

'Nothing.'

'Well, was she OK?'

Dan stares at her in the way that he does.

'Oh never mind,' says El, but he has formatted his reply.

'She didn't say if she was OK.'

'Thank you, Dan. Thanks for the message.' She spends a couple of hours finishing off her grant application; then she looks for some food and finds that they are out of bread and milk and cheese, and goes to the corner shop for bits and pieces because she can't face the supermarket. She does have a better conversation with Dan over food, which is good. He seems mercifully unperturbed by his father's absence, and agrees to being given his train fare to go back to his room at college and get on with his work, because there is nothing useful that he can do here.

She *can* talk to the children, she reassures herself, she can. It's just that Con is around at home more so he's the one they naturally go to. But it's easy for him and the kids to write her out of the domestic history. She and Con shared looking after the kids, for heaven's sake, and she had them on her own while Con was in America. She remembers enjoying the rare occasions when she was able to spend time alone with one of them – which seems to happen less and less, bizarrely, now they are all grown up. She thinks about Megan, who has flown the nest most successfully; immersed in her theatrical world, concerned about Con, yes, but not pestering, not emoting all over the place. El ought to make time to go and see her latest play; Con said she was very good in it. What was it?

But Megan won't mind if she goes or not; Megan understands the imperatives of a busy life. She rarely comes home, she has inherited El's driven genes. She doesn't demand attention from her parents in the ways that Paul and Cara do.

El suddenly remembers how easy it is to talk to Megan, and wishes that she were here. It is a long time since she has had her to herself. In fact the last time she can remember clearly is back when she took Megan to London for her RADA audition. El had arranged a meeting with a research partner from Cambridge, and she and Megan rendezvoused in the late afternoon at Wood Green tube, near the home of El's friend who they were staying with. It was a bright spring day and they decided to wander through Alexandra Park, following the curving paths up to the old Broadcasting House as they talked, watching the view of London unroll before them. There was a dusty, scruffy air to the park, and scaffolding on Alexandra Palace – it had all seen better days, El thought, but she could see that Megan was enchanted with everything to do with London. Her audition had gone well, she was confident they would take her (correctly, as it turned out) and bubbling with excitement at the prospect of life in London.

After El had quizzed her about the other applicants, and the staff she had met, and the first year students who had shown them round, and after Megan had described the photos and reviews from the previous year's shows, and the three theatres and rehearsal rooms she had seen, and they had found a bench to perch on to discuss the merits of hall of residence versus room in a shared house, Megan suddenly asked El about *her* day. El's meeting had been to review adjustments to the medium they were testing for lines of primate embryonic stem cells. She sketched out the research rather tentatively to Megan; none of the kids were interested in her work, and why should they be? But Megan suddenly said, 'Is that how they made Dolly the sheep? She's a clone, right? Did they grow her from a bunch of stem cells?'

El laughed. 'Not exactly.'

'But it's the same kind of thing, isn't it? Are you going to grow an animal?'

'No. We're interested in perfecting the *medium* the cells are kept in, so they can go on growing and we can go on splitting them and keeping them in their primordial state.'

'But why? What's the point?'

'OK, the point is to get this right so that we can go on to establish the best medium for *human* embryonic stem cell lines, which will be fantastically useful for research.'

'How?'

'Because they'll be able to test drugs on them. It'll be possible to see precisely how new drugs affect the health of the cells; and it'll also be possible to use them for tissue repair, say for someone with terrible burns. Maybe even one day, to repair or replace diseased organs. And there are particular illnesses, Parkinson's and diabetes are two, where healthy stem cells should be able to help slow or even reverse the disease.'

'That's pretty amazing.'

'Yes, I think so.'

'So Dolly the sheep is nothing to do with this?'

'Well, no, she *is* to do with it, because she was grown from a somatic cell and that shows that we could, in theory, grow tissue for an adult patient from that patient's somatic cells. Which would resolve the problem of rejection.'

'Somatic?'

'Normal body cell. Dolly was grown from an empty egg, that's an egg which they had removed the nucleus from, and the nucleus of a cell from the udder of a six-year-old sheep. You know why she's called Dolly, don't you?'

'Pass.'

'Dolly Parton.'

Megan began to giggle. 'Is it a boobs reference?'

'Correct.'

'Will you be able to do it soon?'

'What?'

'Cure Parkinson's, repair burns—'

'I don't know. You can never tell how long something's going to take, in science. Could be months, could be years.'

Megan smiled. 'I can see why you like it.'

'Good. I do like it. I love it!'

It is the only time El can recall talking to any of them seriously about her work, and now she hugs it to herself – she knows Megan is like her, hungry, ambitious – but at least Megan doesn't hold her in the contempt in which, she remembers now with vivid shame, she used to hold her own mother.

At 6.30 she cleans her teeth and puts on some make-up and heads off to meet Louis. There are four cars in the car park at the Golden Hind, none of them his. She has just settled herself in a corner with a tomato juice when he arrives. He waves and goes to the bar, and she watches him buy his drink. A small wiry man in a well-fitting suit, there is something about the tension in him, the coiled-ness of him, that draws the eye; has always drawn Eleanor's eye. His right foot is pedalling the bar footrest; his fingers drumming a rhythm on the bar. He is only still when he sleeps. As he turns to walk towards her their eyes meet and he smiles, deepening the creases that run from the sides of his nose to the corners of his wide mouth. His smile has always had a whiff of shared secrets and complicity; it is impossible not to smile back at him.

He kisses her lightly. 'No news?'

'Nothing.'

'Heard from Cara?'

'Dan has. She's going to hospitals. If she finds anything I'm sure she'll—'

Louis nods and sips his drink. Eleanor finds his urbanity distasteful. He sits here, smart and dapper, on his way home, untouched.

'How did it go with Michael? Is he jet-lagged?' she asks.

'Fine. He's full of beans. We did the MRC meeting then lunch with the great and the good, and he's been talking to Kirsty and co this afternoon while I was teaching. I've invited him to dinner tonight.'

'Oh Louis, that's kind. I'm sorry to dump him on you.'

'Don't be ridiculous.'

'The stupid thing is, I could have him to dinner. I mean, I'm not doing anything, just hiding. It's like I'm in purdah.'

'You don't need the strain of making polite conversation.'

'You mean people don't need the strain of seeing someone who might be upset.'

'I don't think people…'

'Is everyone talking about Con?'

He shrugs. 'A bit. Of course.'

'I don't know what to do.'

'There's not much you can do, is there. If you don't have any idea—'

'You know I don't have any idea. What idea could I have? He's never done anything like this before.'

'That's what I was saying.'

'No you weren't. You said it as if – as if I *should* have some idea. Or even as if you thought I was having an idea but keeping it secret—'

'Eleanor, stop it.'

'Don't tell me to stop.' To El's horror, she has to swallow a choking sob. Tears have leapt to her eyes.

'Is there anything I can do?' Louis says kindly.

'Like what?'

'I don't know. That's why I'm asking.'

'Well, what would you suggest?'

'For God's sake, El, I haven't made him disappear.'

'Maybe we did. Maybe he just got fed up of this and thought sod it, why should I live with a woman who's seeing someone else, why should I—'

'Eleanor, if he was going to run off because of you screwing someone else, he would have done it a long time ago.'

A part of Eleanor's brain observes that this is a very unpleasant thing for Louis to say, and that it reveals a level of contempt for her that she can do without. Putting that to one side for a moment, she analyses the content. Though superficially true, it is also wrong.

No one gives their definitive reaction on a first offence. No. Surely it is the cumulative weight of numerous offences, a build-up of insults, a continual, cynical battering, which finally triggers a reaction. El knows this – and feels for the first time a piercing certainty that this is what has happened. That Con has left for precisely this reason. Attrition. He can no longer imagine or make himself believe that things might get better. He has given up on her.

And now she can't suppress the tears. Picking up her bag she runs out of the pub and has locked herself in the car before Louis can get to her. He tries the door as she starts the engine.

'Eleanor. Stop it. Stop! Don't be—'

His words are lost as she reverses wildly, swings round and out onto the mercifully empty road. She can hear her own throat roaring for air between sobs, she can see the road in bursts between gouts of tears, like driving through a thunderstorm. Con has gone because of her. She has finally driven Con away. Of its own volition, it seems, the car drifts towards the kerb and stops moving. The engine stalls. El leans her head on the steering wheel and cries.

Cara rings soon after Eleanor gets in. 'Mum? Have you heard any—?'

'No.'

'I've been to all the hospitals. And the police – a woman told me all the places they've checked. He's not anywhere public.'

'Well, come home, Cara. Get the first flight in the morning.'

'I've just – I've been walking. You know, round the streets near his hotel, just looking at the people. There are so many people in the streets. I just keep thinking I'll see him if I keep doing it, I'm going to see him, he's going to be one of these people coming down the street—'

'It doesn't make sense. If he was there, and all right, he wouldn't just be walking down the street, would he. He'd be on a plane coming home.'

'What about amnesia? He might have had a bump on the head and—'

'Then he'd be in hospital.'

'But he might be all right. Not realise. Just be walking about—'

'He'd have to be staying somewhere, using money, showing his ID…'

The line crackles over their silence. 'Come home, Cara. When's your return flight?'

'Tomorrow night.'

It suddenly seems to El that getting Cara home quickly is more important than anything. 'Change your ticket. I'll pay. Get the morning flight.'

'I'll see.'

'Please, Cara.'

'Bye, Mum.'

Louis calls a couple of times and she switches off her mobile. The second time he leaves a message. 'Ring me, Eleanor. This is silly.' She is not going to ring him.

Paul returns, hears that the police have not rung back about the computer, and goes down to the station himself the following morning. As a result of his efforts a tall, diffident detective sergeant materialises on the doorstep in the late afternoon. He accepts El's offer of tea and the three of them sit at the kitchen table talking through the case. It is immediately obvious that very little is being done. Someone is going through Con's computer today and it will be returned tomorrow. They are willing to liaise with police in Munich but if he has left Munich he could be anywhere – anywhere in the world.

'He could have come back to England,' Paul says suddenly.

'Of course. By some other flight. Or Eurostar. He could be anywhere.'

'And is there no mechanism for—'

'For what? Finding one person, who may be deliberately concealing his identity, in the whole world? I'm sorry if that sounds harsh, but it's true, there's no way we could find him. His bank account hasn't been touched since the Saturday of the conference; he withdrew 250 euros that morning, from the cashpoint opposite his hotel. If he uses the card again the bank will tell us, but so far...' He shrugged.

'If he's not withdrawing money, he's not spending it.' Paul's voice is light and reasonable.

'Correct.'

'The only way you don't spend money is if someone else is looking after you. Or if you're dead.'

'Or if you've already transferred some to a different account, perhaps under another name. We'll be checking back with his bank for movement of funds in the recent past.'

El knows she can do that immediately. His statements are in the blue ring-binder on the bottom bookshelf in his room.

It is refreshing that the detective offers neither reassurance nor sympathy; he is simply going through the facts. El appreciates his business-like attitude. Nevertheless she is taken aback when he drains his tea and says, 'Now I'd like to search the house, if I may.'

'This house?'

He nods.

El is conscious of Paul's eyes on her. 'Of course. Where d'you want to start?'

'I'll start in his study. It'll take me a while, you can get on with whatever you were doing.'

She will leave the bank statements till he's gone. She feels a strong need to keep whatever investigations she herself may make separate from his. It feels as if he is looking for something different from what she is seeking. He's looking for evidence of a crime – committed by Con, or her – even murder, committed by her. He's looking for big obvious things and would therefore misuse or misinterpret such hints and whispers as she might find.

'Mum?' Paul has been upstairs for something and now has his coat on.

'You're going?'

'Are you all right with him here? D'you want me to stay?' He seems embarrassed.

'No, no, it's fine, you go.'

'It's just, I haven't really got anything to do here, and there's a mountain of work—'

She laughs. 'There isn't anything to do here, you're exactly right. Go!'

'I'm picking Cara up at 8, I'll bring her straight back here.'

Cara. Of course. 'Right. I'll make us some food.'

'Good idea. See you, Mum.' And he is gone. Belatedly she feels herself stir, start to raise herself from her chair, as if to offer him a kiss. They don't really kiss much, only at times like New Year. But it should be possible, surely, in these straits, to show a little affection? The front door bangs shut. It occurs to El that she ought to talk to Paul. It's up to her, after all, to take the initiative. Of course he's awkward with her, he knows she's holding back.

She must talk to both of them, Paul and Cara, when they come back tonight. The policeman enters the kitchen, gives her a quick nod, and begins opening the cupboards, crouching to peer into each one. What on earth does he imagine finding inside them? Parts of Con's dismembered body? When he looks in the freezer she realises that that is indeed what he is looking for. She is a suspect. She imagines the case against herself. Eleanor Evanson in cold blood plotted with her lover of three years' standing to murder and dispose of the body of her husband Conrad. She wished to claim that he had vanished in order to benefit financially from his disappearance, and to free herself to indulge more fully in this adulterous affair.

Does she stand to benefit financially? Only if Con is proved to be dead, surely? An insurance company isn't going to pay out for someone who might turn up any day. Anyway, she earns twice as much as him and is not short of cash.

She hears the policeman moving lightly up the stairs. He's doing their bedroom next, she guesses, and wonders dispassionately if he will check the sheets for evidence of harmonious marital relations. She might have been expected to change the sheets, though. Maybe if he found such evidence he would take it as proof of more recent (illicit) sexual activity. Can they date it? she wonders. Anyway, there are no stains in the bed. There has been no sexual activity in that bed for quite a while.

The key to this, the clues to this, will be in her own head. In her memory. She needs to dismiss the whole idea of this Mad person. She needs to approach the problem more rigorously. If Con has deliberately gone – or done something stupid that means he can't return – the most likely reason for it is her. *Done something stupid* flickers in her mind for a moment. Would he? Not unless he was much much more depressed and unbalanced than she realised. He would never put the kids through that. Knowing the fragility of the younger two, especially his beloved Cara – he would never inflict so much harm on them.

But… the dwindling thought kindles to brief life again… if he made it look like an accident? A slip, a fall, a drowning?

This is nonsense. Cara has visited the hospitals and morgue. Con is not dead.

No. Con has gone somewhere else, because of her. Yesterday she thought it was because of attrition. Because of knowing about her and Louis, because she'd finally worn away the last threadbare rags of his love and the past that had tied him to her – but today that seems too simple and too sentimental an analysis. Eleanor has never much liked thinking about the past. Firstly it is a terrible waste of present time, in which there is always something better to be done. Secondly it leads people into nostalgia and even outright grief. But Con is gone. It is as simple and absolute as a child's reading book. Janet sees John. Con is gone. She has lived her life as if people were responsible for their actions, so now she must make sense of this.

In the beginning they had Paul. Well, before that they were going out together, but she could have been going out with almost anybody. It was from that accidental pregnancy that the individual identity of their life as a couple sprang. It seems to El that she had hardly noticed Con till then. She had talked with him, made love with him, danced, walked, eaten, drunk, slept, argued, laughed, sat in companionable silence with him, but he had not really struck her, nothing about him had made a lasting impression or singled him out from the other three men with whom she had also done all these things, or the seven with whom she had done some of them. Until she told him she was pregnant. On her way, more or less, to the abortion clinic.

But Conrad had wanted the child. Against all sense and reason; she about to head north to start her house job at Oldham Royal hospital, he doing poorly paid research in the Cambridge lab and casting about for a career path. She was so bright and shiny then, she had hardly thought about telling him. Mentioned it in passing as they grabbed a lunchtime sandwich at that pub near the bridge.

'By the way, I'm pregnant.' In her head it was already taken care of.

It seems to her now that was the first time she really saw him, saw Con; standing looking awkwardly away from her into the canal, slightly flushed, letting the words drop like stones: 'Why don't you have it?'

He walked behind her along the towpath as they talked about it and she felt the solid weight of him at her back. It mattered to him. Suddenly she felt flimsy, lightweight, and as she cycled away, was so ashamed that she couldn't face her lecture and cycled straight to the student clinic and sat in a queue of grim-faced girls until it was her turn to be sighed over by the doctor and told she would regret it forever if she abandoned her career now. El was astonished. It had never occurred to her to abandon her career. That night she and Con talked properly. He had become more sure of himself and less embarrassed; he wanted them to get married. The career/motherhood conflict had not entered his head either. They would manage childcare between them. He would apply for jobs in the Manchester area, he would get work near her.

His quiet certainty was irresistible. As if the light had been switched on, El saw the beautiful biological simplicity of accepting what had happened, the elegance of there already being a baby inside her, which could grow and be born and be theirs; which she could welcome, not rip out and destroy. There was a great pleasure in knowing everybody else was wrong. None of them could believe how such an intelligent girl, etc. etc., and she and Con knew it would be perfectly all right, and she was filled with boundless energy which enabled her not only to sail through her finals and start at Oldham hospital, but also to redecorate with Con the little terraced house they'd found with views of the distant moors.

Everything went as they had planned – they led a charmed life. Baby Paul was not only perfect and beautiful but also slept long regular hours; within three months she was back at the hospital, and Con had adjusted his lab hours so that he finished at 4 every day and could pick Paul up then, in exchange for working Saturday mornings. No one's work suffered. Everyone gained. Con had been right and she honoured him for it.

She remembers cycling home from the hospital, her breasts heavy and prickling with milk for Paul. Sitting in the soggy old kitchen armchair with Paul on her tit, chatting to Con as he sliced onions, peeled potatoes. At the hospital Mr Steptoe had

had some success in fertilising eggs in vitro; this was the run-up to the birth of Louise Brown, the first test tube baby. The suspense and tension at the hospital, the heightened vitality, was echoed in their life at home. Everywhere, life was taking a new shape, being *re*shaped by people.

She remembers the heady pleasure of knowing she would never be like her mother, she would always have her work. She and Con were conspirators and their lives a revolution; soon everyone would wake up and realise what they were missing, that it was possible to have everything, everything at once without anyone making any kind of sacrifice at all, and without exploiting anybody.

El becomes aware that her face is stiff; that she is holding her lips in an unnatural grimace. She doesn't want to cry. There is no need to think about those times, really. They were simple, nothing lurked in the corners. She can scroll through them, just keeping an eye out for the first broken thread, the moment when it all began to unravel…

But if she's going to cook tonight, some things will need defrosting. She goes out to the garage to look in the big freezer. And here's a shock – the freezer is virtually empty. All there is is a stack of horrible ready meals for one: lamb tikka, moussaka, fish pie. Who eats these? It can only be Con, he's in charge of shopping and cooking. But where are all his frozen veg from the garden? Every year he grows three different kinds of beans, peas, spinach, carrots – he grows them and freezes the surplus in neatly labelled bags, for winter use. He freezes raspberries, black-currants and gooseberries. He has a big well-tended kitchen garden, behind the honeysuckle trellis. Over the years all the kids have helped him with it. She remembers him kitting himself up in waterproofs and wellies on wet Sundays, going out to dig. 'You can take the boy out of the farm, but you can't take the farm out of the boy,' he would say to her and grin. Have they already eaten everything this year? Surely not. She runs out into the sodden garden, across the overgrown lawn and past the trellis. The veg garden is bleak indeed; a few gone-to-seed cabbages, some tilting bamboo canes with dead brown tendrils clinging to them, yellowing weeds, and leafless, spiky-looking bushes. Of course there's nothing here, it's winter. But does it always look like this? So desolate, so abandoned? She makes her way back to the house and changes her soaking shoes. He has not grown any veg this year, he can't have done. But it is unknown in their history. The year he went to America he fussed endlessly over choosing the right person to take over the garden, from several willing neighbours. It is part of the ritual of his life, ordering seeds, the planting out, the weeding, the harvesting. The sight of the freezer with its shop-bought pap which she knows he doesn't like – which she can't even imagine him buying, let alone eating – makes her feel weak. How is it she has not looked in the freezer, or the garden, for so long?

Chapter 10

CONRAD SLEEPS, WAKES, sleeps, losing track of days and nights. He traces and retraces the streets of Bologna, lost in a maze of memories. Time has gone haywire. How many days has he been here? Looking up from his trudging, he notices that he's outside a restaurant. A couple in the window are tucking into full plates. He stops. Just for a while, he could stop being such an idiot. He could have a proper meal. Why not? He knows that why not is because he's trying to conserve his cash, but he'll have to get some from a cashpoint soon anyway, and besides, who the hell cares where he is? He probably hasn't even been missed yet. He opens the heavy door and is met by good smells. He hasn't had a proper meal since the conference, for God's sake. A waiter seats him and he studies the menu, relishing the warmth, the comfort of the seat, the prospect of food – the sudden transition from being a freezing and aimless vagrant, to being a purposeful diner. The clarity of his role here is as satisfying as being an audience member in a theatre – what he has to do is simple and straightforward. Which makes him question, again, the complicated mess he has got himself into. Is he really on the run from Maddy? Is she the real reason he is rattling about alone in Bologna? Surely not. Didn't he make up his mind, definitively, to leave Eleanor three weeks ago, just as he has made up his mind to leave her, repeatedly, in the more distant past? It has just taken Maddy to push him over the edge.

Three weeks ago he went to see Megan in *The Winter's Tale*. It was a promenade performance in a warehouse space in Camden. Con arranged to go to see it on a Saturday night so they could have some time for an exhibition or walk on the Sunday. The only way to see Megan was on her own territory; she rarely came home, and was restless when she did. He was reminded of Eleanor with *her* mother; the duty visit, the impatience.

There is no time to see Meg before curtain-up; he collects his ticket and is shepherded into a holding area. The voluminous space is empty of décor and his heart sinks at the cheese-paring which deprives them of a proper set. But then there is music and a sharp brilliant pool of light in the darkness up ahead, suddenly illuminating the tableau of Leontes' court. As the audience are ushered forward into a circle around them, he sees how intimacy and voyeurism might work for the play. The frozen actors are grouped like a waxworks display and it is not until they come to life – clockwork figures moving to a tinkly, music-box tune – that he realises Megan is among them. He's assumed she was playing Perdita. But here she is, in regal crimson, supple and willowy now she is released from immobility, her face glowing with a tender smile for Polixenes. She is Queen Hermione, flirtatious, mature, poised. She is so like El that it is uncanny; a reincarnation of the El he first met. Mesmerised by her face and rapid, graceful movements, it is a while before Con tunes into the play.

'Inch-thick, knee-deep, o'er head and ears a fork'd one!
Go, play, boy, play: thy mother plays, and I
Play too; but so disgraced a part, whose issue

Will hiss me to my grave.'

The jealous king. The all-consuming, never-ending inventiveness of jealousy, colouring everything; transforming happiness to grief, contaminating the world. The remorseless logic of Leontes' words are a rallying call. This is how a betrayed man behaves. As if things mattered. As if something of value has been lost.

'This jealousy

Is for a precious creature: as she's rare,

Must it be great.'

Something of value *has* been lost, but Con has never allowed himself to play that part: to rage, to destroy. Watching the distilled purity of Leontes' jealousy, Con is shamed. He has not even been jealous, though he has all the factual grounds Leontes lacks. Hasn't El taken up with Louis – continued with Louis – because Con has connived? Given up on her, not cared enough to be jealous? As beautiful, defiant, innocent Hermione/Eleanor/Megan defends herself to Leontes' jumped-up court, Con's lips move with Leontes'.

'My life stands in the level of your dreams.'

'Your actions are my dreams:

You had a bastard by Polixenes,

And I but dream't it.'

Banish the babe, kill the queen, slaughter all who would defend her: let black rage smash the world. In swallowing his own rage, he has made El's behaviour excusable. If he doesn't care enough to break with her, then he doesn't care enough to deserve her. What has he done? Compromised, prevaricated; thought of the children, thought of the disruption. Tried to pay her back by *not caring*. Death in life: she was right to despise him. Of course she despised him. Of course she betrayed him. He's invited it.

In the interval he paces the street outside, compelled by the desire to make a change in his situation. His emotions have been so plastered over and papered up that they have lost all meaning: he has duped himself into the life of a vegetable.

The warehouse is transformed for the second half. Blossom-laden branches hanging from the roof make a pink canopy, with dappled sunlight filtering through. The freshly green-carpeted ground is confetti-strewn with petals; daffodils and tulips spill from overflowing tubs. Shepherds and shepherdesses dance among the audience. There is birdsong, spring and innocence, and Perdita and Florizel's love turns the world anew.

In the shameless sentiment and prettiness of the staging, and Autolycus' and the clown's foolishness, Con rediscovers his composure. It is only a play, after all. The decisions not to rage, not to leave, not to pull the house down around her ears, were painfully made and made for good reasons. Unfortunately he can see now that they were not the right decisions. Because as long as a thing is patched up, it will continue to limp along. Destruction is what's needed for life to spring anew. The freezing obliteration of winter, annihilation by ice of all that tangled growth. It is a cycle old as the seasons; a time of growth and plenty will be succeeded by darkness and death. Out of darkness and death, new life rises. His way of living has been as unnatural as his work, eking out the life of an ailing thing, instead of embracing destruction and trusting spring to come.

By the time the play reaches its sweetly cyclical ending, Con is at peace. It is rare to feel such clarity. He must end this. Walk away. Walk into the freezing darkness and out the other side. He will be able to do it now.

He takes Megan for a late dinner. She is still wrapped in the glamour of the part, still an uncanny double for El. She has a film audition in the offing, plus a term's work with a Theatre in Education company if she wants it. After eighteen months surviving on call centre work, chorus in a panto and crowd scenes in adverts, her career is taking shape and they can both drink to that.

'Will Mum come to see it?'

'I'll tell her she ought to. But you know how busy she is.'

'She didn't see *The Dream Play* either.' Accusingly.

'Not my fault.'

'Why didn't you ask her to come with you?'

'She's more likely to come if you remind her yourself.'

'I've invited her once. If she doesn't want to see me it's up to her. Other people's mothers—'

'Other people's mothers don't have such important careers.'

'Pah!' said Megan, exactly as El might have done. 'I don't know why she bothered having so many children.'

'Why, how many do you propose to have?'

'One, max. So I can look after her properly.'

'You weren't looked after properly?'

'OK, we were, but not by Mum. More by the au pairs than Mum. More by you than anyone.'

'Am I such an inferior option?'

'Oh the poor old thing!' She gave him a wonderfully theatrical kiss. 'Don't be so touchy!'

'Your husband could also look after your children.'

'I'm not having a husband, thank you. Much easier living alone.' She glanced up at the stream of people coming through the restaurant door, to see if anybody recognised her. He remembers thinking calmly that it would not hurt her, or affect her in any way, when he left El.

His Italian is virtually non-existent but still he can tell there is a lot of meat on this menu (*Braciole di maiale*, *Saltimbocca alla Romana*, *Brasato al Barolo* are the three main choices on the board). He doesn't object to meat of itself, but he tends to cook and eat vegetarian to honour Paul and Megan's demands. And right now, there is something quite repulsive about the idea of meat. He settles for tomato and mozzarella, followed by pasta marinara.

It is because of him they are vegetarian, of course. He made a bad mistake with Paul when Paul was nine. It happened just after Dan's birth, in July. Dan was a week early, and Con had to go back to work for a couple of days before taking off his three weeks for the Spanish holiday that they had planned. El was exhausted after a long and difficult labour – Daniel was breech – and while Megan and Cara were happy in the care of Lisa, the latest au pair, Paul was fractious and difficult. Con offered him the option of going into the lab, provided he could read quietly while Con was busy, and Paul leapt at the suggestion. He was pleased to be singled out.

Conrad had a project meeting at 9 then needed to check a colleague's changes to an MRC funding application. In the late morning he became aware of Paul industriously draw-ing at the other end of the bench and offered to take the boy down to the animal house. Here the rodents and primates being used in departmental research lived in wire cages, in a brightly fluorescent-lit, windowless, breeze-block construction. Con was so used to it he didn't stop to think how it would strike Paul, and to begin with the boy didn't ask any questions. He pored over the cages of rats and mice, marvelling at their pink eyes and bald, squirming litters. He dabbed his finger end at their water bottles to make drips fall, and speculated on how those with shaven patches and wound dressings had hurt themselves.

Then one of the monkeys at the other end began to scream.

'Dad? What is it, Dad?'

'Just a monkey. They can be noisy, can't they?'

'Can we see them?'

'Sure.' They walked on past the rabbits to the monkey cages at the far end; at their approach the monkeys began to hurl themselves frantically round their cages; only one sat still on the floor of his cage, staring balefully at Paul and picking at a wound scab on his abdomen.

'Are they frightened, Dad? Are they frightened of us?'

'Well, they don't get many visitors. They get excited.'

'Is it like a zoo?'

'No. Not really.'

'Is it a hospital? Are you making them better?'

'Not exactly.'

'What then?'

'They help us with the experiments. We need them to help us work out how to make ill people better.' The monkeys were calming down, they came to rest on their perches or the floors of their cages, grimacing and staring tensely at Con and Paul, a couple of them chattering angrily to themselves.

'What do they eat?'

'Special monkey food. And oranges. They have fruit for a treat sometimes.'

'But can't they ever come out?'

'No.'

'Do they have names?'

'Not really.'

Paul took a couple of steps closer to the cages.

'Don't go too near, Paul. They bite and scratch. They can be very bad tempered.'

'They look sad.'

Con saw how stupid he had been to bring Paul here. The monkeys all looked fine. Those that had been operated on recently were behind locked doors in the sterile lab; you certainly wouldn't take a visitor in there. 'Shall we go?'

'Why do you have to keep them here?' As Paul turned towards him Con realised that the child was close to tears.

'It's not that bad. They're safe here. They're warm and dry and fed—'

'But they're not free. They can't go swinging through the trees or play—' Paul swiped angrily at the tears on his cheeks.

'Pauly, Pauly, come on—' Con gave him his handkerchief. They passed in silence through the ranks of rabbits, rats, mice, to the outer door.

'Why can't you let them go? Why can't you?'

It was a relief to breathe fresh air again. Con led them towards the canteen. 'I told you, we need them to help us work out how to make ill people better.'

'How?'

'Well, sometimes things go wrong with bits of people's bodies and doctors can't cure them because they don't understand what's happening. Or because they need a new kind of medicine.'

'Are all the monkeys ill?'

'Things can be tested on them. To see if they would work on humans. New cures we've never tried before. When we go back to my lab I'll show you down the microscope, the little cells I'm battling with.'

'You make the monkeys ill, to test the cures?'

'Well, I don't, I work with rats. But some of the scientists have to work with monkeys.' They had reached the canteen. There was silence between them as they selected cutlery and slid their trays along the rail.

'Can I have sausage and chips?'

'If you like. D'you want a pudding?'

Paul chose a white iced bun and Con led them to a corner table.

'What do you do with them afterwards?'

'What?'

'The monkeys. When the experiment is over?'

'Nothing.' As far as Con knew they either died or were euthanised.

'You should let them go.'

'Most of them were bred here, Paul. They couldn't fend for themselves in the wild.'

'Send them to a zoo then, where they can go outside.'

'That's a good idea. Maybe we should.'

After lunch Con switched on the electron-microscope and showed Paul some slides of antibodies swarming round a pathogen. Explained, in simple terms, the battle the body wages against an intruder; explained why sometimes the body's defences need inhibiting, to manipulate a cure. 'Your immune system is what protects you against diseases, or bad things from outside – wounds, infections, viruses. But sometimes we have to try and turn the immune system off, so we can help the body in other ways; help it to accept treatment for cancer, or a transplant, like a new heart. And that's my job. Trying to stop all these little swarming soldiers running wild and filling the bloodstream...'

Paul was curious, and quick to understand. At the end of an hour Con slipped the slides back into their box with a feeling of relief. He had shown Paul why this was interesting. He had shown him what it was really about; that microscopic battle in the blood, which they were going to win. The battle against death. He had at least attempted to redress the balance. Now he knows how signally he failed.

The following week in Spain he took Megan and Paul to the nearby little lake for a swim one afternoon, leaving El and the au pair, and the two little ones, to their siestas. It was hot – too hot to be out, really – but the prospect of cool water enticed them, and he wanted to get Paul and Megan out of the house to make some peace for the sleepers.

The lake – actually more of a pond – was in fields, and surrounded by marsh grass and prickly shrubs. They followed the beaten path through the undergrowth and came to a small baked-mud beach, where it was possible to wade into the murky water without pushing through reeds. There was a bad smell and Con worried briefly about the water, but the lake was recommended for swimming by the owners – it was one of the reasons they had chosen this particular self-catering villa. Paul was first in the water and halfway across the pond when he shouted, 'What's that?' He was pointing at a large pale brown barrel-shaped thing floating in the water at the far side. It was a moment before Con's eyes could make sense of it. A cow. A drowned and hugely bloated cow in the water, stinking of death. Paul realised what it was seconds after Con. Con imagined it bursting in the heat and splattering the whole pond in rotting meat.

As they scrambled out of the water and dragged shorts and T shirts over their wet skin, the smell intensified. It was overpowering; Con couldn't believe he'd let them swim in that. Megan wanted to go closer and have a look; she was curious but not disgusted. Whereas Paul, Con could see, was as sickened as he was. As they walked back, the stink clinging to their skins, the two children speculated on how the cow could have drowned. It must have been drinking, it must have slipped. Or maybe it just died and someone threw it in there. Maybe it was ill…

At dinner that night Paul announced he was not going to eat meat any more. 'It's cruel to keep animals just to eat them.'

'For heaven's sake!' Eleanor was impatient. 'They're only alive because someone wants to eat them. If we didn't eat meat, half the animals on farms wouldn't even be born.'

'We should eat the things we don't have to kill them for. Milk. Eggs. Wool.'

'And what are you going to have for tea? Wool sandwiches?' Over the baby alarm came Daniel's thin wail. Eleanor pulled a face.

Con rose to his feet. 'I'll get him. If Paul really doesn't want to eat meat we should respect—'

'As if there aren't enough faddy eaters in this house. No baked beans for Megan. No vegetables for Cara unless I hide them in a shepherd's pie. No red peppers for you. And now we have to have a vegetarian option!'

'El—' He touched her arm, and she stopped. 'We'll talk about this later,' he told Paul.

When the children were in bed they had a row. He told El about Paul's reaction to the animal house and she was irritated. 'You should have warned him in advance what they were for, that they've been bred specifically for research, that they only exist to save human lives. Stands to reason he's going to start feeling sorry for poor little furry things if you haven't already given him a steer on it.' She tutted at Daniel and moved him to the other breast. He was a poor feeder, dropping off to sleep after only a few minutes on each side, then waking again hungry an hour later.

'I didn't think, did I. Stupidly, I didn't work out in advance all the possible ramifications of taking him into the animal house, as you would have done.'

'I think he should be told he can choose what to eat when he's older. It's all very well virtuously respecting the fact that he's developing his own values, but it's a nightmare as far as cooking goes.'

'It's not that bad. We already have cauliflower cheese, scrambled eggs…'

'We eat meat five nights a week. Have you got time to work out five balanced alternatives? 'Cos I haven't. This child is driving me mad—' Dan was asleep again.

'Pass him here. Paul can have what we're having and just skip the meat; make sure he has plenty of cheese and nuts.'

'It doesn't work like that, does it.' She was busying herself with the breast pump. 'The juice of the stew is meat juice, the roast veg are roasted in beef dripping; are you going to pretend to humour him then lie to him? Either he eats meat or he doesn't.'

'I don't see why you're so angry with me.' Dan lolled limp in

Con's arms, the whites of his eyes visible beneath his half-closed lids. 'This boy's out like a light.'

'Can you try him with a bottle tonight? If I don't get some sleep soon…'

'Sure. Why don't we all become vegetarian?'

'How much do you know about vegetarian cookery?'

'I could find out.'

'Fine. Whatever.'

It was a miserable holiday. Everyone was angry, and after the pond, the nearest place to swim and cool down was a crowded outdoor swimming pool half an hour's drive away. When they got home Con started cooking veggie meals, offering the kids the option of what he had cooked or some of El's big pots of lamb stew or bolognaise. They tended to eat what he had made.

But Conrad never managed to erase that anger in Paul. Megan joined him as a card-carrying vegetarian but she did it with sunny ease, she did it lightly. Con remembers her, in her teens, becoming fascinated by H. G. Wells' *The Island of Dr Moreau.*

'Could this happen?' she wanted to know. 'Could you chop and sew together animals like this?'

'Why would anyone want to? The only point of the work I do is its human application – we're not out to create freaks.'

'But you are a vivisectionist.'

'Well, I wouldn't call myself that but—'

'You do cut up animals.' By now he was working on the monkeys.

'Under anaesthetic.'

'And transplant bits from one to another.'

'Hearts. But we're doing it for a reason.'

She grinned. 'If you put a monkey heart in a person, they might fall in love with a monkey.'

'They might. Unlikely, but you never know.'

'Do you think it's cruel, Dad?'

'I don't know how else we're going to be able to help people with heart problems.'

'OK. I'd rather have a monkey heart than no heart. And bananas are my favourite food!' She slipped away to do something else, leaving Con smiling. Megan was as easy as Paul was difficult.

When Cara asked to go to see where he worked, he managed it very carefully indeed, never mentioning the animal house, confining her to the lab and a collection of beautifully stained slides of cells in varying stages of health and sickness; that and a visit to the anatomy teaching labs, where she could marvel at the skeletons and the models of hearts and intestines. He kept her well away from the animal labs and dissecting rooms, away from meat, alive or dead.

Which takes him back, of course, to Maddy.

After his first meeting with Maddy, the relationship is normalised by the exchange of friendly emails. She does not pester, but emails every ten days or so, wondering how he is getting on, giving the odd detail of her life. She describes a two-person picket outside a local beauty salon where animal-tested products are used. 'It rained heavily and it turned out that no one in town actually needed beautifying that day. I had to remind myself that it was all in a good cause.'

Con spends a long time composing his email to Carrington Bio-Life, carefully itemising the problems with their animal care. It is important not to sound too shrill. It takes nearly two weeks for their reply to come: 'Thank you for your comments, CBL is committed to improving animal welfare.' It is not even signed. In a rage he phones their office, where a helpful answerphone message assures him he will be rung back. He realises that the weekly reports on his animals – on his experiments – come from the CBL office but are never ascribed to a person with a name. He's never even thought about that before; after all, the reports are factual, scientific, they cover the range of information he has asked for – and he has always assumed that they are compiled by different technicians on different shifts. But there is nobody named whom he can get back to.

He goes in to discuss the situation at CBL with his head of department, Gus. Everyone in the department is using Carrington Bio-Life now the university animal house has closed down. But Gus is frantic, with a massive funding application deadline, plus a student from India flying in that night for a supervision on Ph.D. work Gus has not yet read.

'Bad, yes, bad,' he nods, when Con shows him the photos. 'But don't do anything yet, let's check where we're all up to first. I've got a couple of monkeys only a week in, I'd like to get some results before we take any action which may affect the running of the place.'

'But they're transplant monkeys.'

'Yes.'

'So they could survive up to sixty days.'

'I bloody hope so.'

'But that's two months, Gus.'

'Look, I've got to dash. Just sit on it for a bit, will you?'

Con puts out feelers to colleagues in other universities who are using CBL. Responses are all similar: an unwillingness to disrupt experiments in progress, plus fatalistic shoulder shrugging at the suggestion of abuse. 'Everyone said it would happen when the universities closed their own animal houses; farm it out and you can't keep an eye on it.'

'But I have kept an eye on it,' Con protests. 'And I'm telling you what I saw.'

'There are laws and regulations. An inspector has to go in there at least twice a year. You probably hit a bad day.'

Con considers going to the press. If he writes a statement one of the papers surely will pick it up. But what stops him is the issue of anonymity. They'll need to name him as a whistleblower and there will be the resentment of all his colleagues who have kept silent; their experiments will be closed down and no one will be willing to work with him in the future. And the confidentiality clause he signed – how would Kneiper react? Could they prosecute him? Or worse? Surely he could gain the same result, exposure of the abuses and action to put a stop to them, anonymously, through Maddy?

After six weeks (during which he himself has been forced to send instructions for a new set of immunosuppressant trials – his work cannot stand still, after all) he agrees to Maddy's request that they meet on neutral territory in Birmingham, where she has a job interview the following day.

At New Street station his eyes single her out as she comes through the ticket barrier, but he holds his position at the café they have designated, watching her. She is wearing a red skirt and black boots; she looks younger than he remembered. He feels a kind of glee, that El, if she cared to look in his wallet, might find a train ticket to Birmingham and perhaps a receipt for drinks and a meal for two, and wonder what is going on.

When Maddy sees him she smiles and he automatically extends his hand to take her shoulder bag. 'That looks heavy.'

'It's just my smart clothes for the morning.'

'Where will you stay?'

'They've booked me a hotel. Is it OK if we go there to talk?'

'Have you eaten? I've come straight from work, I thought we might grab a bite.'

'Well, won't there be a restaurant at the hotel?' She sounds uncertain.

'Sure, let's head for it.' When they emerge from the station approach she seems to hesitate. 'D'you know the way?'

She recites a name and address. Con knows the place, it's a ten-minute walk. He leads them across the road. 'So are you nervous? About your interview?'

'I think it will be all right.'

'What's it for?'

'HR. It's not very exciting, but the pay is better.'

'Well, that's always a plus.' She seems cowed, as if the size and noise of the city – or maybe it is meeting him – is too much for her. He dredges for things to chat about, feeling awkwardly avuncular. Again he finds himself wondering about her age. Thirty-five? Forty? Yet she has an almost girlish quality, as if she has never been anywhere.

'I'm really grateful to you for agreeing to meet me again,' she tells him. 'You can help the campaign so much.'

The hotel restaurant is adequate, with a respectable scattering of diners, but she reads the menu with an anxious expression and he wonders if she is bothered about money. 'My treat,' he says. 'Were you even planning to eat at all?'

'I had a sandwich on the train.'

'Have something nice now, go on,' he urges. 'And will you drink red or white?'

'Oh, I don't know, I don't think I—'

'There's a good New Zealand sauvignon on this list, you'll have a glass surely.'

'Well, just a glass.'

He orders a bottle, why not.

Once they've placed their orders she seems to relax. She takes a little notebook and pen from her bag and leans towards him. 'You haven't been able to make any progress?'

'No, the problem is that everyone has ongoing experiments, no one wants to upset the apple cart, and CBL themselves are blanking me.'

'So the only way to stop them is through protest.'

'I'm forced to agree.'

'Who did you write to at CBL?'

'The director of research.'

She is writing in her little book. 'What's his name?' She looks up and smiles. 'I'm assuming it's a him.'

'You won't get anything out of him. He's not replied to my letter or email.'

'No, but I just need to know his name,' she says quickly. 'They tell you to get every scrap of information you can, because it might help the campaign one day, in some way.'

Con tells her he doesn't even know the guy's name and points out to her that it will be necessary to withhold his own name from his statement. He's written it the previous evening; a deliberately undramatic account itemising the ways in which the state of the animals contravenes the law.

She reads it in silence then glances up at him. 'The photos?'

'I'm not convinced the photos are necessary.'

'I've been told that they are. A picture is worth a thousand words, you know. People join the protest when they see pictures, it's so much more immediate.'

He thinks about her nameless instructors and wonders if she sees herself performing for them, in her head. 'Names, pictures, dates, don't let anything slip.' She reminds him of a little girl at school, with her notebook. 'Well, I need to think a bit longer about the photos. They may well have CCTV footage of me taking them.'

'You weren't breaking the law. They were.'

'Yes, but they can ID me from the CCTV footage. Bang goes my anonymity.'

She nods doubtfully. 'OK. Who are the people you've talked to so far?'

'How d'you mean?'

'The other researchers. Your boss, your colleagues.'

'You don't need their names.'

'Not to use in the public domain, of course not. But it really helps the cause if we can build up our information banks, like just knowing how many scientists are involved, their names and universities…'

There is no point in withholding names, seeing as she knows his and knows where he works. She could find out from the university website anyway.

When she has finished writing she thanks him and puts her little book away, his statement carefully folded inside. And then they just chat and eat. She wants to know about his family, his children, but when he asks her in return she shakes her head,

wide eyed. 'Oh no, I've never been married. I'm not in a relationship.' She asks about El's career, and what the children all do.
He realises that he has drunk most of the wine and that he is
talking a lot, but it is pleasant to sit in the glow of her attention
and to hear her murmurs of admiration when he explains that
he has looked after the children on a more regular basis than
El, who has a more important career than he does. It is pleasant
to paint an attractive picture of his life (and it is, after all, an
attractive life, a privileged life, of secure income, loving family,
interesting work). She seems to him almost a beggar at life's
feast; an only child of working-class parents already dead – living
alone, a wanderer who has taught English as a foreign language
in half a dozen different cities, never settling, developing attach-
ments to pets rather than people. 'I had such a beautiful clever
cat in Granada, it broke my heart to leave her. She used to tap
on the window for me to let her in at night, and my room was
on the third floor. That cat could have climbed the Eiffel Tower.'

He finds himself searching her words and face for clues to
her solitariness. She's attractive enough – much more attractive,
indeed, than she seemed at their first meeting. She's kind-
hearted. Why has no man – or woman – snapped her up? When
it is time to go for his train he pays and carries her bag as far as
the lifts. 'I'm sorry,' she puts her hand on his arm. 'I need to go
up the stairs. I have a stupid thing about lifts.'

He carries her bag up two flights of stairs and at the fire
door at the head of the corridor he passes it back to her. 'Thank
you so much,' she whispers. 'I've had a lovely time. And you
will make such a difference.' To his surprise she stands on tiptoe
and pecks him on the cheek, then turns with a smile that is de-
cidedly flirtatious, and moves off down the corridor.

He has to run for his train. But her sudden hot breath on his face, and the knowing tilt of her smile, stay with him rather disturbingly. Poor girl. Woman. Poor, lonely woman. And yet there is more to her than that. He finds himself basking, rather, in a sense of his own attractiveness.

Chapter 11

EL ENDS UP rushing to the supermarket for food for Paul and Cara. But once she is in there she might as well stock up on stuff like toilet rolls and washing powder, because she can't remember how much they have left of anything and it would be stupid to run out. She decides a chicken will be easy and only remembers Paul is vegetarian when she is in the queue for the till. Then she ends up drifting aimlessly up and down the aisles unable to think of a single vegetarian meal apart from omelette. She tries to conjure the things Con makes for them, with beans, lentils, nuts, feta cheese. She can't make a Con-type meal, though, even if she could remember one. Pancakes? They would stick to the pan or tear. Soufflé? Too tricky. It needs to be something she can make in advance, not have to fiddle about with while they sit in the kitchen watching her critically.

Since when is she incapable of cooking for her own children? The division of labour has been very marked in recent times. Con cooks, El works late. But surely to God she can throw something together. She ends up buying eggs, green lentils, tins of kidney beans and chickpeas, and pine nuts. Plus salad stuff. She can look for a recipe at home. Here in the crowded brightness of the supermarket her brain is refusing to function at all. Why is it so busy? It is Saturday, she remembers. When she has loaded her food into the car she remembers fruit for dessert and has to go back again to buy overpriced and probably tasteless strawberries, the only soft fruit on offer.

Back at the house she checks phone and emails, nothing, and sits down with the Rose Elliot cookbook. The phone rings – Megan.

'Mum, I could come home first thing tomorrow. But is there anything useful I can do?'

'I wish there was. I don't know what to do myself. None of us do. Cara went to Munich but she's coming back empty-handed.'

'Have the police—?'

'No. Nothing.'

'But have you tried *everyone* who knows him?'

'Yes. Paul's been through his address book.'

'Can't they trace mobile phones?'

'Only if he uses it.'

There's a silence. El thinks she should ask Megan about her play, but she can't remember what it is. 'To be honest, Megan, it's pretty pointless you coming home. Unless you want to.'

'Well – OK. I'll ring you in the morning and see. Bye, Mum.'

When the line goes dead El sits staring at the grain of the kitchen table. She doesn't know what to cook. She doesn't know what play her daughter is performing in. She has not even opened her emails today, and she doesn't want to now. Sitting staring at the table is about as much as she can do. She thinks of her colleague Linda at work. Linda's husband died recently of something short and sharp. Peritonitis, maybe. And Linda was off work with compassionate leave. When she came back she sent an email round to everyone in the department, thanking them for their kindness and support, for the beautiful flowers and for the much-appreciated home-cooked meals and cakes people had brought round. El had not done that. She had contributed to the flowers, but she had not made cakes or meals; it seemed to her rather voyeuristic fussing, to go noseying in on Linda's grief, bearing food. She thought Linda would be better off keeping herself busy doing her own cooking; it would provide her with a distraction.

Now El sees that what she needs more than anything is a friend to come round with a home-cooked meal, and that she is such a cold and heartless woman that she never even made any attempt to understand Linda's distress – or indeed anyone else's, ever. Even Louis, who she thought was fond of her at the very least, cannot be bothered with her. No wonder Con has left her: she is a monster. She hasn't tried to understand how he feels, she hasn't put herself in his shoes, she hasn't done anything at all to deserve his love and loyalty. And now she is crying with self-pity, which is the most despicable emotion of all.

The phone rings; the police, wanting to ask about Con's computer. There are a few emails in a folder called MAD. Was Eleanor aware of them? Yes, she says, and no, she doesn't know who they are from. If there's nothing else, please can she have the computer back? They promise to return it shortly.

El spends two hours making a lentil dhal which turns out to be almost inedibly hot, rice, salad and hard-boiled eggs. When Paul and Cara arrive Cara refuses all food.

'I just need to go to bed, I'm tired.'

'But you must eat something, Cara – you must.'

'I'll have a banana, OK?'

Bananas are, of course, what El has failed to buy. The two in the fruit bowl are almost black. 'It's all right,' says Cara, 'stop fussing.'

'Did you – was there anything you—?'

'No. It was completely hopeless. I've just been telling Paul, I can't face going over it all again. Ask him.' Cara stamps off upstairs as if El has offended her. And El and Paul sit awkwardly over the unappetising food.

'She didn't tell me much more than that,' Paul concedes. 'She talked to the people at his hotel and the conference centre, and no one had noticed anything. I think she spent a lot of time just pacing the streets. You know what she's like, she was expecting some kind of sixth sense to lead her to him.'

'She looks terrible.'

Paul shrugs. 'Oh, she went to the British embassy too, and they kept her waiting for hours and nobody did anything.'

'Megan might come tomorrow,' El offers.

'Police been back?'

'They've searched the house, you know that. They rang and said they're bringing his computer back soon.' If the police find anything of interest about the MAD emails, that will be soon enough to tell him. She cannot cope with a rant from him about how badly she and Con behave. Paul toys with his food in silence. She wishes he could be kind to her, she is about to cry for lack of kindness.

'I don't know what to do, Paul.'

He looks at her, and she feels his anger relax a notch. 'There has to be something. If everything at home and in his room has been checked, then someone has to go through his work stuff. Have the police been there?'

'I don't even know.'

'Well, if I can get a key, I could go tomorrow. I'll see if I can go through his work desk and computer. Will you phone Gus to ask about access?'

'Of course.'

'What are you doing about work?' he suddenly asks.

'What d'you mean?'

'Shouldn't you get a sick note or something? You've hardly been in this week, have you.'

'Well no, but—'

'We can't keep on acting as if nothing's happened. There's no point in pretending you can carry on as normal – you can't.'

'But there's nothing for me to do at home.'

'Are you up for going into work?'

El hesitates. 'No, I suppose not.'

'Right then. Go to the doctor on Monday.'

El realises this is the closest her son can come to being kind to her. When he leaves she clears up the pointless meal and goes to knock softly on Cara's door, but there is no reply.

She remembers the question of money, raised by the policeman, and spends an hour going through Con's old bank statements. There is absolutely nothing untoward. He earns and spends the same amount each month, and every three months or so he shifts any surplus into his savings account with the bank. He has £27,000 in his savings account, and has not drawn anything out of it since they had the roof done five years ago.

This leads her to depressing thoughts about access to bank accounts, and wills, and she takes herself to bed, thinking that if she can't sleep she will read. But she is unable to find a single book which looks interesting.

She has a shower and lies in bed with the light off, knowing she will not sleep. OK, she won't sleep. She'll think, then. She permits herself to consider, again, where things went wrong. It is hard to find defining moments. Things shift slowly, imperceptibly, over years. Accretion, accretion, the slow accretion of tiny details of speech and action like specks of dust which gradually bury the partners in a marriage and make movement, change, impossible. At the point at which you notice change, it has already long ago occurred. Con's souring, his silting up, his loss of enthusiasm and energy, she had already known it for a while when she first *noticed* it. But she remembers when she noticed it most recently: it was when the animal libbers went to the press with a lot of allegations about the animal house used by his lab. That was a defining moment; a moment where she could measure the gap between his position and the position she might have expected him to have.

The first she knew of it was an item on the news as she drove to work. 'Allegations of incompetence and negligence have been made against Carrington Bio-Life animal facility…'

'What's going on? Did you know about it?' she asked him, that evening.

'Yeah. It's nothing serious.'

'Have they got evidence?'

He shrugged. 'Probably made it all up.'

Taking her cue from Con, El dismissed it from her mind. But next morning the paper carried a grainy picture of a pitiful monkey with a pig's heart grafted to its neck. Cara shrieked in horror. 'Dad? Is this what you do? Dad? Dad!'

'You know what I do, Cara. I'm working on stopping one animal from rejecting another creature's heart, in the hopes of developing a better range of drugs to prevent organ rejection in human transplants.'

'But on its *neck*!'

'What do you want us to do? Carve its chest open and take out its own heart, to put the pig's in there? We can monitor the new heart's health, on the neck – we can see quickly when things go wrong—'

'But it's vile!'

'Shut up, Cara.'

It was rare for him to be harsh with Cara. The picture revolted El too, but she told herself she was being squeamish; this was necessary. Lives would be saved by it. 'I don't understand where they've got the picture from,' she asked him. 'Those swimmy lines on it – it looks like a still from a video.'

'The press have got the pictures off the internet.' He put on his coat and went to work before she could say anything else. The story accompanying the picture provided all the details. The anti-vivisection group had been given info by a mole working in the animal house. Key facts were bullet pointed in the article on page 19:

- regulation monitoring procedures were not followed;
- entries on records of inspection of post-op animals were forged;
- clearly distressed moribund animals were not being euthanised.

This was not a random animal lib attack on wicked vivisectionists cutting up our furry friends. They argued that unacceptably high rejection rates of grafted organs were not being properly reported, in an attempt to prolong research which would otherwise be terminated. There was a whiff of authenticity to the whole thing. El recognised the information as being uncomfortably close to what she already knew: the pig/monkey heart transplant programme was posited on the notion of an imminent breakthrough in immunosuppressant drugs. Yet Con had been working on it – she calculated – nearly nine years. Were they any nearer a breakthrough now than when he started? He hadn't mentioned it, if they were.

At lunchtime she went to the PECA website and read the entire document. From the beginning of the story – the dodgy purchasing and importation arrangements for monkeys (in cages smaller than the minimum legal requirements; and after two, not six months' quarantine, meaning that they could be carrying the Aids-related virus or other viruses which might be equally dangerous to humans) to the unacceptably high death rate in surgery, to the failure to properly record and monitor post-op progress, to the total unrelieved failure rate – not one monkey survived with any quality of life – the catalogue of wretchedness seemed all too plausible. No wonder Con didn't talk much about work. No wonder he was depressed. Why on earth didn't he get out?

She raised it when she got in at 10 that night, after a long course-planning committee meeting that was followed by Louis and her needing to get something to eat together. 'I don't know why you stay at the lab, Con. I mean, what's the point in doing something that's going nowhere?'

'Because mostly we think it isn't going nowhere. We hope it's going somewhere. That's why we do the research, El.'

'Don't be sniffy with me. If there have been no advances and this heralded breakthrough is still as elusive as—'

'Who says there have been no advances?'

'That website—'

'Since when did you believe a bunch of rabid animal libbers?'

'It seems an intelligently argued record, Con. Haven't you looked at it?'

'What am I going to learn from some piece of hysteria?'

'It feels convincing. Whoever wrote it either works there himself or is in very close communication with someone who does.'

'I doubt that, my dear know-all, because it would be more than anyone's job is worth to release details of the work to the press; it's classified.'

'Maybe someone doesn't care about their job – maybe they care more about the blatant abuses that are clearly—'

'I'm glad you have such a high opinion of my work.'

'Con, please, just look at the site and see what you think.'

'The drug companies invest millions in this. How do you think they would deal with an employee stirring up bad publicity?'

'Sack them, I suppose.'

'You are an innocent, aren't you.'

'What do you mean?'

'Whoever hits the immunosuppressant jackpot – and there has to be one, eventually, there has to be a cocktail of drugs which make the pig heart transplants possible – will become one of the richest companies on earth. Imagine. Every hospital in the world wants a supply.'

'Go on.'

'You think sacking is the worst they'd do to a person who threatened their research programme?'

'You're being melodramatic.'

'OK. Then why doesn't this alleged mole, whoever they are, why doesn't he or she go public, instead of this cloak and dagger stuff? Why doesn't he go properly to the papers instead of to a bunch of anti-vivisectionist nutters?'

'You think a mole has to hide behind the animal libbers?'

'I think it's all a load of shite.'

'But Con – just look at it and see what you think?'

He left the room without replying, and she didn't raise it again until the following weekend, lying in bed with the Sunday papers, where an in-depth piece about 'Who are the real Animal Liberationists?' was touted in the magazine. 'Did you look?'

'At what?' He was pretending to read the sport.

'The website.'

'I glanced at it.'

'Well?'

'There's a lot of unsupported claims. It's easy to make an animal research lab look bad.'

'You don't think it's authentic?'

'Not for a moment.'

And that was the end of it. The press dropped the story after a couple of days; there was no indication that the claims were being pursued either by police or funding bodies; the issue seemed closed.

But Con's indifference to the claims struck El unpleasantly. At some level, she thought, he had given up; had become so firmly chained to his job and his pension that even if the work was dehumanising and going nowhere, he would stay with it, because it required more energy and imagination than he could muster to get out. She began to feel a degree of contempt for him.

Then came the flare-up before Christmas. They were supposed to be going shopping. El had had a run of evening lectures and work-related social events which Con had boy-cotted, declining the role of what he termed 'celebrity spouse'. She was uncomfortably conscious of the number of evenings he must have spent home alone. She found an empty Thursday evening in her diary and suggested meeting in town for late-night shopping and a meal.

When the kids were little Con had been an inspired Christ-mas shopper, hunting down wonderful toys for each of them, and going to great lengths, as they got older, to find the latest album Paul wanted, a particular brand of make-up favoured by Megan, a jacket patterned with parrots which Cara wore till it was rags, computer games even Dan had not yet tracked down. El remembers how good he used to be at buying her clothes: he had bought her the green silk skirt she still wears from time to time for dinners; he chose her blue wool jacket, and the little black top with sequins at the neck. But no more. As if he is a firm being modernised, retrenching, cutting back on services, he has stopped shopping; now offers money or a token instead.

So the impulse to take him shopping was, she knew, con-taminated: he would read it as her attempt to jolly him along, to rekindle some dying ember of past pleasure, and he would be as recalcitrant as a sulky kid. But if she just left him at home to rot, how would that help either of them? She had to do *something*. If they started where he could find something pretty for Cara and Megan – Monsoon or Kookaï – then he might get into a better mood and...

Forlorn hope. El herself was late to meet him, thanks to a Ph.D. student who responded to criticism by bursting into tears and revealing that her partner had cancer. Con received her excuse in silence and walked out of Kookaï after two minutes complaining that the music was too loud and the clothes over-priced. El found an embroidered bag for Megan in Accessorize, but Con barely glanced at it, took no notice of the beads and earrings that might have been good for Cara, and requested that they stop and eat before progressing to the bookshop.

It was in the buzzing gloom of La Tasca that the argument flared. The place was full of late-night shoppers and service was slow; El realised the shops would be closing by the time they were done. But there was no point in shopping with him anyway, in this mood; she would do her own shopping in half the time, and if he wanted to behave like an old person, that was his lookout.

Intolerable, though, to sit in silence, with raucous Christmas drinking parties and excitedly chattering shoppers all around them. So she unthinkingly asked him how he'd got on at work today. His tone was light and unpleasantly ironic. 'Oh, the usual, you know. The last two animals from the November round were euthanised this week so I'm analysing data from the post-mortems. Then I'll write up the report explaining why our success rate is no higher than it was last July.'

'I can't understand why you're still doing this, Con.'

'It's my job, dear, they pay me on a monthly basis, rather well.'

'You don't have to do it for the money.'

'Really? Let's see, what else could I do? How can I choose between the army of employers beating a path to my door, all eager for the services of a fifty-year-old man with highly spe-cific and increasingly redundant research experience?'

'It's not redundant.'

'It is. You know that as well as I do. You know it better than me, you little hypocrite.'

'Con, I don't see why—'

'Let's get to the bottom of this, shall we? For once and for all. In case you hadn't noticed, you earn twice as much as me.'

'Yes, but that doesn't matter—'

'To me unfortunately it does. Which is one reason why I'm unwilling to give up work which is at least half-decently paid, in order to return to being some tin-pot researcher's lab boy.'

'Money's never been an issue.'

'No, indeed, but when all else fails there is at least a kind of dignity in earning.'

'You don't need to do this.'

'What do you know about what I need to do?'

'To be working at something that's going nowhere, day in day out, it's enough to depress anyone.'

'It's how most people spend their working lives.'

'But—'

'You think the majority of the population find their work rewarding and fulfilling? Processing peas, assembling car parts, digging holes in the road, checking tax returns?'

'There's some point at least to most jobs, something useful's being produced.'

'Well, you know, Eleanor, there was some point to my work – many would say, a quite significant and valuable point, certainly not a harmful one – making more hearts available for transplant is not a harmful one: but my dear, in research as in the rest of nature, the fit survive and the weaker specimens go to the wall.'

'Are you trying to blame me?'

'Not personally. We both had choices. I chose a blind alley, and you have followed your clever little nose to success. And the irony will not have escaped you that now your success helps ensure our failure. Because the obvious way, thanks to you lot, to develop transplant organs is via stem cell growth. Why would anyone continue to fund a Neanderthal pig-to-human transplant programme when the shiny prospect of own-cell grown human hearts is being dangled like a carrot?'

'You think *I'm* making your work invalid?'

'Not personally. It's just the luck of the draw. Your research is the main channel. Mine was a promising-looking backwater. The history of science is littered with the corpses of good research ideas. Who's to know whether it might not have worked, in the end? We've been nearly there for a long time. A bit more enthusiasm, a bit more funding, a bit more fucking luck and we might have broken through. But it's too late now, stem cells have all the good press, they're the obvious way to go. And we're dinosaurs.'

'I haven't been working on stem cells out of malice, to do you down!'

'Of course not. You just lead a charmed life.'

'There's no point in saying things like that. But if you're agreeing that the transgenic research has no future, surely you can agree to leave?'

'Why should I? Kneiper are still putting money into the programme – there may well be other applications for these drugs. And if they decide to pull the plug they'll have to pay decent redundancy money. Given that there's nothing else I'm fit to do, it would be idiotic to leave.'

'You're *fifty*. You've got years of working and thinking ahead of you. You could even retrain, do something completely

different – I can support you. What good will there be in clinging to the wreck as it goes down?'

'*You* can support me? Given that a shred of dignity is just
about all I have left, wouldn't you say I ought to hang on to it?'

The waiter brought their order and they ate in silence. So
that was the way he saw it. Her success ensured his failure. As if
there wasn't enough shit between them, her work must destroy
his.

But Con hasn't gone because of this – has he? It's old news.
It's sad, it's bitter, but they're not work rivals. She's always worked
harder than him, they both know that, and his lack of ambition
has allowed him to do other things. There is always a knowledge
which contradicts observed fact. He was jealous and contemptuous when comparing his career with hers; damaging words
were said. Nevertheless she knows it was not the most important
thing. It was not even, necessarily, a very important thing at all.
He doesn't take work as seriously as her. Which has made all
sorts of things possible: his chief-carer role with the children;
easiness over money, with neither of them caring who earned
or spent the most; a generosity in recognising and honouring
each other's differences. The work rage is not a root cause of
anything. More, a manifestation of unease, a symptom of some
other, deeper wrong.

She is drawn back again to Cara's birth. That time of happiness. Back again to the golden centre; follow the thread from
there, to find out the heart of the rot.

El remembers being seduced by Con's sweetness after she
told him she was pregnant. Once Hélène had left he seemed
to take over the entire running of the house. He brought her
breakfast in bed and shielded her from the children's tantrums,

he made love to her with renewed intensity and frequency.

'You only like me when I'm pregnant,' she joked.

'I like that you're different. Your body forces you to slow down.'

'You like me handicapped with a big fat weight.'

'Maybe. Yes. I like the fact that you can't just put it down. I like how primitive it is. Pregnant women are different from men.'

'Unlike nasty, everyday, non-pregnant women, who're out there pretending to be men.'

'Absolutely. Fecundity rules, OK.'

The birth of Cara was a bridge which they crossed to find one another, to find the two golden years that led to Daniel's birth. If it was guilt that made her love him – well: it didn't make the love any less real. Nor the love with which he responded. If ever good can come from bad, then surely that was it.

El tells herself it is necessary to be clear about that time. Not to mythologise. Because of what happened afterwards. She must know she is not deluding herself. OK, one of the effects of Cara's birth was to bring Con into focus. She had accepted him before as a fact in her life. Husband. Father of her children. And yet, as she had said to him in an early spat, 'You could marry anyone, within reason.' He chose to take that as a slight, but what she had meant simply was that the creation of a long-term partnership and environment for raising children was not dependent on infatuation or lust: as the half-population of the world who live in arranged marriages could attest.

'How romantic,' he said wryly.

'I think it's probably good to be unromantic. I haven't got unrealistic expectations.'

'It wouldn't make any difference to you if you were married to someone else?'

'He would have to have similar educational and probably class background, similar aspirations. Which an arranged marriage would take care of anyway.'

'And the marriage would not be any different?'

'Of course it would be *different*, because he'd be a different person. It might be worse or better. But it wouldn't be impossible.' Her sense of it was that she had learned to love Con as a husband firstly because she had been physically attracted to him and then because of his persistence, because he seemed to know *he* loved *her*; and then because of qualities like tolerance and open-mindedness and an interest in ideas; because he was, in many ways, like her. And the ways in which he was not like her were more or less complimentary. 'I'm not insulting you!' she scolded him. 'It's real, it's based on usage and knowledge, it's not some fantasist's *true love* that will last about a week.'

He made a mocking bow. 'Next time round I'll marry a poet.'

Her sense of the marriage was that although she loved him (of course, it went without saying) he hardly impinged on her: he was there in her life, a major figure, like the children – but he could also be not there. Her identity was still single.

After Cara, that changed. Because guilt and emotional anxiety made her more susceptible? Because the marriage anyway would have developed into a new and deeper phase? Or simply because of logistics; in the year after Cara's birth they spent more time together? The last was the most plausible answer. But it could have been a mixture of all three.

What happened was that she became more aware of him. Of his physical presence; the way he handled the baby, the way he silently anticipated what El needed and where she was going, lifting/shifting/opening/closing/mediating the world of objects around her so that what she needed was always to hand and her movements around the house, from house to car, from car to clinic or wherever she went, were eased and lightened. She noticed the space and quiet order he created for her to be in; it was as if he gave her a special world. But she also remembered how this had irritated her when Paul and Megan were born: his careful thoughtfulness and manoeuvring had filled her with impatience, so that she had snapped, 'I'm not ill, you know, I'm perfectly capable of opening the door for myself!'

Now in this time of lucid happiness, it was possible to examine that. 'I used to think you were being sexist when you opened doors and carried stuff for me before.'

'Used to think?'

'I like it now. Can I still call myself a feminist?'

He grinned. 'A pampered feminist.'

'More to the point, can you still call yourself a feminist?'

'Naturally. I am lightening a woman's physical burdens in order to facilitate her intellectual pursuits.'

'You're sure you're not suggesting I'm a weakling who might snap if I had to carry my own bag to the car? And reinforcing the stereotype that you are my big strong protector?'

'Think of it more as a master–slave role. You're the superior being and I'm the brute.'

'OK, I'm happy with that.'

'You can pay me back. This is strictly baby-linked. It will cease the day you stop breastfeeding.' She breastfed Cara for eight months.

She became more aware of his mind. Noticed, almost with

surprise, his clarity. It was over this period that she decided to get out of IVF. The intellectual sparring – the articulating and being listened to – the working out of a new position and learning to defend it; the testing of it in argument, was all down to Con. His persistent, rigorous opposition forced her to make her ideas watertight; she tested them against him till she knew they were true.

When El remembers this now it drenches her in sadness. That is what's been lost. How long since they have argued like that? Neither of them has become stupid, senile, uninterested in ideas. So why have they stopped making each other think? Why, for the last however long, has there been nothing to talk about?

She remembers the night she went to hear Gena Corea and Robyn Rowland speak about reproductive technologies. Paul and Megan were both miserable with colds, and Cara was niggling and hadn't fed properly. El had half a mind not to go. Con persuaded her that Cara would settle better if she was out of the house, which was almost certainly true. But although this would be a set of arguments she knew she ought to hear, she had little appetite for a gaggle of lesbian feminists moaning about evil men in white coats, and had told herself she would stay no more than an hour.

The venue was depressing – a dingy church hall with a FINNRET banner drooping across the doorway: Feminist International Network on the New Reproductive Technologies. She resented the fact that they had appropriated the word feminist, as if to oppose them were to be non-feminist. The Feminist International Network had managed to conjure a full eleven women out of the Manchester gloom to listen to this American star, so already El's slipping-away-early plan was foiled. But once Corea began to speak, that didn't matter. El was riveted: this was not some poky little organisation of man-hating separatists and conspiracy theorists. Corea was stunningly well informed, able to paint a convincing picture of the progress and effects of IVF on a wider geographical and political scale than El had ever contemplated. She made no false claims or assertions; her arguments were all about interpretation. What she did, as El realised later, describing the evening to Con, was to drag out into the daylight all the half-formed anxieties and objections that had been lurking in the depths of El's mind for the past eighteen months.

'She started with success rates. Claims of success rates, and actual live births. You know the Norfolk Clinic has the best success rates in the world – well, it's still only 13 per cent. And that's five and a half years after Louise Brown. The success rates are not improving.'

'You knew that.'

'I sort of knew it, but it gets obscured, doesn't it, by successful ovarian stimulation, and successful fertilisation, and successful cleavage and success of embryo transplant – but after all these successes, the whole thing still fails more often than not.'

'OK.'

'So then the argument is, women are being offered children. Yet this is a highly experimental, 87 per cent failure risk procedure, involving many direct threats to the women's health and well-being, and they are being asked to pay for it.'

'No one's forcing them. If you can't stop people spending money on getting pissed out of their heads, you can't stop them spending it on making babies.'

'Right. It's being offered as a choice to childless women. But in fact it's not a choice. Because eighty-seven out of a hundred of them will come away without the thing they chose.'

'Well, you could argue that the success rates should be honestly revealed, but after that, it is free choice.'

'Take a step back. The point of feminism is to give women freedom. Freedom to live their lives as they wish – equally with men.'

'In so far as men are free.'

'OK, OK. Within the constraints of being human. But that freedom must be freedom from social pressure to conform to biological stereotyping.'

'In what sense does an IVF programme constitute social pressure?'

'By its very existence! It says to childless women, it is your destiny to bear children, so don't consider making a life without them – come and try again to have them.'

'It can say what it likes – women don't have to listen.'

'But it's the underlying assumption: if you can't have children you're incomplete, and must be willing to sacrifice any amount of money, time and health in order to try and get them. Instead of saying to the childless woman, OK, there are a million other things you can do, go off and find one that interests you.'

'El, no one obliges them. Childless women can say that to themselves. But they don't. They queue up for IVF programmes.'

'But the *existence* of those programmes creates social pressure.'

'It is scientifically possible to go to the moon; that doesn't mean all men feel obliged to try and go there.'

'It's not reckoned to be a defining part of your identity as a male that you should go to the moon.'

'I should adventure and explore—'

'Bollocks. You know about amniocentesis in India?'

'Go on.'

'Used for sex selection. They find out the sex of the foetus and then abort girls. Corea had some figures, I wrote it down. Listen. An estimated 78,000 female foetuses have been aborted in the last five years. Of 8,000 abortions in Bombay last year, 7,997 foetuses were female.'

'Terrible, clearly. But your argument?'

'My argument is that the use of amnio in India is not progress. It is the opposite. It is like genocide, it is like the holocaust, only it's men and women—'

'The people who have the amnios and abortions are women.'

'And do you think they do that of their own free will? You don't think their husbands and society pressurise them?'

'OK.'

'So it would be best not to have that option. It would be best if there was no amnio.'

'You can't undo medical progress. You have to educate people so they can make the right choices. Presumably they've been smothering female newborns for generations.'

'But the choice – here in this country, the pill has given more women control over their own fertility, deciding to work, choosing to parent or to be childless – and then along come the scientists with a procedure which basically says, "If you don't have children you're ill and we can treat you." It says infertility is a *disease*.'

'This would all be so much more convincing if it came from a childless woman.'

Of course, he was right, and that took them on to biological determinism, and how far it is ever possible or desirable to try to overcome that; on to the male impulse to impregnate as many females as possible; the female desire to bear children by the most powerful, successful male available. 'Both of which, to some degree, humanity has overcome in the interests of social stability and a better environment for our young – thus proving we are not slaves to our biology, and that our lives are better for not being so. Game, set and match to me!' she crowed.

Revisiting these debates, El is aware of her own past actions in a way that it was easy not to be at the time. Glenn was younger than Con, more ambitious. She thought she'd simply had some fun. In fact she'd mated with the most powerful and successful male available, and got a child out of it.

She finds this analysis repellent, has always seen biological determinism as an insidious, cobwebby set of puppet strings to be swiped through wherever possible. And so has Con, although he's always been willing to offer her a run for her money in an argument. But what if they've both been wrong, all along? What if every choice and decision they think they've made in their lives has been no more than their genes tugging at their puppet strings? What if she has spent her time, ever since turning against IVF, arguing futilely against a force which is as unstoppable as the incoming tide: the overriding desire of females to have children?

Has she pretended people can choose how to behave in order to shield herself from a much uglier reality – a reality Con, maybe, has been learning to embrace?

Chapter 12

WHEN HE HAS finished his pasta marinara Con orders another glass of wine. Silly, it would have been cheaper to get the bottle in the first place. He drinks it slowly, telling himself it is his sleeping draught. He'll sleep tonight and then tomorrow he'll be able to make some sensible decisions. Sitting here drinking alone makes him feel as if he is on holiday, waiting for someone; waiting for El and the kids to join him, turning over in his mind what they might do tomorrow. His real life, that competent slightly weighty machine of responsibilities and routine, of planned-and-saved-for-treats and familial interactions perpetually animating him, continues in another dimension unstoppably, since by definition it can have no end, being what Conrad is, being Conrad's life.

How can his life have ended before he has?

He should be on his way. He pays, hauls on his coat and sets out into the cold again. He seems to have wandered away from the main drag; the street is dark and narrow without shops. He turns right towards what seems to be a road with more streetlights. It is raining now in earnest, thin stinging drips that hit his skin like shards of ice. Maybe that last glass was a bad idea, he feels a little fuzzy. Emerging from a couple of turns at the end of the street, he finds himself at a major road. Three lanes of traffic in each direction. Did he cross this to get here? He has a memory of traffic and a dog, but wasn't it a smaller road? He finds the lights have changed and a green pedestrian sign is urging him to cross. It must be right because on the other side the covered pavement begins again, the vaulted brick roofing which is so distinctive in the city centre. It is good to be out of the rain. He has been going for a while when he realises he's climbing a hill. There's no hill in the centre of town; and it looks darker and darker up ahead. This is wrong.

As he turns to go down he sees a figure fall back into the shadows. Someone was following him. Quickly climbing down from the high pavement into the road, he crosses to the other side. His eyes can make out movement – indistinct movement, down in the street below. People walking up the hill? He rubs at his eyes which are blurred by rain or sweat, but they refuse to focus. Lights are set into the brickwork of the vaulted arches overhead, he is lit up and on display. He moves on up into the dimness midway between lights, and leans against the wall, feeling the vibration of his heartbeat. Still can't make out what's moving down there. Then he sees that it's a monkey. There's a monkey staring at him, standing up on two feet in the middle of the road. Definitely a cynomolgous monkey, its grey fur is haloed by a streetlamp lower down the hill. Its eyes gleam in its black face, it is very still, it's watching him. He wants to turn and run but he knows how fast they are. It would be up his back in seconds, clawing at his head and neck, chattering with rage. If he keeps still maybe it'll get distracted. He blinks and the monkey's gone. His eyes scour the dimly-lit pavements and dark roadway, ears straining for the click of its claws upon the stone.

He is trying to quiet his breathing, he is trying to see where the monkey has got to, he is already instinctively pulling up his collar to protect his vulnerable neck, when a male voice further up the hill barks, '*Chi e quello?*'

'*Scusi.* I am lost. *Inglese.*'

'English?' The man approaching Con is walking with a stick, slightly stooped. As he moves into better light Con sees his face is fierce and intelligent.

'Yes, I have taken a wrong turning. I'm looking for my hotel.'

'Where is it?' His English is fast and good.

'City centre.'

'You are on the via di San Luca. You must go back down the hill.'

Maybe the monkey will be scared by this man's voice. By his stick. If Con can walk down the hill with him he'll be protected. 'Thank you.' He waits for the man to fall into step beside him.

'What is your hotel?'

'It's – it's—' The name has gone.

'Street?' says the man. 'Street of your hotel?'

Con has no idea. He just knows what it looks like. If he can get himself into the right neighbourhood he will be able to find it. 'I've forgotten,' he concedes.

'You are tourist?'

'No. I'm a scientist. I've been to a conference and I, I had some bad news. I came to Bologna for, for a rest.'

'Sorry for your bad news. I am Alberto.' The man is gravely courteous. Con offers his name and they shake. There is no sign of the monkey and Con's hot sweat is now freezing on his skin. If he can get back to his room and shut the door he'll be safe, he can take off his wet coat and have a warm bath. Alberto is a saviour.

'Your English is very good.'

'Hah!' Not quite a laugh. 'My wife was English. She is now two years dead.'

'I'm sorry to hear that.'

'I go to evening mass for her. You know the church, of the Vergine di San Luca? But you should not to walk this hill at night, we have not so much light here. Sometimes the robbers come.'

Con is not concerned about robbers. He is concerned about the monkey, which is back in the road ahead, keeping to the dark centre of the street, keeping pace with their speed, glancing back at Con over its grey shoulder every few seconds to check that he is following.

'What is the matter?' asks the man.

'There—' Conrad points. 'You see?'

'What is?'

'A monkey. We have to be careful, they are vicious.'

Alberto stops and ferrets in his pocket. For a moment Con hopes he might take out a gun and shoot the monkey. But there's bound to be more. 'This is where I live.' He has a key in his hand. 'I wish you good night.'

As Alberto unlocks the door Con notices that the monkey has stopped going downhill and has fully turned to look at him. Another burst of scalding sweat erupts through his skin and he puts his hand to the wall to steady himself. Alberto opens his door and steps inside, switching on a light. He turns to look at Con again. 'You are unwell? You like a glass of water?'

Wordlessly Con nods and follows him into the hall; as the door closes behind him relief unstrings his limbs and he crumples to the floor.

★

Later he is in a small dark blue bedroom with posters of racing cars on the walls, and a lamp glowing beside his bed. He is aware, through memories which are shifting like sliding glass doors, of a series of things. This is the bedroom of Alberto's grown-up son, his headache has returned tenfold, there are monkeys after him. He is shivering and yet his skin is slick with sweat. Alberto gave him a glass of brandy as he lay on the hall floor, and he doesn't know where his hotel has gone. He is in bed in his clothes, he hasn't even got pyjamas. The lamp is giving off flakes of light, more like bubbles in fact, bubbles of light which seem to float up towards the ceiling. It soothes his itching eyes to watch them. And then to let his lids fall shut.

After a period of blackness he opens them again to find the same scene. He feels secure, almost as if he has reverted to boyhood, to the age of the son who decorated this bedroom with his racing cars. And he has a son of his own, too. His flickering thoughts turn to Paul's room, Paul's posters, of owls, pandas, polar bears and whales. Paul is the one person he would like to tell what he has done. He would like to win Paul's approval, at last, after all these years. It is only Paul who has maintained an unwaveringly critical attitude to the use of animals in research. It seems to Con now that he patronised the boy by rooting it all in that first unhappy monkey house experience. Why insult Paul by implying that his seriously held beliefs are simply the after-effects of childhood trauma? Say rather that that first visit to the monkey house planted a seed of intelligent questioning.

Con remembers Paul's arguments and the arrogance with which he demolished them. He saw arguing with Paul as sparring, as play. He realises now that Paul must have guessed this and felt belittled by it. As he grew older he moved from emotional (in Con's head, soft) arguments, to hard: to questions of cost and political choice. Here it became more difficult to demolish him, and the arguments ran on from one conversation to the next.

Con remembers taking him out to practise for his driving test, soon after Con had started working for Corastra. His new work had been the subject of conversation in the house all weekend, and Paul had made his disapproval clear. They were on country roads, driving towards Halifax, and Paul continually drove just a little too fast for comfort. Con had to check himself, after he'd exasperated Paul by twice asking him to slow down. He kept his eye on the speedometer and vowed to himself not to mention it again unless the needle touched 60. It didn't, Paul's speed was perfectly calculated; Con knew it was being used to wind him up. They came to a lay-by with a mobile shop and he suggested they stop for a coffee. Paul parked and Con got out into the damp air to buy the drinks.

'I think the research you're doing is unnecessary, politically suspect and immorally cruel.' Con realised that Paul must have been rehearsing the sentence in his head as he waited for Con to return with their coffee, selecting and rearranging the charges for maximum impact.

He tried for lightness. 'Oh, is that all?'

'I'm serious.'

'OK. Unnecessary because you think people with heart problems should be left to die?'

'Yes.'

'Politically suspect because the money should be spent on starving children?'

'Yes.'

'Immorally cruel?'

'You chop out pigs' hearts, you stick them in monkeys, the pigs die, the monkeys die.'

Despite himself, Con was needled. 'I'm not doing it for fun.'

'Maybe. But you are doing it for money.'

'For God's sake, Paul! You don't even understand the basics of what I'm doing, yet you set yourself up—'

'Tell me then. What makes it so different from what I think?'

'The reason we're using monkeys—'

'Start with the pigs. Go on, explain it.'

'Right. We want to make a pig heart that can be transplanted into humans. Pig hearts because pigs breed easily in captivity and have large litters – a lot of hearts can be supplied.' His anger began to subside. 'D'you really want to hear all this?'

'Sure.' A rare grin from Paul. 'Give me the ammo to whop you.'

'You know the big problem with transplants is rejection.'

'Yes.'

'Well, the more divergent the species the more ferocious the rejection. If you put a normal pig heart in a human you get hyperacute rejection, which means the antibodies of the host's blood attack the antigens on the surface of the alien heart and reduce it to a black swollen mass within minutes.'

'Ugh.'

'So, the pig is genetically modified, which is to say a very small number of its 50,000 genes are modified to alter the surface antigens of the pig's cells so that they more closely resemble human antigens. So then when the pig heart is transplanted the human immune system is tricked into seeing the pig organ as human and not attacking it, OK?'

'OK. Does this have to be done to every pig foetus?'

'No, the transgenic pigs breed naturally and their offspring inherit their genetic make-up.'

'They're not slowly going to grow more and more like people?'

'Only in science fiction.'

'Then what?'

'Then we transplant the hearts to monkeys.'

'And what happens?'

'We treat the monkeys with immunosuppressants, to help prevent rejection, and we monitor their progress with a view to transplanting hearts like these into sick humans in the near future.'

'How long do the monkeys survive?'

'Anything from a few hours to sixty days.'

'So the best you could offer anyone is sixty days?'

'At the moment. If you consider that HAR takes six minutes, sixty days is not bad going.'

'So in the hope of one day producing a heart and drugs that will keep a human alive for longer than sixty days, you kill – how many pigs? How many monkeys?'

'The pigs are irrelevant, since we breed them specifically.'

'OK. Monkeys are our closest relatives in the animal world. They can remember, love, hate, play, feel pain and rage—'

'This is the furry friends argument.'

'You know a mother monkey will grieve for a year or more over the loss of her baby?'

'The belief that human life is more valuable than animal life is a principle of all research involving animals.'

'That's speciesism.'

'No argument.'

'It's wrong.'

'We'll have to agree to differ.'

Of course he knows it was cruel. His ability to work depended on him effectively blocking out that knowledge. How easy to be a bleeding-heart sympathiser. He has a physical sense, now, of how tightly he screwed himself up against that sympathy, how he locked up his feelings, and the cost at which he did it. He had to make himself feel nothing. And what he locked up has broken out now, flooding his system with grief and shame.

Something is shaking. Con opens his eyes reluctantly and sees Alberto tugging at his shoulder. 'You drink now. Drink or you will dehydrate.'

Con pulls himself up in the bed; his body is strangely heavy. He takes the glass of orange from Alberto. 'Thank you.'

'Now water.'

Con obeys again. Alberto watches him drink. 'I'm sorry about this – you are very kind—'

'No problem. You have the flu I think. Headache?'

'A bit.'

Alberto points to the bedside table, there is a box of paracetamol. 'Take two.'

Again Con obeys; there is an ache around the bridge of his nose which he is afraid will turn into tears of gratitude. How can a stranger be so kind to him? When he looks up again, after painstakingly swilling the tablets down his constricted throat, Alberto has gone. Con lies back on the bed, too exhausted even to shuffle down properly under the blankets. When he's better he'll organise something. Buy Alberto a present. He allows his eyes to close.

How long did it take, that shift at work? That slow sub-terranean movement from optimism, conviction and discovery, via endless knock-backs and tiny inchings-forward, to the dull acceptance that this was it, nothing much was changing? The animal rights people gave them a year's grace by letting out the pigs. That put the whole programme back a year while they bred up a new batch of pigs, ironically instilling in Con a renewed sense of optimism and purpose. Maybe with the next batch of pigs there would be a breakthrough. And then when the new pigs were ready, nothing worked any better than it had before. Always this cycle of hope and of being slapped down.

He was naive; naive and gullible. Ditto with Maddy. Soon after their Birmingham meeting she asked to meet him in London, and he organised a visit to Megan's play that evening to make sense of the journey. Maddy was waiting for him at Euston and led him to a basic-looking Indian restaurant five minutes away, on Drummond Street. It was a sweltering August day.

'I'm not sure I fancy Indian for lunch,' he tells her.

'Oh, but it's vegetarian and the food is very good. Please give it a try. I always come here.'

It is on the tip of his tongue to suggest sandwiches in Regent's Park, or a pub with a beer garden, but she looks so distressed that he goes along with it. The food is spread out on a long table; following her, he helps himself to random spoonfuls until he has far more than he wants to eat. He has never been able to understand the point of eating hot food when you are hot. They settle at a table. 'So how was my statement received?' He knows it has not appeared on the Prevent Experiments and Cruelty to

Animals website, because he's been checking it regularly.

'There are problems with the group,' she tells him. 'Real problems, everything has been held up.'

'What's gone wrong?'

She shakes her head. 'Relationships. Turns out the man who does the website has been having an affair with Lindy, who is Tom's partner. Lindy and Tom are the founders of PECA. When it came out there was a huge flare-up and nothing has been done on the website since. He's got it all password protected, none of the rest of us can touch it.'

Con nods. They are cranks. The idea that anything will get done via Maddy is simply a waste of time.

'I'm so angry with them all,' Maddy confides. 'If you believe in a cause, a cause like this, the animals should come first – not petty things like family and relationships. All that has to be put aside. It's a crusade, we need to fight together.'

'Did you show them my statement?'

'Yes – yes. But they're carping. They're saying, *Where are the photos?* and *This is useless without his name on it.* They're so petty and negative and they gang up together…'

Con realises she is near to tears. 'Don't be upset. And you were right, this dhal is excellent, so is the – the green curry.'

'I will be upset. Of course I will. Just because they've all known each other for longer than me, because it's *their* group that *I've* joined, I'm like a kid they can order around.'

Con is really afraid she will cry. He is annoyed with himself for not realising, before this, how flaky she is. Now he comes to look at her properly, she is a mess. She's wearing a crumpled, off-white shirt and faded cords, on the hottest day of summer. Her hair is greasy and her skin grey. 'You're not at work today?' he asks.

'I'm on holiday.'

He thinks she has lost her job. 'Listen, your people at PECA will sort it out. Of course they will. People are always selfish when they're upset. When the dust settles they'll update the website, don't you worry.'

'Everything I do,' she says, 'is for the cause. If I can't make a difference I might as well be dead.'

'Come on now, Maddy, don't talk like this. If you've really fallen out with the PECA bunch, have you thought of starting a group of your own?'

'Me and whose army?' she says bitterly. 'Everyone's afraid. Will you give me those photos?'

'Well, there's no point right now, is there? With the website not working.'

'The point is then at least they'll see I mean business.'

'But Maddy, I don't want... the photos can't be a pawn in an argument between you and your friends. I mean, I can't just—'

'You can't just help me. No. Of course you can't. Why should I expect that?' Her voice is getting louder. She has not touched her food. 'Why should I expect help from a scientist?' She pushes away her dishes and stands up. She is at full volume now. 'Why should I expect help from someone who has everything he ever wanted handed to him on a plate?'

'Maddy—'

'My life is nothing but shit.' She turns and slams out of the restaurant. A waiter grins at Con. After a moment of embarrassment, he realises how relieved he is to be rid of her. He has made a stupid mistake, and he vows he will not make it again.

But then, of course, he does.

★

With what feels like a physical effort, he shifts his thoughts away from her. He doesn't have to go back. He never has to go back there, it is over. Sleep, like black water, closes over his head.

Alberto comes into Con's room bearing a tray of food. Soup, bread, a peeled and sliced apple. Con shuffles himself to sitting up again and takes a couple of spoonfuls of soup. The spoon is so heavy he can barely lift it.

'Alberto, thank you.' His voice seems to have become a whisper. 'But I can't – I'm sorry…'

Alberto nods. 'Try the apple. You must have something. It will be three days now – you must eat.'

Conrad forces down a slice. His throat is sore and swollen and the shreds of apple are like splinters in it.

'OK, I will call doctor.'

Maybe wise, thinks Con. This is an illness. Has he really been here three days? He is ill, in a stranger's house, he can't even shift himself back to the hotel. He must give Alberto some cash. He fumbles through his wallet but there doesn't seem to be any. He remembers paying with a 50-euro note at the restaurant – was that the last of his money? He hands Alberto his bank card, and laboriously writes his PIN on the back of an old receipt. Alberto tells him, with dignity, that he does not require money, but he will agree to fetch 250 euros for Conrad.

'You will telephone your wife, perhaps?'

Con glances at his switched-off mobile on the bedside table. It lies in a forlorn heap with his hotel key and loose change; Alberto must have emptied his pockets when he put him to bed. 'Yes, of course. Thank you.'

Alberto removes the tray and returns with another glass

of water. As Con's heavy eyes close he hears Alberto moving around the kitchen and then the front door softly opening and shutting. Con squints at his phone. He could call El. Tell her he's ill. The whole episode could be put down to his illness and there would be no need to explain any of it.

No. He does not want El to rescue him, with her impatient efficiency. Is she always impatient now? The now Eleanor is a woman he does not really look at. He knows how she looks: the slightly stiff posture with the deliberately straight back; the defiantly jet-black hair which seems, when she is tired, too dark and vivid for her face. He suggested to her a year ago that she should stop dyeing it and she laughed incredulously. He thinks silver or grey or whatever combination are now threading their way through the black would soften it and be kinder to her pale fifty-three-year-old skin. But it's not so much the posture or the hair or even the clothes, which are smarter and more discreetly formal than he likes, which identify her as a certain type and class of woman; it is the closed-ness of her face. She is intent on other things; her work, her own busyness, her lover – intent on anything but Con.

But is that what his grievance boils down to – a plea for attention? Is this why he does not look at her? Because what he sees when he looks negates him?

No – there's another reason for not looking at her. Because he wants her to know he is angry. The withholding of eye contact is the withholding of himself. He's saying she's not worth looking at. He's negating *her*.

And does she look at him? When she does, he dislikes the way she does it. It is as if she knows in advance whatever he is going to say. She finds him both predictable and slightly disappointing.

So he is not looking at her because he doesn't like what she projects back to him, a sense that he is slow and that she has more important concerns. She is not in the least interested in what of herself he reflects back to her. She doesn't care what he thinks, because his thoughts are irrelevant to her. This is why he doesn't look at her. Because she has negated him far more effectively than he has negated her.

But where are the other Eleanors, the ones before this one he cannot look at? He can only think of photos, as if his memories have been stolen by them, or distilled into static moments. Their wedding photo. The best one; the one that the kids used to pore over wonderingly, savouring the notion of 'before we were born'. Eleanor is radiant. She doesn't look pregnant; she is smiling straight at the camera, her hair lifted slightly back from her face by the breeze outside the register office, and her lips are slightly parted as if she is meeting something, like a swimmer breasting a wave, she seems to be afloat upon the moment. Anyone who sees the photo knows her smile is about Con. It is connected to her fingers entwined with his, to their facing a future together.

The picture of her breastfeeding Paul. Con still carries this in his wallet; it is tattered with age. She is looking at the photographer – Con. She is smiling a complex smile. A fraction of it is almost shamefaced. It says what a ridiculous cliché for you to take my picture feeding our baby – she is smiling at their cheesiness. But overcoming the hangdog look is a great beam of happiness that says, I'm glad you're looking at me and it doesn't matter ever what anyone else thinks because we both know this is wonderful. It is both public and secret, shamefaced and proud, again, it is Eleanor faring forward.

He tries to think when she stopped looking like that, when she stopped drawing him into complicity with her own reactions (or knowing he was already complicit). Might it have been that *he* stopped understanding *her*? Might that have been the beginning of her impatience?

But she stopped offering him things to understand. How could he understand if he didn't know? And in the history of all that, her affair with Louis is not, in fact, very important. It is symptomatic, not causal. Things were wrong a long time before.

It comes back to the America trip. That's where things started to go unstoppably wrong. When Dan was four, Con was invited to go to Cornell for six months. His old friend Max had a decent grant for further research into arresting the production of antibodies in lymphocytes; it was a good overlap with Con's work. Con told Eleanor in a moment of self-indulgence, pleased to have been asked.

'Why don't you go?'

He instantly regretted telling her. 'I don't think it would be a good idea while the children are so young, do you?'

'Why not? I don't think it would be a problem at all.'

It would so obviously be a problem that he was defeated. If she was really oblivious to how much time he spent with the kids, to how much he did in the house…

'I'll take some unpaid leave,' she said.

Con sat down.

'I've been thinking about it anyway. I need some proper time to work on the book.'

Of course. The book.

'You should go to Cornell. It's a good opportunity.'

He felt a strange despair, which he knew he must conceal

from her, because it was composed of things he could never admit. Firstly he didn't want to go – but if she knew that she would know he'd told her about it for effect, which was humiliating. Home was the place he wanted most in the world to stay in, with the children, with her. He would make no sense, away from home. And even if she did take unpaid leave, she wouldn't look after the children properly, she wouldn't do all the things he did. But the received opinion between them was that he did more childcare than her because she put her work first, so if she was now generously offering to put *his* work first, he should embrace her offer with open arms. He was ashamed at his lack of enthusiasm. It should be good, working with Max; it should be exciting, being in America on his own. He would have to go and pretend to be pleased. And the lie would have to be maintained both here and there, before, during and after. 'It is,' he said. 'A good career move, probably. But won't you feel rather lumbered?'

'Of course not. Home all day, and with an au pair to do the running round – luxury! I'll actually have time to think.'

She would have time, she would be home – and he wouldn't be here to share that. It was a thing he had dreamed of since the golden time with Cara, them being home together again, cooking for each other, having time to put the children to bed together or take them to the park on a summer evening. Little luxuries her work schedule never permitted, because on the rare occasions she was home early she insisted he make the most of it (by which she meant, work), and if he resisted, pointed out plaintively that she was surely entitled to an evening on her own with the children. She assumed being home was easy. Relegating all his time at home to the level of self-indulgence, something for which she had no need to feel respect or gratitude. She would find time to write a book. Proving her greater reserves of energy and efficiency. There was no escape.

Max met him at the airport. So little had Con been able to believe he would actually make the trip, that at the first sight of Max lounging against the pillar grinning from ear to ear, Con was shocked and wondered what coincidence had brought him here. It was impossible to look at Max and not smile. From the mirror glasses pushed up into his wiry black hair to his sardonic grin to the turquoise shirt covered in bronzed surfers to his elephantine, wrinkled grey jeans, Max was a piece of mockery and self-mockery. 'O-Kay?'

The grin was so big and the implications packed into the two syllables so vast that Con couldn't reply, only nod his head quickly and smile and, like a kid, swallow down the great lump in his throat. Then they both had to laugh at the weight of questions and answers spawned by their meeting like this.

Max's car was as big as a tennis court and shell-pink. He shrugged as he swung Con's case into the trunk. 'If you're going to live among the gas-guzzlers you have to keep your end up.'

The sun was still bright although it was nearly 7pm, and the remains of what must have been a hot day lay around them as they headed into the city: the babble of car stereos through open windows, the baked smell of the blacktop, as he was instructed to call it, bronzed bare arms resting on wound-down windows, as relaxed drivers steered single-handed; and when they came off the expressway, a girl in a red halter neck waiting obediently for a pedestrian crossing signal. Max pulled up and they watched her hesitate then cross in front of them. The lights caught up and changed to red as Max accelerated away. 'Food?' he said. 'Drink? Drink then food?'

'I've been eating and drinking for the last eight hours.'

'In-flight crap. You can have something good now. Vietnamese? Thai?'

Con glanced at his watch. It was midnight UK time. Max caught the movement.

'You gotta stay up. Then you'll sleep through.'

'Till when?'

'Till late. We'll get a drink. Something to eat. Go to a couple of bars,' he wiggled his eyebrows at Con, 'pick up some girls.'

'Yeah yeah. I have to phone home.'

'They'll be asleep. Do it just before you go to bed.'

Con imagined 6am and Eleanor snuggled in bed with Dan curled beside her.

'I didn't think you'd make it,' said Max.

'Why?'

'All that domestic bliss. How is your lovely wife?'

'OK.'

'And the tribe of offspring?'

'Thriving.'

'She doesn't mind you coming?'

'She pushed me out of the house.'

'OK, so you're going to have a good time. A bachelor life again.'

'I hated being a bachelor.'

Max tutted and shook his head.

So began six months of homesickness, ill-defined anxiety and sleepless nights. He rarely phoned home because the time difference was so awkward, and there was always such a mob of them at the other end wanting to talk that the conversation often revolved around the unfairness of how long the previous speaker had taken. If he phoned late afternoon on the weekend, the kids would be in bed and he stood a chance of getting El on her own, but Max was determined to show him the country, and weekends were often turned into excursions in which long-distance phone calls had no place. He resorted to airmail letters – long, regular, detailed ones for El, and amusing roundings-up of where he had been and what he had seen, enclosing postcards, for the kids. What came in reply was pretty thin: hastily scrawled aerogrammes from El, occasionally a longer letter with a page from Paul or Megan enclosed. Once he received a delicious fat envelope from the four of them, with drawings from Dan and Cara, and letters from Paul and Megan.

When Conrad came home, Eleanor drove to meet him at the airport. He had thought she might bring the children but then of course they would all have been hanging round if the flight was delayed. Also, El said Cara wasn't very well, claiming to have one of her headaches again. The doctor couldn't find anything wrong, but while she was droopy like that it was best to keep her in.

'Have you had her eyes tested?'

'Yes, Conrad.'

'Sorry.'

'Well, it is the obvious thing to do. How tired are you? I told Greta we'd be back later, I thought it would be nice to have you to myself for a little while before the mob descends.' She grinned at him. He felt almost overwhelmed by her physical presence. Her thick black hair was stylishly cut, shorter than he'd seen it before, tapering into the nape of her neck in a wedge that made him think of the cropped stems of cut corn. He couldn't imagine touching it.

He almost started to tell her how much more he'd enjoy a drink together after he'd said hello to the kids, how the thread of anxiety over them which had spun from his entrails when he flew away was now stretched so taut he could hardly move, but he was aware that she would think him mad. And be, quite rightly, offended. He creased his stiff face into a smile. She seemed bigger and more vivid than he remembered, her cheeks pinker, her lips redder, her breasts under her shirt voluptuously swollen. He was simultaneously attracted and repelled by her; it was astonishing that this glossy female was his wife.

'You look tired,' she said.

'I've not been sleeping very well. Excited about coming home, I guess.'

'You have a slight twang, you know. A very slight American flavour.'

'Really?' It seemed to him he'd hardly spoken to anyone but Max.

El pulled in at a big featureless pub on the main road back from the airport. It was almost empty and had a canteen-like foody smell. He expected her to wrinkle her nose and reject it but she didn't, and he was glad because the sooner they did the drink the sooner they could get home. There was the obligatory plastic Christmas tree in the corner (ten days to go!) and he remembered with satisfaction the presents he'd tracked down for them. Cara's in particular was brilliant: a pop-up tent she'd be able to use in the garden. They settled in a corner with their beers.

'So how was it? Overall?' she asked.

'Very strange, being away from you and the kids for that length of time. I wouldn't do it again. And Max – I couldn't live like Max.'

'You couldn't drink a vat of alcohol and pick up a new girl every night? He must have been very disappointed in you.'

'And you, overall? You didn't miss me?'

'There hasn't been a lot of time. Between the book and the kids and the work things I really couldn't wriggle out of, I've had more to fill my time than you.'

'You're looking good on it. You're looking amazing!'

She smiled. 'There's interesting work stuff. Lots I want to tell you about. You know the MRC grant I applied for last week?'

'Tell me about the kids first.'

'You'll see for yourself. They've grown.'

A silence. He shouldn't have stopped her talking about work.

'They're still getting on OK with the new au pair?'

'Greta's fine. The other one – Catherine – did I tell you about the week I asked her to leave?'

'You told me she was scatty.'

'She was late for Megan and Cara. Not just once, repeatedly. They came home on their own a couple of times.'

'Over the main road?'

El nodded. 'I gave her a warning and she ran out in tears. Then Paul said she'd been coming into his room.'

'When?'

Eleanor grimaced. 'Evenings. When I was out.'

'Doing what exactly?'

She frowned.

'Not you – her.'

'I don't know. Paul started backtracking as fast as he could. Nothing, he said. Just knocking on his door and asking him things.'

'What sort of things?'

'Meanings of words. If he wanted to watch telly with her. Nothing important, he said.'

'You think there was more to it?'

'How can we tell? I mean he's thirteen and she's nineteen. If she made some kind of sexual advance to him he's not going to want to tell us. The only practical thing to do is get the damn girl out of the house.'

'Why didn't you tell me? How long had it been going on?'

She shrugged. 'I didn't want to make a big thing of it. I told him I was sacking her for being late for school. But then when she left she took stuff.'

'What?'

'My silver chain. And Megan's birthday money.'

'For God's sake.'

'What can you do? I suppose we've been lucky so far, we were bound to get one bad 'un.'

'Did you tell the police?'

'No, I told the agency and they've taken her off their books. I wrote to her parents asking if they could return the necklace, but there was no reply.'

'And is Paul OK? You don't think he's been affected?'

'How can anyone tell? He's a sulky hormonal teenager. I don't suppose she's damaged him irreparably but he's hardly at his best anyway.'

'Did you replace Megan's money?'

El rolled her eyes.

'Sorry. D'you want another drink?'

She held out her glass and his heart sank. Even as they sat here the unknown Greta might be opening Paul's door, or Megan's – might be initiating any one or all four into some dark revolting rite. Why did they have to leave their children with strangers? Why was it not possible to tell El he wanted to go home? Because then she'd know he'd rather see the kids than her? Or because it would offend his own notion of himself, proving him to be an overprotective parent rather than a free spirit happily reunited with the woman he loved?

He took the drinks back to the table. This time would pass. Like the deserts and continents of time he had traversed in the States, heading with the idiot persistence of an insect for his distant home.

'Is Dan's bedwetting sorted?'

'It's still rather hit and miss. So, what was the best bit?'

'The Falls and New York were the highlights, like I told you. I was thinking we could have a great holiday there with the kids one summer, that eastern seaboard is a good mix – beaches, old whaling ports, swimming and history. We could rent a car—'

She nodded. 'Well, I've been invited to a conference in Texas in June, we could start there and—'

'They don't break up till July.'

'We could take them out of school for a couple of weeks.'

'It's not fair to take Paul out at this stage. And given they have six weeks off anyway, why break into school time?'

Eleanor shrugged. 'Shall we go?' She drained her drink abruptly.

It annoyed him, to go like this after he had put in the time in the pub. They got into the car in silence and he debated with himself whether to put his hand on her knee. She might just brush it off. But it might make her smile. He put it there and she ignored it so he slid it slowly up and between her thighs. She glanced at him and he grinned, and she smiled back.

'You'll have to wait till tonight now.'

'What d'you mean, "now"? Were you suggesting a quick shag under the table at the pub?'

'They had rooms.'

'Rooms?'

'There was a big sign in the car park. Rooms £30.'

'But we're going *home*.'

'Like I said, it'll have to wait.'

'Why didn't you say something?'

'It was just a thought.'

'But I'm not a mind reader.'

'If it wasn't in your head it doesn't matter.'

'That's not fair!'

'It's OK.' She laughed. 'Forget it.'

When they arrived at the house Daniel and Cara ran out clamouring to the car.

'Oh, we're better now, are we?' Eleanor remarked to Cara, who fixed herself, limpet-like, to Con's back.

'Leave her be,' he said before he could stop himself, and El walked away into the house.

Six-year-old Cara was heavy and he had to make her drop off before he could get his bags out. Hugging her he noticed that her face was pale and there were dark circles under her eyes. She didn't look well. Dan on the other hand was inches taller, chubbier and more solid, bellowing his welcome. The baby, now all of four years old. Megan appeared on the doorstep and came running down to hug him too. The relief of seeing them was so intense he had to lean against the car to get his balance. 'Where's Paul?'

'At Steve's. He's always at Steve's.'

Con was momentarily hurt by his older son's absence, then ridiculed himself. Here they all were, here were three warm solid perfect children welcoming him and Paul would soon be home too. And Eleanor, who had come to meet him with lascivious thoughts and with whom he had failed to click. He must make things right with Eleanor.

Paul, when he returned for tea, had changed more than any of the others. It was as if the bones in his face had shifted under the skin; he had the protuberant, knobbly face of a youth now, his childhood was left behind. He blushed and nodded when he saw Con, backing away from physical contact. Con felt a sudden piercing sympathy, remembering the excruciating embarrassment of walking across the quad in his first year at King's, feeling rows of eyes watching him from the first-floor windows. How many years of embarrassment must the poor boy endure, now he had entered that zone?

Cara was clingy, and in the middle of the meal she burst into tears because she wasn't allowed to sit on Con's knee. When Eleanor's thin patience snapped and she sent Cara to her room, it was all Con could do not to run after the wailing child. They continued their meal without her, Megan glowing with older-sister self-righteousness and Eleanor responding monosyllabically to Con's bright questions about her book. Greta the au pair ate silently with downcast eyes and disappeared to her room as soon as they were done. Only Paul, sealed into his bubble of adolescent angst, and Dan picking carefully at the acceptable parts of his meal, seemed unaffected.

Con bathed Dan and read him a story, then went to see Cara, who was lying under her duvet fully dressed, sucking her thumb and hiccupping. He made her wash and get into her nightie, then sat on her bed stroking her hair rhythmically until she dropped to sleep. He could have fallen asleep himself, but there was still Megan and Paul and Eleanor to go. The sound of the TV drew him into the sitting room, where Paul sat in silence and Megan giggled over a comedy programme he'd never heard of. He sat with them till it ended, cuddling Megan, then went to look for El. She wasn't in the kitchen so she must be in her study. He poured them a glass of wine each and carried hers in to her. She was on the computer, her fingers swift and methodical on the keyboard. He watched her save before she turned to him.

'Thanks. Thought I'd take advantage of you dealing with the kids. I gave Greta the evening off – I'm assuming that's what you wanted?'

He nodded, feeling he had failed some kind of test. El turned back to the screen. 'I'll be done by 9.30. Just want to finish this chapter.'

From then on, it seemed, they could hardly get in step. There were repeated moments of crackling incomprehension and distance, which had to be deliberately smashed by touch or laughter. It was as if they were angry with each other for not knowing about each other, and having to tell, to talk and explain, was cause for further irritation, because of the assumption that they did know already. They had been apart for too long to just pick it up again. It was the sort of irritation you might feel with a deaf person who has deliberately turned off his hearing aid. Each knew the other could understand, would easily understand, just didn't seem to be trying. And as time went on, and Con began to unearth various problems with the kids that El had not dealt with as thoroughly as (he believed) she should have done, the cycle of misunderstanding and blame between them became steadily more entrenched. He found out from Cara's teacher that she was best friends with a girl who had been caught stealing from other kids; and sure enough, the thefts Catherine the au pair had been charged with were down to Cara's friend – as Cara admitted when he talked to her. Dan would not play with other kids at nursery, or indeed at home. He barely communicated with anyone. A new battery of tests was instigated by Con. Paul was away from the house far too much; only ten-year-old Megan seemed on an even keel.

The trip to America was a mistake; it opened a fault line between them. He knew it at the time, and he knows it still.

At some point he must have drifted into sleep, because the next thing he knows is Alberto banging the front door and hurrying into his room.

'This number. This number was wrong. I am sorry but the bank, they keep your card.'

Alberto has typed in the wrong PIN – most likely Con has given him the wrong PIN. He has done it three times and the machine has swallowed Con's card, and there is no way for Alberto to retrieve it.

'You must ring your bank. I think they can post you a new card. But it will take time.'

Blearily, Con tries to focus on the problem. He has no money and no way of getting any. But he can't just lie here, helpless in a stranger's house. Obeying Alberto's instructions he switches on his mobile, which bleeps its 'battery low' warning and dies. He knows how it feels. He shakes his aching head at Alberto and mouths the word 'Sorry'.

Alberto leaves the room and Con closes his eyes. The bank will try to contact him at home, with news of a card misused in Bologna. The game is up.

Chapter 13

CARA IS HEROIC in her resistance to food. El is struggling miserably to remember how Con coaxed her out of her last anorexic bout. Tempting morsels are not having any success, neither are begging and pleading. It is inconceivable that Con can be knowingly doing this to Cara. A year ago, maybe – when he found out. But despite the shock waves that rocked them both then, his behaviour towards Cara never changed a jot.

It was idiotic bad luck that he did find out. Maybe that's the cause of it after all. Maybe he's simply had a very delayed reaction.

It started innocently enough, one of Cara's altruistic impulses. She decided to become a blood donor. Both El and Con agreed privately that she was probably too thin. 'But let the nurse tell her that,' argued El. 'Otherwise it's just us moaning on.' Their hope was that if she was rejected because of her weight, maybe she would become interested in eating enough to build herself up. She said she was nervous of going on her own and Con said he would take her and be a hand to hold. To his surprise, the nurse simply noted Cara's weight along with her other details, and began to collect the blood.

And it just happened, it so happened, as the nurse was dealing with Cara, and Con was standing benignly by, admiring his daughter's courage – it so happened that Cara asked what blood type she had. To which the nurse replied, type A. Con, overhearing, stepped forward helpfully to say, 'That's not possible.' It was not possible. Con and El were both type B. Their children could only be B or O. Never A. He got as far as opening his mouth to tell the nurse, and then he closed it as the truth dawned. It was possible. It was entirely possible, if Con was not Cara's father.

That evening he waited till El was alone in the kitchen then asked her, 'Who's Cara's father?'

'You, you fool.'

'She's blood group A. B plus B does not equal A.'

'She's yours. You were there when she was born, you've raised her, you've looked after her, you've loved her – she's yours.'

'But I wasn't there when she was conceived.'

'Con. This was nineteen years ago.'

'I'm curious.'

'It wasn't important. Look, I didn't even know she wasn't yours until I saw her. I mean, she could have been yours.'

Silence.

'I'm sorry, Con. I didn't know what to do. The affair ended long before she was born and it was never—'

'Does he know?'

'What?'

'Her father.'

'Of course not. No one knows and that's the way it should stay. It's irrelevant, she's nothing to do with him.'

'You must have thought I was thick. The hair. The eyes. The eczema.' He makes a noise like laughter but he isn't laughing. 'The low IQ.'

'Stop it.'

'All the others managed university. They *are* mine, I take it?'

'For fuck's sake stop it, Con. She's yours.'

'You must have found it ironic, the trouble she's given me.'

'I didn't find it anything. She's yours, she's like what she's like, she's herself. I never even thought about it, after the first few weeks. She's our child, yours and mine, she loves you and I love you and the fact of her conception was simply random.'

'Of course. Sorry I mentioned it. Bit crass of me to notice, really.'

'Please, Con. I know it's a shock. I know it was wrong. But I agonised about it and there was nothing to be gained by telling you. Look how you love her now. Look how she loves you.'

'Blue eyes, recessive gene, with brown-eyed parents.'

'That's possible—'

'I trusted you.'

'I'm sorry. Look, it was a long time ago.'

'So who was the stud? The blond blue-eyed Viking daddy?'

'You didn't know him. I don't know him any more, it's in the past.'

'Which makes it all right.'

'No. No. But—'

'Have you *ever* been faithful to me?'

He went upstairs, El remembers, without waiting for a reply. He was upstairs, quiet, she didn't know what to do. She wanted to beg him never to tell Cara, not that she thought he would, but she wanted the reassurance, and she knew that in his current state he would not reassure her about anything. When she went up to bed he was not there and she realised he had gone to Paul's old room. There was nothing to be gained by pursuing him at that time of night.

She left before he was up in the morning, and then it was there, between them, when she came home at night. He would not return her greeting when she came into the kitchen. Then he said, 'There's nothing left. Not a vestige of decency in twenty-six years of marriage.'

'You know that's not true. You know we were happy. After Cara was born was the happiest year of our lives.'

'Because you lied to me and got away with it,' Con replied.

'Because we loved each other and our children. Think of the things we did then – the holidays, the games we used to play, the parties. Don't you remember that weekend we went away for your birthday?'

'Don't I remember how you manipulated me, how you used your great charm and cleverness to create the illusion of love, which like a sad fool I imagined to be real? Don't I remember how it was our best time, the time you were busy hoodwinking me? Don't I remember how you've made a fraud of everything that matters?'

'Don't trash everything just because you're angry.'

'It's not me that's doing the trashing. You're the one that trashed it by fucking someone else and bearing his child and lying about it, lie after lie after lie.'

'I am not lying now. It was the happiest time of my life.'

'Knowing you had betrayed me and got away with it was the happiest time of your life. Yes.'

'No. I was happy because I loved you.'

'Guilt.'

'Love.'

'Guilt. And then we both got paid back with the birth of Dan.'

'Don't say that.'

'Why not? Aren't we in the throes of Greek tragedy here? The wife pollutes the bloodline and the foolish cuckolded husband loves her all the more for it and she luxuriates in her moral squalor. Until the gods bring punishment in their own good time: the next child born to this blind, arrogant and mendacious couple is solitary and friendless, afflicted by the gods for his parents' wrongdoings.'

'Con, don't say things which can never be put right. Don't destroy everything.'

'Why not? You did.'

'You're mad if you don't know when we were happy.'

'Cuckolded. Unsuccessful. Mad. Have you finished?'

How could she talk to him? There was nothing she could say. And neither of them could sustain that level of hostility. After a while Con stopped sleeping in Paul's bed; he came back to bed with El, and neither of them said anything about it. It was an untouchable subject – like Louis, who Con also knew about. There were chasms in their marriage, which they skirted without comment. Was it to keep up appearances? For the sake of the children? For self-protection, because to do anything else would be too traumatic? But Con has chosen to leave now, after all those months of going through the motions of a normal married life.

Lying in his bed in Bologna, Conrad has no real sense of time. Alberto brings him drinks and food with regularity, and sometimes switches on the little bedside light. But Con is not sure if he has been ill for hours or days. He is sweaty and light-headed but his memory continues to unspool, and he can focus on that, and forget all about the clammy sickbed in the blue motor-racing bedroom.

The saga with Maddy continues, of course. A few days after the distressing scene in the Indian restaurant, she sends him a very long and sane-sounding email. She apologises for her behaviour and reveals that she suffers from chronic insomnia, which sometimes reduces her to 'a really pathetic state'. She knows she was rude and silly, and she is sorry she spoke so disparagingly about her fellow PECA members, who should be respected for the years of selfless work they have devoted to the cause of animal liberation. She is mortified to think that she insulted him. She can't live with herself until she knows that he has forgiven her. She doesn't want anything from him but forgiveness. Please please please can he reply, just to let her know he doesn't despise her? And so she can pay him back for the lunch she wasted.

Of course he replies, telling her that he knows what it is like to feel as if the world is against you. And that his daughter Cara has suffered with insomnia. Maddy replies with gratitude, and reveals that PECA's internal strife is resolved and that the website is up and running again. 'You will find your statement here,' she writes, and the link is pasted in. Con clicks on it and finds his list laid out in a rather indigestible slab of yellow type against a turquoise background. On the plus side, it is all there, no one has tampered with his words. But he has to wonder how many people have troubled to read it. The PECA web man's design skills are clearly limited. And it is obvious that the addition of photos would improve the page considerably.

It does not surprise Con when Maddy raises this in her next email. Could they just meet to talk about the photos again?

She doesn't want to pressurise him but he must recognise that nothing has changed for those poor monkeys since he first visited CBL in March. Words alone are never enough to persuade people. It is photos that make all the difference. Please, can they meet; she will come to Manchester, he doesn't need to travel anywhere, she will come to a hotel in Manchester and meet with him, and he doesn't need to worry about the way she was last time because she's got some marvellous new sleeping tablets and she's feeling on top of the world. Con wonders if he should advise her that her sleeping tablets were almost certainly tested on animals. But it would be petty, and is beside the point. He fobs her off for a while, but when she sends him an email with a date and the suggestion that they meet after he's finished work, in the bar at Malmaison, he agrees. It is not as if he is doing anything else to try to change things at CBL; Malmaison is new and he quite fancies a look inside; and if she is flaky, well, so is he, and half the rest of the world. Before he goes to meet her he deletes their entire email correspondence.

Malmaison is an odd choice of venue for her, he thinks, but maybe she has chosen it for proximity to the station. He finds himself rather excited by the thought of seeing her again. And her appearance justifies his excitement. She has clearly made an effort. She is wearing a silky black top with a scoop neckline that reveals the swell of her breasts. Her hair is glossy, and her walk more swaying – he realises it is the first time he has seen her in heels. 'You look so well,' he says. 'Are you here for work?'

'Yes. Meetings. You know, clients.' She leans forward, exposing more cleavage. 'Conrad, we really need those photos.'

'Maddy, I've explained—'

'You've brought them, haven't you. Can I just have a look?'

She knows he has. But he feels unwilling to concede so quickly. He will let her look, and then they can discuss it. He passes her the envelope. While she shuffles slowly through them he orders drinks, keeping an eye on her face, afraid of her distress. When she's done she puts them face down on the table and rests her head in her hands.

'Maddy?'

'They're vile.'

'Yes.'

'How can you think it's all right to keep this quiet?' When she raises her face, a deep flush has spread up from her throat.

'That's why I didn't want you to look before.'

'We need to pick half a dozen to go online. Now, without wasting any more time.'

'But—'

She is rising to her feet. 'I've got a scanner in my room. We can blow them up on screen.' She is on the move, her wine glass held aloft, her flushed cheeks and glittering eyes blazing a way through the milling drinkers, and he is following her like a child towards the lifts where she walks in without hesitation, pressing the button so swiftly that the doors almost slam on him.

In her room, which is oppressively swathed in black and red, she sits at the desk at her open laptop. She feeds the photos one by one into the scanner, which is alongside. Con perches awkwardly on the vast bed. It is strewn with her clothes; he has to shift a bra and tights to make a space. She is copying all of them. He hasn't even agreed… he seems to be in a trance of indecision. He stares blankly at the deep red wall, while she taps busily on the keyboard, ignoring him. It is taking a long time. Then she unplugs something and brings her laptop to the bed and sits beside him. 'This is the best, lying on his side, because you can see the hopelessness in his face. The vomit one, obviously. This one, clawing at the neck? I know it's not totally clear, but if we use the next one too…'

He has not looked at the photos since he showed Gus. He knows what they are, he has seen the real thing. But now his stomach churns as he sees them with her eyes and understands that it is beyond the pale to keep them secret. On the computer the pictures are bigger, brighter, more detailed. If it means losing his job, so be it.

When she has made the selection she returns to her seat at the desk and he watches mutely as she works at the computer for another few minutes, saving material and firing off an email. She closes the laptop and turns to face him. 'Well,' she says. 'That's that.'

Suddenly she is beside him on the bed with her hand on his thigh and her face very close. 'Thank you,' she says. She leans in and kisses him on the lips.

It is a shock and not a shock. Her hand slides up his thigh, her breast presses against his chest, her body is glowing with heat. He responds automatically but the images of the monkeys are still in his head. After a moment he leans back and takes her hands in his.

'Maddy, listen. You don't have to thank me. I mean, you don't have to thank me like this. It's not a transaction.'

'Isn't it?' she says, looking up at him. 'Isn't it a transaction?'

He begins to smile foolishly, raising a hand to smooth her hair, but she stands up. 'Why did you come up here with me then?'

'Because you wanted to copy the pictures.'

'Really?' She laughs.

'Really.'

'You didn't come with me into my hotel room because you thought you'd get a chance to screw me?'

Con doesn't understand why she is speaking to him like this. 'We were meeting about the pictures.'

She rolls her eyes. 'Why wouldn't you let me have them last time we met?'

'Because I hoped there might be another way of doing it. Because I was worried for my job.'

'So what's changed?'

'Time has passed, and I've realised that like you said, the statement alone doesn't have enough impact.'

She shakes her head contemptuously. 'It wouldn't have made any difference what I wore or did?'

'No. Why would it?'

She perches on the edge of the desk, ferreting in her handbag. 'You people make me sick,' she says.

Conrad is sitting on her bed, his thighs sinking into it, surrounded by her discarded clothes, and nowhere to put his hands. 'Which people? Scientists?'

'Scientists, husbands, middle-class wankers. Smile.' She raises her camera and takes his picture.

'What are you doing?' Con stands up, blinking. 'I don't know what I've done to annoy you but—'

She gives her fake laugh again. 'Oh, where shall I start? In Birmingham, you think I'm so stupid I don't even know where I'm staying and you have to lead me there by the hand.'

'But you *didn't*,' he starts, vividly recalling leading her across the road.

'But I *did*,' she mocks, 'only you assumed I was thick.'

'I was trying to help,'

'Why do you think I need help? Because I'm not as clever as you?' She continues to snap him as she talks, and he holds his hand in front of his face, idiotically, as if she were paparazzi and he some kind of criminal celebrity. 'You have to show me what a big strong male you are by carrying my bag and holding open doors. You tell me what to eat and drink—' Con recalls offering her wine. He feels nauseated. '—as if I'm too much of a child to have any tastes of my own.'

'You asked me to carry your bag upstairs,' he protests. 'You said you didn't like lifts.'

'Does that give you permission to be a sexist wanker?'

'You just got in a lift,' he blurts.

She laughs in his face. 'From the start you've been stringing me along with little bits of excuses about your important job, which consists of torturing helpless animals. You tell me I'm looking well when what you mean is, sexually available. When you can see a bit of tit, suddenly you are open to persuasion. When you think you'll get your end away, you give me the photos you should have given me three months ago.'

Con sits again. Anger is beginning to burn inside him. At himself, of course, as well as at this crazy bitch. 'Then why aren't I fucking you right now?'

She shrugs. 'Because you're a hypocrite?'

He adjusts his clothes and heads for the door.

'Or maybe you just can't get it up,' she adds. He closes the door on the sound of her sniggering.

Con's analysis of this encounter changes, depending on his mood. He has been low enough at times to believe everything she says, acknowledging her itemisation of his failings. At other times he recognises that she is insane, because frankly, why would she turn on him when he has actually given her what she wants – assuming the photos are what she wants? Was she offended that he didn't want sex with her? Surely not. The point is, he might well have done, if she hadn't been so crass. But doesn't that prove the accuracy of her analysis? Did he only shy away from sex because she presented it too bluntly as a transaction, offending his delicate sensibilities? He would have liked it perhaps, if sex had been an added extra, with some pretence at her being attracted to him. Is that it – she offended his vanity?

No doubt about it, she has succeeded if her aim was to undermine him and fill him with self-loathing. She has succeeded very well. Beyond all this (which is, he reminds himself, trivial, because it is only about his own feelings, which don't actually matter to anyone else) there is the larger issue of her malevolence, and the power she has to do harm.

Which is revealed very quickly. In succession, the home of the director of research at CBL is daubed in red paint with *ANIMAL KILLER YOUR NEXT*; Gus's car windscreen is smashed with a brick bearing the taped message *DEATH TO VIVISECTIONISTS*; and two of the colleagues Con named to her receive parcels through the post containing blood-sodden menstrual towels labelled *HIV POSITIVE*. That's to say, two colleagues admit this has happened to them. There may be others who don't care to make the information public.

He goes over what she knows. About El and the children. She knows where he lives. What will she do to his house and car? What will she send him in the post?

He needs to go to the police, and he needs to tell El.

No one is making the connections. No one is connecting him to any of this, not even Gus. His complaints about Carrington Bio-Life seem forgotten. The pictures have gone viral with no reference to him. They are attributed to 'a mole on the CBL staff'.

Con lies awake at night waiting for Maddy to strike again. But nothing comes, not so much as an email. He tries to tell himself that the red paint and brick and sanitary towels are not her but some more extreme member of her protest group, acting on the information she has delivered. One of the photos makes the *Guardian* and El points it out to him with distaste. 'Don't you and Gus use CBL? This looks a bit horrid.'

'Yes. I don't know,' he says. 'They must be subject to routine inspections, surely.'

Then El starts badgering him to resign. He comes within a hair's breadth of telling her. But she makes him furious. With her revulsion and her holier-than-thou and her always knowing better than him. With her great career. He gets angry and says things which should not be said. He defends his research and the animal house to her. Why? Why? Because it is not up to her, it's up to *him*. And if she had an ounce of imagination, and real interest in him, wouldn't she guess that the mole must be him? Wouldn't she understand immediately how hateful this is to him?

He endures a couple of weeks in which time passes in slow motion, and he patrols El's car, his car, the children's movements, the lab car park, as if only his own assiduous attention has the power to protect them.

Then comes an email. *Don't worry, I haven't forgotten you, wanker.* He deletes it instantly then moves it from the deleted folder into a storage folder which he calls MAD. It is evidence. He should go to the police. But it is as much as he can do to drag himself from home to work and back again, and fuel himself with oven-ready pap from the freezer before crawling into bed again. A kind of grey mist is closing in on him.

He has to tell El because there is a threat. But what would he tell her? That he saw abuses at CBL and was too ineffectual to get anyone to take them seriously, so gave his photos to a crazy animal rights woman? That he has given her enough information to track down various players including his entire family, and that she has already attacked people and property on the basis of what he told her?

But this is not the reason for not telling El. It is not because it will make him look bad – though of course it will. The reason for not telling El is her El-ishness; she will briskly consider and then pronounce that the best course of action is X. And X will be a course of action that he doesn't want. It will probably involve calling the police and escalating the level of danger. Or El may decide to contact Maddy herself and talk some sense into her. Yes, that would be El's preferred line of attack, and then Maddy would give her version of Con's behaviour, maybe worse, and show El the picture of him sitting on her hotel bed surrounded by her underwear, and El would be contemptuous of him, and either be at personal risk of violence from Maddy, or (more likely) succeed in reasoning with her and prevent her from causing any further mischief. At this moment Con cannot tell which would be worse – for El to be hurt, or for her to solve the whole situation with calm and reason. Both would be insufferable, and both would prove him spineless and despicable.

A few more emails arrive – they are all short, and all menacing.

She is certainly planning something. As day follows day, action becomes less and less possible, because if something needed doing, why hasn't he already done it? He rings the children in rotation, one per night, calling Megan early before she leaves for the theatre. He's practised at gleaning their news and movements while implying that the ship of Home sails smoothly on, bearing El and himself towards a happy sunset. 'There's no news,' he repeats. 'No news is good news, eh.'

Beyond this and the rare functional exchange with El, it is possible not to speak to anyone at all, one day blurs into the next. It is by pure chance that he catches a news item on the radio while driving El's car to the garage for its service. It is about activists and an animal research facility. A woman and two men have been arrested for vandalism and threatening behaviour. Cars have been defaced with red paint and individuals have received written threats. The accused cannot be named...

He knows it is her.

He scours the internet for more information but there isn't much. Two individuals have been apprehended with cans of red paint on private property, and the third has been identified as a result of questioning. Bail is refused, the trial will take place in December. A month away. She is in prison for at least a month.

The wash of relief does not last. They can't put her away for long on 'vandalism' and 'threatening behaviour'. She'll probably have served her time before it comes to trial. And what use is any of it? The protestors are the villains, and the research facility is an innocent victim – no one is doing anything about conditions there. As for what Maddy might tell her lawyer – Con realises that he will almost certainly be named. He might get called as a witness. It will be impossible to keep it secret from El.

Is it around this time that the nightmares begin? It seems as if he has lived with them for years, but that can't be true, because Maddy figures in them. She is in prison, in a cage, exactly like the cages in the animal house. She is chattering with rage, like the monkey. She is tearing at her own flesh, with razor-sharp nails, tearing, lacerating, screaming in his face, and he stands there splattered with her blood, unable to move a muscle. There is no key to her cage. He wakes slick with her warm blood, but when he wipes his face on the sheet it is nothing but his own oily sweat.

As the trial approaches he remains in suspension, waiting for the email, the phone call, that will drag him in... but nothing. Is it possible she hasn't named him? Why? Is she saving him for worse punishment? On the day they are found guilty the three are named: John Hogan, Tom Masters, Rebecca Vine. Rebecca Vine? There are no photos. It has to be her, who else could it be? The woman's sentence is the longest, six weeks in prison and community service. She has already been held for four weeks. She walks free.

Con checks his email obsessively, forty, fifty, a hundred times a day. *What punishment is good enough for what you've done? I should rip your heart out*, he reads. He no longer trusts himself to drive; shapes of other cars seem to rush towards him from the edges of his vision. He has to slow down and pull over to the kerb and people hoot and gesticulate. At roundabouts he waits and hesitates until he can wait and hesitate no longer, and then he plunges out into the path of oncoming vehicles, accelerating wildly. He arrives at work sweating, his heart pounding. Better to take the train. And there is a twenty-minute walk either side of the train journey; exercise is good for sleeplessness, he's told Cara often enough. It makes no difference, in point of fact. But at least he's not behind the wheel and about to kill someone. *Long distance torture is easy, eh. What the eye doesn't see. You will see, shitface, trust me.*

There is a strand of him, always, who is Con, observing his own behaviour with detachment; assessing him like the subject of an experiment, noting that he is suffering panic attacks and other symptoms of stress; that his sleeplessness is a form of depression; that his appetite and libido are significantly reduced, that he is losing weight, that his hair is now entirely grey, his eyes dull, his skin dry and flaky. If he was an animal, he should be put on a different regime. *See you soon, sweetie.* Not if he can help it.

He sets off for the conference on automatic pilot. A month earlier, he would not have been able to allow himself to go, because his presence at home, checking, checking, for the safety of El and the children and his colleagues at the lab, was essential. But now time has warped it and he can see that his checking is ineffectual. His presence near those he would like to protect is not only no protection but quite possibly an added risk, since he himself is target number one and proximity to him may cause them to suffer collateral damage – when she strikes.

He is almost demob happy, packing for the conference. He will be leaving her behind along with all his other woes. Different rooms, a different city, decent meals; people who know him, knew him, knew the confident and amiable social being Conrad Evanson. (Was he confident? Was he amiable? He cannot begin to imagine how they saw him. But surely not as this trembling semi-transparent wreck, not as someone incapable of holding it together...)

Everything goes well. He takes the train to the airport, his flight is on time, his hotel room is on the third floor with a view of trees. He is able to perform the conference camaraderie and feels humbled by the commitment of his colleagues to their research. It is a long time since he has been able to imagine that what he is doing is important. On the Sunday evening, the mood after dinner is convivial. He sits with Park, a Korean who did his Ph.D. with Gus and worked in the cubicle next to Con's lab. Park fell in love with an Irish girl, of whom his family disapprove. The girl doesn't want to move to Korea, but Park's career there is really taking off, he's second in department, it would be crazy to leave now. They want to marry, but what sense does it make if they don't even live in the same country? As he and Park drain their wine Con listens and advises with keen interest. Afterwards, he realises he has actually forgotten about Maddy. He has spent the whole evening not thinking of her once. But then comes the walk back to his hotel.

It is a short walk from the conference centre in Munich to Conrad's hotel. Park is staying with friends a tram ride away. Con walks with him to the tram stop then turns the corner towards his own hotel, away from the brightly lit main thoroughfare.

This is a quiet residential street; on the corner there's a building site enclosed by hoardings, then well-to-do houses, with brass nameplates of dentists and lawyers, shuttered windows, small coiffured shrubs in planters. The streetlamps are heritage, resembling gas lamps and giving as little light. As he moves towards the end of the empty street Conrad hears a lighter step behind him. He glances back. There's a squat tree between him and the nearest streetlamp, and the shadows of the branches reach across the street. A woman is coming towards him through the shadows. Her.

Chapter 14

ELEANOR IS LOST. If Con was delaying coming home to teach her a lesson, this is too long. If he is with another woman called Maddy, it is implausible that he has not contacted the kids. If he is kidnapped, there's no ransom. If he's ill or dead, someone must know. This silence, extending for days, stretches her nerves taut and keeps her awake all night, making her heart flip every time the phone rings. Her work is going to pot; Cara is keeping nocturnal hours and not eating; Paul comes and goes at random, so angry he barely speaks to her; Megan is on stage every night, and Dan is Dan. El has sent Louis an email asking him not to contact her, which he is respecting. She didn't imagine he would do anything else – what *could* he do? But still maybe she hoped. It makes her all the more solitary and unreal. She is a ghost. Her urgent vivid life has become a painted backdrop against which she sees herself standing immobile, with no lines and no direction. How will this end? How can she make it end? Sometimes people are missing for years. Then it would be up to her, by main force, to wrestle her life back into some kind of reality. But where will the cut-off point be and what will signal it? What will stop this grey succession of helpless, passive hours? How can she regain control?

She hates it when the phone rings. Some people are avoiding her but others want to offer their support and ask how things are going. She hates rehashing the same worn phrases; no, no news yet, the kids are being very good, thanks; no, there's nothing you can do but very kind of you to offer. Even the smallest task she sets herself, such as cooking something tempting for Cara, becomes overwhelming. She sits indecisively flicking through recipe books, then has to search cupboards for ingredients and make a shopping list, then worries about leaving Cara alone or missing a vital phone call. Yes, everyone has her mobile, but the home phone is the real one, the one Con would ring. Being in the house for when there is news is the only positive thing she can do, so then it's back to the recipe books to find something which can be made from ingredients already in the cupboards, or trying to decide whether to phone Paul and ask him to shop. And she is doing no good staying in with Cara because Cara hides in her room and when El knocks on the door with a drink or a snack, Cara thanks her mechanically but doesn't talk, answering only monosyllabically when El dredges up some-thing to say to her. She can't communicate with Cara – not in this state – Con is the only one who can.

El cleans the house automatically. It is distressingly filthy, she has not cleaned it properly for months, and neither, despite the agreement that he should, has Con. Cleaning, washing the grime off the paintwork, polishing the soap residue off the shower cubicle, reaching down all the ceiling cobwebs with a broom, gives her the sense of accomplishing something. But she cannot bear to use the vacuum, because its noise may block out the sound of a phone call. She creeps backwards down the car-peted stairs with a brush and dustpan, brushing each step clean, raising small clouds of dust. She tests herself by trying to set a date when she will return to work, but the tide of matters she is already behind with feels so daunting that she wants to duck and avoid it. And beyond that, she can't see the point. What is the point of going to work? What is the point of all those things she was so busy busy busy with?

She is cleaning kitchen windows when the phone rings. She reaches it on the third ring. The police. Conrad's bank card has been used in Bologna, Italy.

'So he's in Bologna?'

No, his bank card is. She is reminded that it may have been stolen. There may be difficult circumstances. The bank card was used with a wrong PIN, it may not have been used by Conrad. Eleanor is advised to contact the bank where it was used; she is given the number and the name of someone who speaks English.

Now there's a blur of activity, now everything shifts. The Italian man she speaks to, having requested Con's account number and other lengthy verification, tells her the person who used the card was Alberto Carpazo, who has left his name and address, and has explained to a bank clerk that the owner of the card, Conrad Evanson, is at his house and is too ill to use the card himself. Alberto's address is dictated to El.

'Is there – did he leave a phone number?'

'Madam, he did.'

When she has written everything down El hangs up the phone and sits staring at it. He is alive. In Italy. In a strange man's house. As far as she knows, Con doesn't speak Italian. Relief and fear are enough to paralyse her for a moment. He's found. But he's ill. And, since he hasn't phoned her, she has to assume he doesn't want to see her. Unless he is too ill to phone? What is he – what *was* he – up to? Her impulse to phone Alberto's number dies. She paces the house for twenty minutes then checks flights to Bologna. There's one late this afternoon from Manchester, seats are available.

She goes up to Cara's room and tells her, and suddenly Cara is focused and energised, though tears are running down her face.

'We should phone him right now, Mum. The Italian.'

'That was my first thought. But we don't really know what's going on. Maybe it would be better just to go there. If Con wanted us to know where he was, he would have phoned. His mobile's still off, I tried it. If he's too ill to phone then we can't talk to him anyway. And if this man – Alberto – was lying, then phoning will give him warning that we are coming, do you see?'

'But he's *there*—'

'Yes, and we can be there by this evening. There's a flight at 3.45.'

'Would they have told him? That the bank has contacted the police?'

El shrugs. 'There are too many unknowns. We don't know why he's there, we don't know what state he's in, we only have a stranger's word for it that he *is* there. If we go to the house unannounced – say we get there early evening – he won't be expecting us. We're more likely to find *something* out than if we ring and give him time to vanish.'

Cara is shaking her head. 'But why would he want to vanish?'

'Darling, it's what he's done. We don't know why. But if he started by doing that, we have to assume he still doesn't want us to know where he is.'

Eleanor books their flight. With phoning the other children, and packing, and downloading maps of Bologna and booking a hotel on a street close to Alberto's address, the morning is gone and they are on the plane before there's time to think again. Cara looks terrible, and though El tells herself she couldn't have left her alone at home, she knows she could have asked Paul to stay with her. El's notion that she is bringing Cara for Cara's own good is countered by the knowledge that she is bringing Cara for El's own good. Con will want to see Cara, whereas he might not want to see El. In that sense she is using Cara, and the girl looks on the point of collapse. El will make everything easy. They'll get a taxi from the airport, drop their things at the hotel then go straight on to Alberto's. Whatever happens there, she will get Cara back to the hotel for food and sleep before it is too late. El squashes down the bubble of hope which keeps trying to rise in her chest.

She turns over in her mind whether there might be danger. Whether she might be walking – and walking Cara – into a trap. If Alberto is a front, for kidnappers, say, and El and Cara deliver themselves to his door… But what is the point in kidnapping a whole family? And making no ransom demands? And El has left Alberto's address with the other kids; she has promised to ring them later tonight. Things will swing into action pretty quickly if she doesn't call them.

The problems begin before they even land. The time for their descent into Bologna airport has already passed when an announcement is made by their pilot. 'Weather conditions on the ground are now unfavourable. There is a fog. We will follow a holding pattern and wait to see if conditions improve. On the advice of the control tower we will take time. Apologies for the delay to your journey.' From the babble of other passengers El deduces that this is not uncommon in Bologna and that if the fog persists the pilot will divert to Milan. Cara begins to cry. El puts her arm around the girl's skinny shoulders and tries not to cry herself. She is coming round to believing that this is some kind of punishment: that in every protracted detail since Con's non-return, she is being punished for her heedless selfishness, for her busy careless irresponsible life, for the happy El that she has been. Now she must submit to fate. She has no control.

And indeed there is no situation she can imagine where one has less control than in an aeroplane. Twice the pilot makes his descent, and glints of airport lights are briefly visible through the dense black cloud. But on each occasion he rears back up into the sky, the engines screaming, the passengers silent and white-faced. After the second attempt he announces that the tower reports the fog is lifting slightly and that he will make one final attempt before abandoning and diverting to Milan.

Cara is shaking. El is a seasoned air traveller, she knows they are unlikely to die – and yet that fear is so all-consuming that it has engulfed the entire planeload. They have been reminded that they are in a tin can thousands of feet above the earth and that only those screaming engines and the pilot's skill stand between them and a plummet to the ground. When a suicide attempt becomes real – when the tablets are in the mouth, or the feet balanced on the span of the bridge – how can anyone ever go through with it? El wonders. The will to live is so strong, so intense and unthinking, how can it be annulled? She wonders if Con thought of suicide before he took off. If running away (which is what she now guesses he has done) was a coward's sui-cide? She can't call him a coward, though. Since his absence has reduced her to an abject state. He was conscious of something that she was not prepared to admit. Their failure, their cruelty to one another, the wasting of their lives; she pretended to be oblivious, and Conrad, he acknowledged it. She is in no position to call him a coward.

The third attempt at landing seems to happen in slow motion, the descent taking place through complete blackness. El finds herself physically braced and desperate for the abort, the upward lurch – when the engine sound changes, and with a shocking jolt they are on the runway. The airport lights appear through shifting swathes of fog. They are taxiing along the runway, they are on the ground and heading for the light. As their shock disperses, the passengers begin, raggedly, to applaud.

Everything is slow. Freezing fog lingers in the narrow streets of Bologna. The taxi they have patiently queued for takes them as far as a traffic jam then sits there; the only thing moving is the meter. Glimpses of the streets in the foggy darkness reveal ancient buildings with barred windows, everything shut up and closed against them. At their hotel El decides Cara should go to bed immediately but Cara refuses, and so they are out into the icy blackness again. Their taxi driver, who insisted on payment when they arrived, has gone, and anyway Alberto's address is within walking distance. The hotel receptionist gives them a coloured tourist map of the city and draws in biro the line they should follow. El takes Cara's arm but Cara shakes her off, and so they move singly along the murky street. The streets are more like alleyways, and other dark figures materialise suddenly, their footsteps muffled by the fog. Lamps are visible as haloed blobs, illuminating a few inches of fog around them but shedding no light on the street. El can't see which way up to hold the map, never mind the biro line. The air is cold and heavy with moisture, El is gasping for breath, her lungs half-suffocated. She can think of nothing but danger now. Her own skin and hair are wet, which means Cara's will be too. She's an idiot, she should have waited till morning. Now they are heading uphill under covered arches. In the empty roadway the fog has lifted, but it still drifts under the arches, revealing and then closing off their route. She peers at numbers on the ancient doors; the place is silent and closed up as if all the inhabitants are sleeping or dead. El checks her watch, just after 8pm, it's not late – then remembers 8pm UK is 9pm Italian time. Well, too bad, they are here; they are wet and cold and bedraggled and perhaps asking for trouble, but she knocks hard on the door and stands, shoulders squared, between Cara and the door, waiting for it to open.

When Alberto ushers them into Con's room, Cara runs to hug him. When she has settled, curled on the bed beside him, her head nestled into Con's shoulder, he looks up to meet Eleanor's eyes. She waits in the doorway.

'I'm sorry,' she says at last but Conrad is speaking too, at the same instant. 'What? What did you say?' she asks.

'I said I'm sorry.'

'We're both—'

'Yes,' he says.

Now she's able to move forward and kiss him and take in the unhealthy heat of his skin, his pallor, his red eyes. 'You've got flu.'

'Or something like it, yes. Alberto has been taking good care of me.'

She sinks to her knees on the opposite side of the bed to Cara, and Con reaches awkwardly to put his arm around her shoulders. She is suddenly embarrassed at the thought of Alberto watching this maudlin scene, but when she wipes her eyes and looks up, he is gone and the door is closed. She moves the lamp off the small bedside table and sits on the table, taking Con's warm hand between hers.

'Have you got somewhere to stay?' he asks.

'Hotel, it's quite near. Shall I come and fetch you in the morning?'

He nods.

El knows there is all the time in the world now to talk, but still she can't make herself wait. 'Were you running away from me?'

Con takes a long time to answer and she wishes she hadn't asked, especially with Cara listening. 'It's hard to say. I didn't start with the intention of running at all. No, I didn't start by running away from you.'

El's eyes well up again. What if she had lost him? 'I love you,' she whispers.

Amazingly, Con grins at her. A ghost of the old Conrad grin. 'That's good,' he says. 'I love you too.'

'And me,' comes Cara's muffled voice from Conrad's shoulder.

'And you, my little Cara.' He turns his head on the pillow and plants a kiss on her hair.

The three of them cling to one another in silence.

In the morning it is decided they will stay at the hotel until Con is fit to travel. Cara's constant presence makes it impossible for Con and El to talk, which is good, El realises. He is weak and sleepy and still running a temperature. There are lots of things it is better not to say. It is Cara who asks Con about what happened to him, and his explanation – that he is fed up with his work and wanted a day or two on his own to decide whether to quit – is plausible enough, as is his request that they should take a present of some kind to Alberto, who has played the Good Samaritan.

El leaves Cara with Con and goes in search of expensive chocolates and wine. A work crisis followed by illness and collapse is an explanation that everyone will be able to understand and El wonders if, in fact, she wants to know any more than this. He left without telling her, without talking to her, and for reasons which may not all be to do with her. The issue of Mad – of another woman, if there is or was one – isn't it better to let it lie? Conrad is not with Mad, after all. And that would be the only real betrayal, El realises – if he actually left her for another woman. She can see, they both know, he wanted her to find him. And he must know that she wanted to find him. That any sense of relief at his absence lasted for all of ten minutes. That without him she made no sense – none of them did, the family made no sense without him. If he doesn't know it then she can tell him. But there's no rush.

Chapter 15

PAUL, MEGAN AND Dan are all at the house when Conrad, Eleanor and Cara arrive home from Bologna. Megan has organised a meal to welcome them. Sitting at table, the centre of their attention, Con feels overwhelmed, like a child at his own birthday party. *There'll be tears soon*, he imagines himself saying. Each of them has worried about him and grieved for him; he is unworthy.

'Did you honestly think we wouldn't worry?' says Megan. 'You thought no one would notice you'd gone?'

'Well,' says Con. 'Well, you'd notice, of course. But I suppose I didn't imagine it would upset you unduly… I mean, you've all got busy lives.'

'So busy we don't care what happens to our father,' remarks Paul acidly.

'Paul thought I'd murdered you,' El contributes.

There is a moment Con can't read, as Paul and El lock eyes. He decides to laugh. 'Well, I'm not sure I would have blamed her. I was miserable company.'

'It's not a crime to be miserable,' says El softly. Con really is afraid he will cry.

'Paul said the police will assume it was the spouse. I told him he was being stupid,' says Cara.

Con glances at her thin white face, and at her plate. 'I hope you don't think you've finished,' he tells her.

'For God's sake, Dad! I'm an adult!'

'Then eat like one.'

'Ba – bum!' goes Paul, and Dan pats his palm against the table for applause. El glances at him and laughs. There are so many of them, El and Dan and Cara and Megan and Paul, so bright and big and noisy, Con wants to take in each one of them properly and rejoice in their presence but the conversation keeps jumping on and changing and they fire questions at him which he can't answer and by the end of the meal he is dizzy with their energy and speed.

It is extraordinary to be home. Everything is so poignant – so precious. In the morning, before the children are up, his and El's breakfast mugs and plates wait to be cleared, one last slice of toast leaning crookedly against the marmalade. They woke early and the two of them sat here facing each other across the table and ate their breakfast together. That's when he told her about Maddy. These crumby plates bear witness. The low winter sunlight slants in through the Victorian window he put in on the landing, with blue and red glass in its corners. It stains the white wall of the staircase red, blue, red, blue. The banister rail is smooth beneath his hand; it has been painted white, then blue, then sanded back to the bare wood and varnished, during the years that they have lived here. There is the quiet bedroom where he and El sleep in that big double bed, he with two soft pillows, she with one hard. His garden, desolate and sodden but showing the first hints of spring; a cluster of snowdrops, spears of daffodil leaves, a blackbird singing.

He feels as weak and grateful as a convalescent.

'You *are* a convalescent,' El tells him. 'You've been ill. You need to give yourself time.'

He will. On Monday he'll go to the doctor and get a sick note. It is amazing that he can be here in this beautiful house which belongs to him and El; with his wife, whom he loves; with his children.

It is only after they have all departed on Sunday afternoon that he and El really have the place to themselves. He wanders into his work room and contemplates the gaps left by the removal of his files and in-trays. Presumably the police will return things now he's home. When they do, perhaps he'll have a bonfire. El appears in his doorway.

'D'you fancy a walk? The sun's shining.'

'Good idea.'

'Just a short one,' she says. 'You old invalid.'

'The canal and then back along the old railway line?'

El nods and they put on boots and coats in silence. Once they are off the road she takes his hand. There's a fitful wind and the low sun flickers between heavy clouds. He notices that the hawthorn beside the path has tiny buds like hard little nipples. Out here, in the cold air, it is possible to breathe.

'Well,' he says.

'Well,' says El.

He wants to be honest. 'I'm not very good at answering your questions because so much was wrong. I mean, everything was wrong.'

'I know. That's to say, I didn't know. But once you were gone I worked it out.'

'For you as well?'

She shrugs. 'Work is fine. It usually is. I suppose because it is, I immerse myself in it and I let everything else go to hell.'

'I was a drag on you.'

'Well, you were. But I wasn't exactly treating you well. I mean, the thing with Louis—'

'Tell me.'

'I don't quite know. How it got to that stage. I suppose he's the cleverest person in the department; he understands without me having to explain. He's quick, he's funny—'

'So. What will you do?'

She stops abruptly, pulling Con round to face her. 'I'm telling the truth, you fool. Can't you see we have to?'

'Yes. Of course.'

'I've finished with him. I understand how crap it was.'

Con holds still, forcing himself not to ask how Louis has taken the news. El looks back up the path then returns her gaze to his. 'I want to be with you.'

He allows a grin to break across his face. 'Thank you, my Lady.'

'Idiot,' she says, flapping at his arm with her free hand, and moving on down the hill. 'Idiot.'

'Yes, I am. I could see myself, like a great blot. But it all got so knotted up I could never talk to you about it – the awfulness of the animal house and Gus and everyone ignoring me, and then Maddy and the threats and the damage she was doing, which was all my fault… I couldn't see a way out and I couldn't see a way to tell you. I thought you would despise me.'

'Oh Con.'

'Well, why not? I was despicable.'

There's a silence. They walk on down the steep, gritty path

towards the canal and a string of geese pass, honking overhead. 'I was impatient,' she says eventually. 'I'm always too impatient.'

Con shrugs. 'You wanted me to be a success and I wasn't.'

'I'm not sure that's true. I just wanted you to be as involved in your work as I was.'

'To make it OK for you to ignore me.'

'That's the negative way to put it. You could say, because I was happy in my work and I wanted you to feel the same.'

'I could.' His tone is doubtful and she glances at him.

'Look, whatever you accuse me of, you're almost certainly right. Sometimes I think all I want is for everyone – not just you, but everyone – to leave me alone to get on with my work. To make no more demands on me; to expect nothing.'

'Yes. I felt that.'

'But when you weren't there…' She trails off. They go down the steep steps, cross the road, under the railway bridge and down past the old mill to the canal path. The valley bottom is in shadow. El doesn't speak again till they are by the canal. 'This is the thing that's hard to explain. When I didn't know where you were, or whether you'd come back, I was useless.'

'Well, I imagine it was a shock. And naturally – probably, naturally – you wouldn't want me to be the victim of some nasty accident.'

El shakes her head. 'No. It's hard for you to believe because it was hard for me to believe. I couldn't go to work. I couldn't help Cara. I couldn't answer Paul. I couldn't shop or cook. I couldn't even think of a way to look for you.'

'You were upset,' he says uneasily. An El who is doing nothing is unimaginable.

She shakes her head again. 'It wasn't about being upset. I

wasn't sobbing and tearing my hair. It was about being mean-ingless. Without you.'

Con is stuck for a reply. He thinks about sitting on the train to Bologna with the bass beat of his neighbour's music in his ears and the monkey house stench of orange in his nostrils: he thinks about the dark wet streets of the city with a lurking presence always at his back, and of the bar where he saw the young couple with their baby in a carrier: he thinks of squatting in the shadow underneath the window of his *pensione* at night, so that the revolving orange light in the street would not shine over his face. Was he meaningless? And if so, was it because of El's absence?

'I don't know what to say,' he says slowly. 'It wasn't simple. It wasn't one thing. I mean, all the time I was away, it was for lots of reasons. You were one of them. And I was – lost, I suppose you could say – lost without you. Is that the same as meaningless?'

El laughs. 'It's not a competition! You don't have to have been just as meaningless as me.'

'But it always *is* a competition with us, isn't it?' he finds him-self saying. 'Isn't that the trouble? Over work, over the kids, over caring about each other.'

'*Is* it a competition over work?'

'Not any more, obviously. But I suppose it was at one point.'

'OK. Let's not fight old battles. Not a competition over work. It's not a competition over the kids because you've put in the time with them and you're their main person. Which I knew, but I understand it better now.'

'Meaning?'

'Meaning I understand jealousy is not appropriate and that I should honour you for the things you can do better than me.'

'It's not a question of better, it's just a question of having the time to pay attention.'

'Conrad, for God's sake, accept a compliment! You are a better father than I am a mother and thank heavens for it. They need you. They love you.'

'They love you too,' he says quietly.

'Yes, so much that they think me capable of murder.'

He laughs, and after a beat she joins in.

'When we can talk like this,' she says, 'it's impossible to believe how much we couldn't talk.'

'Things get furred up,' he says. 'Like limescale in pipes. Like cholesterol in arteries. Things get clogged up and then the – the system needs a – a—'

'Good dose of vinegar,' offers El. 'For the limescale, anyway.'

Con looks up and takes in the faint haze of green on the willows, the pinkish red of other twigs and branches. 'When do the pussy willows come out?'

El laughs. 'You're asking me, country boy?'

'Early spring,' he reflects. 'It must be soon. D'you remember when Megan wanted to pick some and we argued?'

'What did we argue about?'

'You said she could and I said she couldn't.'

El pulls a face. 'Conservationist.'

'Not at all. They're practically impossible to pick. You can bend the twigs double before they'll break. And then you have to twist and twist it round to try and snap the strands of bark. It hurts your hands, it's horrible.'

'So who won?'

'I told her I'd go for a walk later with the secateurs and cut some for her.'

'And did you?'

'No idea. I probably forgot. But so did she.'

'Right.' She stops to watch as two drakes skid down onto the surface of the water behind a duck who is streaking away as fast as she can, neck outstretched. 'All the things we've argued about. All the millions of things,' she says.

'Yup.'

'Was that the problem? We more or less stopped arguing.'

'Well, if you think back that's not true. It had got to the point where we only argued. The arguments were few and far between, but that's because we didn't actually see each other very often.'

'All right. Do we need to sit down with a pen and paper to do this or can we do it as we walk?'

'Do what?'

'Draw up some rules. Some do's and don'ts.'

'You're going to fix us with a list of rules?' His voice is more sarcastic than he intends.

'Look, Con. We've both admitted. Lots of things went wrong. It's not going to just all come right again because we want it to.'

'It's not all going to come right again because you make a list of rules.'

'No, but it might help. Anything that might help is worth considering. Number one, make a time to talk every week. One evening minimum. Say Friday. Starting no later than 7pm.'

She is serious so he nods.

'Your turn.'

'God, El, I don't know.'

'Do something together every weekend. Walk, theatre, gallery, outing.'

'Every weekend?'

'Why not? Doesn't have to be all weekend, it might just be Saturday afternoon.'

'I feel like I'm being marriage guidance counselled.'

'That's not a bad idea either.'

'NO.'

'Not a bad idea at all!'

He realises she is teasing him. 'Make a list of rules if you want, and I'll look at them. But I'm not convinced.'

'OK,' she says. 'I will. And you know what my third one will be?'

'No.'

'Sex.'

Conrad sighs. In Bologna there were twin beds in the hotel room and anyway he was sweaty and ill and Cara was popping in at all hours. Last night they curled up together for the first time in their own bed, and although he put his arm around her and she spooned her back into his belly, there seemed to be an unspoken agreement that this was enough for now. That after the flight home and the noisy meal, and with the children in the house, a chaste hug was the most appropriate end to the long day. Anyway he was exhausted. Also, Con thought, I am nervous. Maybe she is too. He couldn't actually remember the last time they had made love.

'Sex,' persists El. 'Because if we can't talk about it – if we don't communicate about it – it's another, I don't know, chasm, between us.'

'Right.'

'D'you want to talk about it now?'

'No.'

'OK.'

They climb up to the old railway line in silence. The sun flashes in their eyes. The trees and bushes alongside the track are more forward than those by the canal; higher up, Con supposes they get more light. There are several bearing pale catkins which do actually dance like lambs' tails in the wind. He points them out to El.

'I know I'm annoying,' she says. 'But you don't understand what's happened to me. I don't think you do, anyway. I was just – incapable. And it makes me want to put solid things in place, so it never happens again.'

'It's funny,' he says. 'We don't talk about love.'

'Love? No, not really. I mean, I don't know how we'd define love. But if it means you don't really exist unless the other person is there, then aren't we talking about it?'

Somewhere along the way they have dropped hands and he reaches for hers again now. It's cold. 'Where are your gloves?'

'Bologna?' She grins. 'You can warm that one, the other's in my pocket.'

'I think we should go home and go back to bed,' he says, squeezing her cold fingers. 'And see what happens.'

El wakes, as usual, earlier than Con. Monday. She will have to go to work. She will have to be sensible and efficient, and affectionately wry about Con's escapade. She will have to be graceful and grateful with those colleagues who have covered for her. Perhaps take in some cakes? Some wine? She will have to tear like a whirlwind through the queries and tasks that have piled up in her absence, and prioritise the urgent ones. She must make sure she arrives home before 7. She will have to be pleasant with Louis so there's no silly atmosphere for other people to pick up on.

But they're all bound to know, she realises. Is it really likely that she and Louis have been talking and laughing together in the department, working late together or leaving together after work, and no rumours have attached to them? Of course people will have linked their names. Did she imagine it was all a secret just because she wanted it to be one? Shame rises like a tide, momentarily flooding her calculating brain. The flotsam that floats on the tide is a question: was I only not ashamed before because I thought it was a secret? She wonders if she finds it shameful now simply because she realises it is public knowledge. She wonders if she has any morals at all.

Con stirs and turns over so his back is to her. She turns to face the same way and bends her neck to rest her forehead against his shoulder blade, a supplicant. With her nose tucked under the duvet like this she breathes in the hot, strong scent of their bed; their sweat, their sex, their sleep. It's how their bed used to smell. It's how it should smell.

She is about to leave for work when Con calls her name. She turns back in the hall, car keys in hand, impatient. 'Con?'

'In my office.'

He is wearing the multicoloured dressing gown, sitting in front of her laptop which she's lent him for the day. 'What is it?'

He points. His email programme is up, the message on the screen reads: *Welcome home. You can run but you can't hide. Looking forward to meeting your lovely wife.*

El stares. She knows without asking that the sender is Mad.

She has the same sensation as when she first discovered the MAD emails: a lurch in her stomach, a physical spasm of fear and disbelief. 'How does she know you're back?'

Con shrugs. 'It was just there when I opened my emails.' He peers at the screen. 'Sent at 6.47 this morning.'

They stare at the email in silence. When Con told her the Maddy saga yesterday morning, El deliberately held back. She found parts of it frankly implausible, and she suspected that he was giving her an edited version. He must have been attracted to Maddy, he almost certainly slept with her; how else account for the vengeful malice of the woman's tone? How else had Maddy got her hooks so deeply into him? A more detailed story would emerge, but at breakfast on his first morning home was not the time. El was conscious of sounds upstairs, Megan taking a shower; soon the kitchen would fill with the children. And it was clear to her that Con was still not fully recovered. His memory was probably unreliable, there were things he must surely have hallucinated when he was running a temperature in Bologna.

She boxed the Maddy story as something to be unpicked at a later date. But now here it is, shoving itself in their faces as they try to go about their daily lives.

'We should call the police.'

Con sighs. 'What can they do? It's not even a threat. You could read it as humorous.'

'There's the one about ripping your heart out.'

'But if she claims I seduced her – she's got photos of me in her hotel room – it's no more than anyone spurned in love might say. It's a reference to the monkeys, anyway.'

El realises he is speaking the truth. The story he's told her is true. 'But Con, she could come to the house anytime.'

'Yes.'

'She could throw a brick through the window.'

'Yes.'

There's a silence. El is suddenly aware of the car keys dangling from her fingers. 'OK. I have to go to work.'

Con pushes back his chair and stands. He folds his arms around her and kisses her forehead. For a moment she allows herself to slump against him and be comforted.

'Are you going to reply?'

'I shouldn't think so.'

'Be careful today – if anyone comes to the door.'

'I'll be careful. Now go.' He pats her on the rump and she goes.

She rings him at lunchtime to check he's OK and to remind him to make a doctor's appointment.

'I'm all right,' he says. 'You don't need to fuss.'

'Any more emails?'

'El, if we spend our day worrying about what she's going to do, she's won.'

'I know.' In fact, El has not spent the morning worrying, but rather rushing from one overdue task to the next, and it was only when she stopped to grab a sandwich that she guiltily remembered Con in his dressing gown of many colours, staring glumly at the laptop. 'I know,' she repeats. 'I've been busy. What are you doing?'

'I'm composing my letter of resignation.'

'Good.'

It is good. Very good, that he is taking such immediate action over work. But there will be problems thrown up by that too.

What on earth is he going to do all day, every day? She wonders if he's thought about it. And catches herself again being rather dislikeable. Why is she patronising him? Why is she presuming he won't have thought about it? In the crisis he has been through it has almost certainly presented itself more luridly to him than it has just done to her.

Is this, perhaps, one of the after-effects that she must learn to live with? The presence of a little nagging voice which undermines her swift certainties, which casts doubt on her assumptions, which suggests that other people may understand more than she has given them credit for? She reaches for a name for the little voice. Self-doubt? Uncertainty? Humility? She's not sure and there's no time now. She notes it for future scrutiny and ploughs on through her day.

By the end of it she's done everything except behave in a pleasant and natural manner with Louis. When she saw him coming down the corridor she ducked into the Ladies and hid there like a schoolgirl until she knew he'd gone. She realises she will have to email him to explain what's happened and why the relationship is over. All she's given him so far is a tantrum and a request not to contact her. As if it's his fault. Driving home, she picks at that and understands that she does blame him for not being kinder or more understanding, and that it is entirely unfair of her to blame him, because both of them have always known full well that neither of their marriages were or would be threatened, and that therefore neither of them would ever make too heavy a claim upon the other. If Louis' wife had run away or died, El would have been equally wary. Of course. Because the last thing she would have wanted to do was to give Louis a false impression of how important he really was to her. Ugly but true. So how on earth can she blame him? She must send an email tonight apologising and being quite clear that it is over.

Conrad has made a smoked salmon quiche. 'I made it earlier. We can have it whenever you're ready.'

She knows he's done that because he expected her to be late. She's not late. They are both glad that neither mentions it. They linger at table after they've finished, with the premonition of a depressing conversation about Mad hovering over them. El wants to compose her email to Louis first, but she doesn't want Con to think she's doing something work-related in preference to talking to him. And it's not just Mad they need to discuss, she remembers. There is unfinished business from their previous conversation.

'Yesterday,' she says, pouring them both more wine.

'Yes?'

'When we were talking. You said it always *is* a competition with us. Over work, the kids, and caring about each other.'

'Yes.'

'We dealt with work and the kids. We didn't talk about caring about each other.'

He laughs and puts his hand over hers on the table. 'Do we need to?'

Making love has set a warm current running between them. When she looks at him he is bigger, stronger, more solid than he used to be. As if she'd been living with the ghost of Con before he went away. 'But I mean it,' she persists. 'I think we should talk about it. It *is* a competition, isn't it? You've always thought I cared more about work than about you. And you've always thought that *you* cared more about *me* than I did about you.'

'And what do you think?'

'I think you care more about the kids than you do about me.'

'So what's to discuss?' He is surprisingly sharp.

'While you were away, I thought you would get in touch with them if not with me.'

'It's a different relationship, isn't it. The kids used to be completely dependent on us. Cara still is in many ways. And you are an independent adult.'

'Of course. I'm not saying any of these things is bad. I'm just wanting to, I don't know, acknowledge—'

'What?'

'Sometimes I feel I have to prove something to you.'

'No one likes being taken for granted.'

'Of course not. But we both *know*, don't we? We both know we're here for the duration, it's not going to be hearts and flowers every day.'

'Hearts and flowers once a year would be nice!' This is a reference to Valentine's Day. He has always given her roses and she has always teased him for the cliché of it. She has seldom remembered to reciprocate.

'Touché.'

They sit in silence for a while but El can't let it go. 'I shouldn't need to prove it to you because you know, you are the bedrock.'

'Not a tremendously rewarding role, being a rock.'

'Well, what do you want? When I rang to ask how you were today you told me not to fuss.'

'True. Leave it. Some things don't have answers. Will you look at my letter for me?'

El reads Con's letter of resignation. He's sending it to Corastra and copying it to Gus. It is measured but truthful, citing his concern about conditions in the CBL animal house alongside his fear that the research may prove to be a dead end, as the reasons for his leaving. It doesn't blame Gus, but it doesn't let him off the hook on the subject of the animal house. She circles a couple of redundant commas and passes it back to him. 'Good. Well done. Will you go back at all?'

'I'll have to. I've got three monkeys still in trials, I'll have to see them through and write an interim report at the very least. But I've got a sick note for a week so there's a breathing space.'

'Very good. What will you do now?'

'El, there's something I have to tell you.'

Her heart flips. She knew. From the minute she arrived home she knew there was something. He's made her a nice meal, he's talked, he's listened, but something – there's been something in his manner, a seriousness, a distance, a – she doesn't know what it is but she's afraid it will be awful. He's made up his mind to tell her the truth about Maddy. Is he going to leave her after all?

'El? Cara came round this afternoon.'

Cara? Cara! But what's wrong with Cara?

'Please don't take this the wrong way. She said she wanted to tell you but she didn't know how to. I'm sure, if it hadn't been for all this—' he waves a hand '—drama, she would have told us both before now.'

'Told us what?'

'She's pregnant.'

Con's not leaving. Cara's not ill. Briefly, El rejoices, before landing squarely on the problem. 'She can't have it.'

'Slow down.'

Yes. That's why Cara didn't tell me. She knew I'd say that. How many times today is El going to slam into her own knee-jerk responses? Suddenly she has a vision of Megan as a toddler, teaching herself to get over the back doorstep. Clutching the door jamb, lowering one leg over the sill and then tumbling as her weight lurched forward onto it and she lost her balance. Not crying. Patiently clambering up and trying again. She must have done it a dozen times. El remembers standing unnoticed in the kitchen watching with fascination and thinking, *this is how children learn. They just keep on practising until they master something.*

Maybe I will learn now, El tells herself. Not to think I am always right.

In the same flash of thought she understands what Con is worrying over; that despite Con's absence, Cara couldn't tell Eleanor and had to wait for her father's return. Indeed, she had to go to Germany hunting for him, before there was a parent sympathetic enough to spill her troubles to. Con is afraid El will be offended. And naturally it hurts. But she has no right to the hurt. It's always been known that Cara is Daddy's girl. And has not El herself played the greatest part in making this happen? If anyone needed it, it is evidence of the success of her insistence that Con is Cara's father and the most important person in her life.

El raises her face to Con. He's leaning forward watching her. 'Sorry. Yes,' she says. 'Tell me.'

'You all right?'

'I am.'

'OK. She's already four months along.'

'Four months? But she's like a piece of string!'

'I know. I know. She says food makes her feel sick. She hasn't told him because she's convinced he'll try to make her have an abortion, and she says she wants to have it.'

'She can't even look after herself.'

'That's true. But there's an argument which says that if she has someone else to look after, someone totally dependent on her… Maybe it will nudge her into being a bit more responsible.'

'Like it has done so far.'

'Look, El, I don't know the answer.'

'What did you tell her?'

'I said she must do what she thinks best. I said we'd give her all the help we can.'

Cara won't have any money. She won't have anywhere to live. Con's point about being responsible for a child is a good one, but not if Cara comes and lives here. Because the care of the child will simply fall on Con and Cara will continue to behave like a child herself. El restrains herself from saying this. There's time enough, and Con will see the sense of it. Better for them to pay Cara's rent on a place of her own.

'Has she been to the doctor?'

'Yes. And I've told her to make another appointment this week to get some dietary advice.'

'And she's been living with that lout all this time? She's going to have to tell him.'

Con shakes his head. 'She's staying at her friend Jenny's. She's been there since New Year apparently. She tells me – I don't know how true it is – she tells me that she's split up with him for good.'

'Well. It would simplify matters, if it was true.'

'Yes.'

They look at each other and El smiles wryly. Con grins back at her.

'So. Grandparents, eh? When d'you reckon to start knitting?'

Chapter 16

IT IS FIVE years later.

Conrad is looking after Cara's children, which he does two days a week: four-year-old Tilly and the baby, Lucas. After a fretful morning Lucas has fallen deeply asleep, and Tilly is happily lining up all her small farm animals, Playmobil figures and dinosaurs in ranks across the kitchen floor. The arrangement never reaches its end, because she continues to move different creatures from the back to the front, and to set others in pairs, instructing them in a half-whispered, sing-song voice as she does so; sometimes making a shift in direction, so that they must all be aligned facing the window, or the door; sometimes creating a carefully selected breakaway group, which is then rejoined by the entire contingent. She can be happy playing like this for hours. Con has tried listening in to her story but all he can glean are fragments: 'You can come with me.' 'No no, we're going this way.' 'The cockadoo is being very naughty, hmmm, hmmm, hmmm.' She doesn't like it if he sits and listens, so he gets on with cooking. El has said she'll be back to eat tonight, but she'll probably be late. He wants to feed Cara when she comes to collect the kids; he guesses that by the time she gets them home and into bed she's too tired to bother cooking for herself.

There has been talk for quite a while of Cara and the kids moving in with him and El, and he's hopeful it will happen. Less driving around for all of them, built-in babysitting and company for Cara, and the opportunity for him to exercise more control over what they all eat. Cara has ballooned and shrunk repeatedly since first getting pregnant, and at the moment she is nothing but skin and bones. There is part of his thinking which still classes plentiful eating with freedom from anxiety; it was hard not to think of Cara as more contented when she was plump: placid, maternal. Illogical, though, if she was comfort-eating. The plumpness was as much a sign of distress as is the skinniness. As he grates the parmesan he ponders the power of physical appearance to suggest personality and mood. And he thinks again of shape-shifting Maddy.

In the days after they returned home from Bologna, it became apparent to him that he would need to see Maddy, for precisely the same reason that a child needs to look under the bed where he thinks a wolf is hiding. He needed to stop her from being his nightmare. He let the idea gather force while he ticked off the other things he needed to do. Like giving in his notice at work. And, after he had actually left, and after long discussions with El, writing a letter to Carrington Bio-Life, copied to Corastra, saying that as a scientist whose animals had been kept at CBL, he had damning evidence of conditions in their monkey house. He listed the problems and requested a meeting to discuss changes they should implement. He indicated that if they did not reply within two weeks he would go to the inspectorate with an official complaint. El agreed that the anonymous release of his photos may not have had much effect, but with his name and his research experience behind it, and with a real rather than a vague threat, they might find him difficult to ignore. Their reply, with a meeting date, came within the week.

And at the meeting, the director of the animal facility greeted him with smooth assurance. There had been a change of regime; he was new in post, he had been appointed to ensure that Carrington Bio-Life's spotless record on animal welfare was maintained at all costs. He took Conrad's points extremely seriously, and he was very pleased to be able to tell him that all the deficiencies noted by Conrad had been remedied. Would Conrad like to accompany him on a tour of the facility?

Grimly, Con agreed, and naturally all was as the director said. Given that the animals were there as subjects of research, conditions were acceptable. Con was sickened by the sight of them but there were no obviously moribund animals being kept alive. The cages were clean, they all had water, their charts were scrupulously detailed and up to date. The director thanked him warmly for his interest and invited him to return whenever he liked. Con was shaking by the time he left, but it was over. He had done his best, and now he could try to forget it.

In all this time Maddy, the threat of Maddy, lurked in his and El's minds. She had sent two further emails since his return, from a MAD2 email address: the first, *Nice try, Houdini*, had badly unnerved him because he wasn't aware of having escaped anything. What trap had he blindly side-stepped? He reviewed his recent movements, imagining her watching from the shadows. The second read: *I know what you're going to do before you even think of it. Don't imagine I've forgotten you.* He guessed she had found out that he had left his job. El still thought he should go to the police. She called Mad a stalker.

One morning he emailed her simply requesting a meeting,

stating a safe time and place: a Costa coffee shop in the centre of Manchester at 2pm on a Tuesday. He and El deliberated whether El should be there too, sitting discreetly at another table, keeping an eye on things. But in a public place, it seemed like overkill. Maddy emailed back succinctly: *OK.*

In the café, Conrad spotted her before she saw him. She was wearing jeans and a black T shirt, with a scuffed leather bomber jacket. She looked hard and lean and dangerous, the very opposite of that mousy librarian he had met at first. Every time he saw her she seemed to adopt a different style. She pulled out the chair and slumped down opposite him without giving any sign of recognition. 'You haven't got a drink,' he said, despising himself for the thought that he might go and buy her one.

'That's because I don't want a drink.'

'OK. I'm here to tell you this has to stop.'

'What?'

'You. Following me. Threatening me.'

She laughed. 'You did an ace disappearing act in Munich. Like a secret agent.'

'I knew you were in Munich.'

'I might have been.'

'Look, Maddy, I am doing what you want, OK? I have resigned my job, I am no longer working with animals, and I am advising CBL on how to improve conditions in their research facility.'

She shook her head. 'You give an inch and pretend it's a mile. You need to talk to all the other scientists whose animals are there, you need to persuade them all that their work is cruel and evil, and you need to get the place closed down.'

Conrad took a mouthful of coffee. It was good and strong

and he realised he was enjoying it. He was back in a world where the taste of coffee could be enjoyed. She was not part of that world. 'That won't happen,' he told her. 'Animal research is vital. I am prepared to work for better conditions for the animals but nothing else. There's no way that place will close down.'

Maddy suddenly leant forward over the table, bringing her face close to his. 'I went to prison because of you. I went to prison because you're such a wishy-washy, two-faced bastard. Have you ever been to prison? D'you know how shit it is? When they take away your clothes, and put you in a stinking little cage and shove disgusting slop at you three times a day – like they do to your animals in their lock-up?' Her voice was low but piercing. Con was aware of glances from other tables. He forced himself to keep his own voice light and conversational.

'You're mistaken, Maddy. I had nothing to do with that.'

'Oh yes you did. You wouldn't do what needed doing, you wouldn't denounce CBL, you wouldn't identify yourself, so I was forced into reprisals against your fellow torturers. I had to take the fight to them.'

'Forced? Who forced you?'

'If you care about something – hah, you don't even know what that means. If you *cared* about the animals, you would do everything in your power to save them. You would plot, you would fight, you would risk your own safety, you would do *anything*.'

'Paint slogans on cars, and put sanitary towels through letterboxes?'

'Anything. Anything for the cause.'

'I don't see how that helps your cause.'

'That's because you've got no fucking imagination. Don't

you think those little men might be scared? Don't you think they might be worrying, oh dear today it's my car but tomorrow it might be me? Maybe I should change my job? Don't I know that the only reason you're conceding anything at all is because I finally got you good and frightened?'

For a moment Con quailed, feeling the power of her logic. No, he told himself. Don't let her do this again. 'You don't know anything about me. I'm not frightened of you because there's nothing you can do to harm me. I've told my wife all about you. After I left Munich I went missing for a few days and the police were involved in finding me. They are still expecting a full account of what happened, and if you threaten me again – if you so much as look at me again – I shall give them your name.'

'Hah!' she snorted contemptuously.

'And your aliases, and your criminal record, and I will press charges.'

'What charges?'

'Stalking. Threatening behaviour. I've got all your emails.'

'You're a dick.'

Conrad took a mouthful of coffee and set the cup carefully down. She watched him for a while then leant over deliberately and grabbed his half-full cup from its saucer. She raised it to her lips and he thought she was going to drink, but she spat into the cup.

'You won't know what's hit you,' she said.

'Maybe not, but you will be prime suspect. As I said, my wife has all the details.' The skin on her fingers, clenched around his cup, was rough and chapped. He imagined her scrubbing herself, trying to get rid of the red paint she had used to daub the cars. Suddenly she seemed to him like an angry kid – defiant, hostile, knowing she was cornered. 'You have to promise never to contact me again. Not to email me or threaten me or follow me. You have to leave me alone.'

'Or what?' she jeered. 'Or Mr Plod will lock me up again?'

'Yes,' he said simply. There was a brief silence. 'And you know you don't like it,' he added.

'You are a pathetic wanker,' she said, setting down his cup.

'Fine. Just promise.'

'Promise? You think I'll keep a *promise*, scout's honour?'

'Promise.'

She was defeated. He knew that. It seemed to him he had known it from the moment she threw herself into the chair opposite him. What did she have? Nothing. All the power was with him. She pushed back her chair abruptly.

'You need to promise, Maddy, or I'm talking to the police.'

'Oh mister wank-face, yes sir, I pwomise!' She sang it out loudly enough for all the heads in the café to turn, and then she was gone, slamming out of the place at full speed. A few people caught Con's eye and shook their heads or raised their eyebrows, indicating sympathy. He nodded at them and went to get himself a fresh cup of coffee. Which he would enjoy from start to finish.

And Maddy had never contacted him again after that; her name never cropped up, she disappeared from view. It seemed as if El continued to worry about her long after she had receded from Con's thoughts – sometimes he would be surprised by El wondering what had happened to her or who she was torment-ing now. With distance Con could see that Maddy had done him no physical harm. She had committed no real crime.

And now – with Cara's two kids to deal with, and the

allotment he shares with Paul, and films to watch with Dan, and the usual shopping and cooking and cleaning at home – that whole crisis of five years ago seems both distant and unreal, as if it happened to someone else, some other, febrile, neurotic Conrad. His flight and El's pursuit of him were enough to shock both of them into temporary good behaviour; into a period of talking, of honesty, of consideration, of nostalgic love. But this phase did not last long. How could it? he reasons with himself. Their lives are too similar to what they were before. El is still following her career, her department is having astonishing success with stem cells, they are attracting major funding, they are in the news. She is sought after, as a conference speaker, as a Ph.D. supervisor, as a research partner, and to sit on policy, prize-giving and funding bodies. If she agreed to all the requests, she would spend half the year overseas. There is no reason for her to give it up; she loves it and she thrives on it. So of course Con is house-husband; of course he eats at home, alone, while she attends glittering dinners; of course he deals with the crises in the lives of their offspring; of course the novelty of his bid for escape wears off. They are what they are, living the life they have always lived together – why should his running away for a few days have any lasting effect on that?

He sometimes wonders how they would have fared in their marriage if El had been the man and he the woman. He guesses it would have made it easier for him to accept his role. The sexism of that thought makes him guilty. By and large they get on. Sometimes they talk, but mostly they simply co-exist, in relatively harmonious parallel lives. She told him the affair with Louis was over and he believes her. They make love together occasionally, rather awkwardly, and both with a sense that this is not quite how they want it to be. At times he tells himself it is a simple question of age, and at other times that they have lived too long together, and known each other too well. He couldn't say if he loves El. But he is her husband.

Eleanor comes home at 8 that evening to find Cara and the children still there, and her dinner in the oven. The house is a tip and she realises again how much she doesn't want Cara to move back. But it isn't fair of her. Conrad is the one who helps Cara with the children, and it is only right that the decision should be his. Cara and the children are company for him and give him a role. If he's happy to have them underfoot all day then that is up to him. She thinks of the times she has come home to find the house quiet and tidy, and him waiting to serve up dinner for two; when they have sat like civilised adults discussing the minutiae of her research, or his gardening, or the next holiday they are planning, or Megan's latest success in the theatre, and then moved to the comfy chairs in the sitting room and buried themselves happily in their respective books. She thinks of the calm mutual contentment of their evenings alone together, which will be disrupted by Cara's dramas, and by children playing up and trying to delay their bedtimes, and by all the mess and muddle of family life. Why isn't she ever enough for Conrad on her own?

And then of course she feels guilty. He needs Cara and the children in a way she doesn't. And the children need a father figure. She has other things: work, her students, her colleagues. Of course he needs to be loved by Tilly and Lucas, and to be Cara's main support. And how much better it would be for Cara if she moved back. Cara could confide in her dad, he could help her pull herself together. El knows that she cannot. She's tried, she has really tried; when the three of them came home from Bologna, when Cara was pregnant the first time. That Easter she took Cara off on an idyllic Tenerife holiday of sun and swimming and delicious restaurants. Cara was silent and tetchy, eating nothing due to (she claimed) feeling sick with her pregnancy, sleeping late and wasting the fresh sunny mornings. El could not break through to her. And if she is jealous because Cara and Con watch rubbish TV together and cackle with laughter, or spend hours discussing the quirks and fads of Cara's children – if she is jealous of those things, then she is an utter bitch. Cara must move in, and Eleanor will be glad. It is Con who has organised the conversion of the attic into Dan's self-contained lair, and that works brilliantly. Now Dan has a decent job in IT, he is even paying rent, and they have the security of knowing where he is, knowing he is safe.

She feels a dull, nagging unease whenever she thinks about the time Con went missing. It was terrible, and she discovered how much she needed him. But once he was back it was hard to remember the urgency of that. Each day, after all, comes down to a mundane domestic sequence of breakfast (eaten separately, El rising a good hour before Con), departure for work (a peck on the cheek), return from work (a peck on the cheek), dinner with maybe a few minutes' chat, clearing up and reading, and bed (a peck on the cheek). How could anyone invest that with the heightened emotion she felt when he disappeared? Of course they are simply furniture in one another's lives – what else could she expect? But it gives her a sense of failure and shame, and makes her even feel that she is recreating the conditions for him to depart again. She realises she doesn't know how to be married. She can't understand how other people do it, day in, day out, for years. And then one of the children comes round, or friends for dinner, and Con jokes and talks about ideas she has never heard him mention, and she is struck by how funny and interesting he is. Afterwards she tells herself he is only dull with her, just as she is only dull with him.

She takes her plate of moussaka into the sitting room and sets it on the coffee table. Cara is on the sofa with Lucas flat out beside her, thumb in mouth.

'Wine for the worker?' Con offers, passing her a glass. Tilly comes and stands on the opposite side of the coffee table, staring intently at El's food.

'Are you hungry, Till?' she asks.

'When's she not?' from Cara.

'Can I give her a bit?'

'She won't like it, but feel free.'

'I'll get you a little spoon, Tilly, and you can have a taste and see what you think.'

Conrad is on his feet before she can move, fetching the spoon. 'She's eaten two dippy eggs, haven't you, Tilly lass? And more cucumber and carrot sticks than she can count.'

'Three five four nine eleven!' retorts Tilly.

'Exactly. Here's a spoon.'

Tilly attacks her side of El's plate, and El eats from her own side.

'Don't spill it down you. We're going in a minute,' Cara threatens.

'Cara and I were talking,' Con begins.

'About a move-in date?'

'Not quite yet. About Megan's old room and how I might reorganise it for Tilly and Lucas. D'you think Meg would mind if we boxed her stuff up?'

El laughs. 'I think it would be entirely reasonable, given that she left home nearly a decade ago!'

'I don't want her blaming me for turfing her out,' says Cara sullenly.

'For God's sake—' starts El.

'I'll ring her,' soothes Con. 'I'll ring her and tell her I want to clear the room. We can fit some of her stuff in our wardrobe. She can come home for the weekend and sort out what she really wants to keep.'

'I like this,' Tilly announces triumphantly, shovelling in another mouthful.

'I can see you do, young lady. There'll be none left for me!'

'Great, now this one's asleep. He'll howl when I try to put him in the car,' complains Cara. El's eyes meet Con's and she allows her eyebrows to rise a fraction of a fraction. *Cara is exasperating.* He smiles back at her without moving a muscle. *She is, but what can we do?* Suddenly El feels like laughing.

'Tilly,' Con says. 'You've eaten so much of your poor granny's tea that she'll be hungry all night. D'you want to come with me and find some more food for her?' Tilly nods seriously and trots into the kitchen after him.

'Won't it be a bit shit for you if we come back?' Cara asks in the sudden silence. 'You won't get much peace.'

'We've never been much for peace,' El tells her. 'Having kids around will be good for us.'

'I know Dad wants us to come but it's different for you. You're busy at work all day, you want to flop when you get in.'

'Am I not flopping?' El asks her. 'Food cooked for me, wine poured for me, world-class entertainment provided? What more could I ask?'

Cara smiles one of her all-too-rare smiles, and Eleanor's heart soars. Con and Tilly come back from the kitchen bearing, respectively, a second helping of moussaka and a tiny lopsided cupcake smothered in hundreds and thousands. 'I made this!' Tilly announces.

Con is grinning at El. *Thank you, yes, you see we can weather Cara and her kids, together.* She smiles back at him. *Yes.*

Mostly El doesn't think about the marriage, because she is too busy, and busy with too many other interesting things. But when she does think about it, in a rational, objective way, she feels slightly resentful and defeated. It is not what she imagined it would be, and it seems likely that is more her fault than Conrad's. She blocks their holiday times into her new academic diary promptly every year. Planning holidays together – and indeed taking them – is an easy thing to do. They can share an interest in a new place, in its culture and history, in walking and in eating different kinds of food in different kinds of settings. They get on well together on holiday. But increasingly El studies their fellow travellers with a jaundiced eye. Most are old, similar to Con and El in age, or older. They sit in couples in companionable or hostile silence, they visit the sights, they take dips in the pool or the sea. We are just the same as them, El thinks, and she hates the thought. All their hope and imagination and love and cleverness – and what are they, at the end of the day? Just the same as everyone else, living the same clichés. She hates it, and she hates herself for having allowed herself to imagine that she was in some way different and should have been able to arrive at a better way of living. She hates the trick of it: you start off young, imagining you can do anything, that life is yours to shape as you will. And then you find yourself trammelled into exactly the same pattern as everyone else. There is the illusion of choice, but no real choice. Just a narrowing funnel.

And then something happens – the birth of Cara's children, for example, or Paul getting married, or Megan getting rave national reviews, or a breakthrough of some kind at work – and suddenly all her resentment is washed away and she realises how happy and blessed she is, and how her own individual life is, certainly, more vivid than anyone else's, and more distinctive and original and important. And she knows that the originality and importance is in no small part due to the exceptional nature of her marriage with Conrad.